AMPHIBIANS:
THE DARK SECRETS DEEP DOWN IN THE BAYOU

Part 1

By: Lannon L. Burdunice

AMPHIBIANS

Lannon L. Burdunice

AMPHIBIANS: THE DARK SECRETS DEEP DOWN IN THE BAYOU.
Part 1

Published by Lannon Burdunice Literature LLC. (LB Lit.™)

588 Hatch Ave. W. #6

St. Paul, MN 55117

www.lblit.com

Library of Congress Control Number: 2022951124

ISBN 9798986903507; ISBN 9798986903514

Dedications and Acknowledgements

This is dedicated to my mother Louise Wesson for always loving me unconditionally; to my children for being my greatest accomplishments in the world; and to my cousin Mel for all of her genuine care and support.

I want to thank God first and foremost for blessing me with the talent and ability to write this book.

Mark Stoltenburg, Jennifer Stevens, and Troy Vincent; Education staff members at the Minnesota Department of Corrections- Stillwater Facility for all of their help in making the computer lab available for me to type up this book.

Prologue

Something strange begins happening to Silk after the blast that should have, and would have, killed an ordinary human-being. Little did Silk know, however, she was no longer an *ordinary human-being*. Her throat, breasts, torso, legs, hands, and eventually her entire body, all start to illuminate and glisten like flames in the rain. Beatrice comes out and apprehensively spots Silk. She tries to throw another blast at her but it bounces right off of Silk and crashes into a huge thirty to forty-foot tall pine tree, splits it in half, sending it crashing down onto Beatrice's home. Furious, Beatrice tries another spell and tries to re-charge her energy to send another blast at Silk, but it's like her power got cut off because she could no longer work her magic energy up. Silk's mouth is moving but her eyes are closed, head hung down, hair wild and frizzled now even in the rain, and she is rising off of the ground. She uncontrollably recites spells of her own, and all of the reptiles of the bayou and swamps appear around her as if possessed by her spells. Beatrice looks on in horror. Silk finishes her spell then points and yells, "Go to hell Beatrice!" a wave of energy entraps Beatrice all around, consuming her, then leads her to the swamp waters where a black whirlpool in spinning viciously pulling her towards the mouth into a portal. She screams until she is swallowed up by the black hole in the swamp. Once Beatrice is gone everything calms down, including Silk, and the thunderstorm also ceases immediately. The amphibians are still poised as if awaiting a command from Silk. Silk's feet reconnect with the earth, and all of the mud and dirt fall off of her body like dead skin. She opens her mouth and Iblis comes out crawling off of her outstretched tongue. The lizard returns to its species and Silk walks away, leaving Beatrice's yet again ruined estate.

Silk now feels guarded by all of the cold-blooded creatures, even the killers, like she is now their new leader, by the way they are watching over and surrounding her now; the same way they used to guard Mama B. She is exhausted and decides it's time to go home, but not before she recites the spell she'd just tricked the voodoo queen out of before her demise. She does it and after feeling satisfied walks out into the dark glossy woods to go home and back to her normal life. Or so she thinks.

Chapter 1

The southern regions of the United States, in states like Texas, Louisiana, Mississippi, Alabama, Georgia, and Florida, are home to many swamps and bayous that are filled with wildlife. Silk Greene lives in New Orleans, Louisiana with her family, all of them were born and raised. Silk visits the bayou often to pick flowers, marvel over the glowing goldfish in the water, and to see the various species of wild animals the bayous provides homes to. This has been a childhood habit of Silk's. Since the age of six Silk has been fascinated with nature, the beauty of the wilderness, and the freedom it provides to both herself and the creatures of the wild. To her the bayou is a place where she can go to be at peace, where she can be herself and find serenity.

Whenever something is bothering her or she just needs to get away to clear her head, Silk always makes her way to the bayou, undetected by anyone in her family or the neighborhood. As a child growing up in the 7th ward of New Orleans, Silk endured a lot of criticism and was often teased for her fascination with animals and the great outdoors. Silk's older sister Roberta and kids from the ward would call her a "freak of nature" or "cave woman" just because she loved nature so much. The teasing and bullying was so overwhelming that they would send Silk off screaming and crying in embarrassment. Although it was a lot to take in, Silk didn't let what the other kids said deter her from what she loved so she stayed visiting the bayou and continued being herself.

Although there are many territories and sections that make up the bayous down in New Orleans, Silk has this one particular area close to where she lives where she visits religiously. To get to this section of the bayou she has to cross several territories that make up the wooded part of the city. Although Silk began touring the swamps as a young child, she never knew who, if anyone, actually owned the land in the woods. There were only two houses that she had ever spotted throughout the large vegetated landscape. Although curious of whether the residences were vacant or not, never had she known anyone to inhabit these two houses since she'd known about the area. Unbeknownst to Silk, these trenches are most definitely home to more than just the coldblooded and wild animals, they are home to two of the most mysterious and powerful of human beings in the world.

Chapter 2

Silk and her identical twin sister Essance both attend St. Thomas High School. They were born three minutes apart from one another on January 2, 2000 at Saint Bonifacius hospital. The twins just turned eighteen and are scheduled to graduate with their class of 2018. Both girls were raised with very strict and disciplined upbringings by both of their parents, DeAngelo and Lashunda Greene, and were hardened on the principle of taking advantage of the free education and programming they are afforded. "It ain't never been a greater time than today for a negro to have an education in America. Bout fifty some years ago black man or woman couldn't even dare walk in, let alone be taught in the same schools as white cherrin. So don't take what you girls got for granted. Take full advantage", is what their father would always tell them and it stuck with his girls because they did just that. Both twins got straight A's and had been in excel classes and on the A honor roll since they attended junior high. The girls were geniuses to say the least.

Although twins, Silk and Essance are totally opposite. Whereas Silk loves all kinds of plants, animals, everything else outdoors, Essance dislikes all of those sorts of things and she has nothing to do with any of it. Essance is more into entertainment, fashion, and sports than

environmental stuff. Both twins are enthusiastic about furthering their education after high school. Silk plans to enroll at Yale University to study Biology and Essance plans to enroll at Southern California University to study Fashion Marketing. Identical twins with totally opposite attractions.

Silk and Essance are walking from breakfast as the bell sounds indicating the last five minutes before the start of the first hour class of the day. The girls walk and talk to their lockers, which are right next to each other. "Hey girl, you missed breakfast. Where were you?" Essance asks when she spots her and Silk's best friend since preschool, Lillianna Hawkins, who they've always referred to as 'Lilli' for short, approaching the lockers. "I know girl, I didn't hear my dang ole alarm go off and messed around and overslept," Lilli answered with a tired yawn. "How y'all get here?" Lilli asked. "Our daddy dropped us off today," Silk answered while getting her Literature book out of her locker for her first class. "And why couldn't one of you heifers call and seen to it that I rode with y'all and made it on time?" Both girls looked at each other snickering waiting for the other to respond first. "See uh uh, y'all hoes is messy I can't even function with y'all today. Uh uh, not this early, ya heard me," Lilli responded to the girls, rolling her eyes playfully while opening her own locker. Attempting to stop laughing, Silk began, "see what had happened was, ya hear me, I tried to call you but ya dang ole voicemail kept getting on the line, and as much as I loves ya baby, I don't want to

keep on hearing yo dang ole voice through a voicemail, on and on again ya hear me?" Silk starts laughing some more her and Essance. "My phone was dead so I'ma gone head and give you this one lil baby. But dang now a bitch gone be

hongry as a bull till lunch come round," Lilli says, rubbing her stomach for emphasis. "No you not girl. We bought you a yogurt, apple cinnamon Danish, and apple juice, your favorite girlfriend," Essance replies, fetching the items out of her strap bag. "Forreal? Oh thanks yus honey darlings!" Lilli thanked the girls cheerfully using a French accent. "You's welcome my dear, you know we got chu woe. But aye, you better eat and drink fast because we got less than two minutes to be in class before the bell rings so gotta go!" Silk replies with emphasis on the last part. The girls all share a playful laugh and go about their separate ways to their first hour classes.

Chapter 3

As the school day comes to an end, Silk finds herself at her locker by
herself. Her sixth hour Advanced Calculus teacher Mr. Evans held
her back to inform her about a Calculus tournament that was
coming up that he thought she'd be interested in participating in.
Silk was full of excitement and joy at the news and gladly accepted
the invitation. Essance and Lilli had already gotten to their lockers
and had left the school building. Silk is putting her books away
when an enormous force rams into her back causing her to fall into
her locker. "Ouch! Hey, what the..." Silk yells in pain. "Shut up
hooka fo I slap the brown off ya lil light skin prissy ass" says the
voice that pushed Silk. Silk immediately becomes full of rage.
Barrika Barnes is a girl that grew up in the same neighborhood as
Silk and her family. Barrika is a brute, standing five foot eleven and
weighing nearly four hundred pounds. The heavy teen put you in
the mind of 'Resputia' from the movie "Norbit" only darker. Like
Biggie Smalls said in his hit 'Juicy,' Barrika is "big, black, and ugly as
ever." The girl hates anyone who is a lighter skin complexion than
her, smaller in size, shorter in height, anyone who is considered cute,
she hates them all both male and female. Because Silk and her twin
Essance
were all of these things, Barrika couldn't stand them from the
moment she laid eyes on them when they all were only
kindergarteners.

Barrika is a bully in every aspect, and the whole school and
even neighborhood knew this. Silk and Essance are Barrika's favorite
victims. She would pull at their hair when their mother would style
them in long braided ponytails, rip their new blouses or dresses that
they wore to and from church, step on their brand-new shoes, steal
their property every chance she got, and any and everything else to
humiliate the two girls just because she was so jealous of them. The

twins always fought the big girl off, but were no match for her even with their strength combined, Barrika always walked away unscathed while the twins went home bruised, scraped and aching.

Silk gets back up to her feet as Barrika tries to shut the locker door on her to lock her inside of it. Silk lunges at Barrika and swings a closed fist as hard as she could muster but misses by inches. Barrika grabs Silk by the back of her shirt and flings her across the floor, sending her crashing into the lockers causing an audible bang. A staff member at the school heard the bang and comes out of his classroom and into the hall to see what the cause of the crash was. "What's going on out here? Hey knock it off, Ms. Barnes get over here now," Mr. Easley yells. Barrika takes off running in the opposite direction ignoring the teacher's instructions to stop. "You gotta come back tomorrow Ms. Barnes, and when you do, there will be a write up for you in the principal's office!" Mr. Easley yells after her before she disappears around a corner. "Are you alright Ms. Greene," Mr. Easley asks Silk as he helps her get up off of the ground. "Yes sir, I'm fine," Silk answers, wincing, indicating pain in her forearm. Mr. Easley observes blood protruding out of Silk's forearm. "You need to go see the nurse Ms. Greene. Come on, I think she's still in her office," he suggests. "No, I'm ok Mr. Easley," Silk rejects as he tries to gently usher her towards the nurse's office. "Are you sure Ms. Greene? That's a pretty large cut and I think you need to report it. As a matter-of-fact I believe its school policy that it be reported. Besides, you don't want it to get infected, you know," Mr. Easley urges. "No really, I'm fine, I really gotta get going. My father is waiting for me outside, sir." Silk counters. "Well alright Ms. Greene, but I'm most definitely making a report of this and so the principal and nurse are likely going to want to hear what happened out of your mouth as well, alright?" Easley concludes with, looking defeated. "Yes sir, I understand." Silk replies. "Ok have a good night and go clean that up immediately, seriously." Mr. Easley ends with and walks back to his classroom. Silk picks her bag up off the floor and proceeds in his direction to leave out the front entrance of the building.

Outside Essance and Lilli are talking to a group of teens from their gym class. Essance notices the irritated look on Silk's face. She also notices the blood pouring down her twin's right forearm and dripping off of her finger. "Oh my god, what happened Silk," Essance burst out in concern. "Man that fat black bitch dat's what happened," Silk snaps. "Who Barrika," Lilli asks. "Yea," Silk mumbles in the affirmative. "Where dat hoe at we finna beat her fat ass," Essance hollers in fury looking around for Barrika. All the girls turn to the sound of loud laughter and spot Barrika's arm hanging out the window of a Chevy Blazer pointing up both of her middle fingers at the trio and sticking out her hot pink tongue. Lilli grabs a rock from the ground and lunges it at the truck completely missing her target. Feeling defeated by her bully yet again, Silk races off without another word to Essance or Lilli. The girls both call after Silk in an attempt to stop her but to no avail.

Chapter 4

Silk runs nonstop, crying the entire way to her safe haven. She gets to her usual spot on the bayou, drops her book bag on the grass, and kneels down at the edge of the river.

She scoops water with her hand using it to clean off the blood and dirt from her forearm. Silk is not paying attention as she cleans her injured arm. The swamps and bayous are home to various land and water creatures including alligators. Her blood dripping into the swamp water immediately attracts the cold-blooded predators. Lurking under the murky water are twelve hungry bloodthirsty gators all hawking down their vulnerable prey. Silk is so emotional and consumed with the task of cleaning off her arm that she doesn't have a clue of the imminent danger looming right before her. Her unawareness is costly and the gators have the element of surprise, but there are more eyes on her than the gators and Silk doesn't even know it. With more and more of Silk's blood dripping into the water making the gators hungrier and hungrier, they all at once make their move at an easy dinner. Out of the calm murky water a twelve and a half foot long, six hundred fifteen-pound monster lunges up in one instant with its massive powerful jaws wide open aiming straight for Silk's head. Caught completely by surprise, she jumps back in shock letting out a terrified scream as she falls to the ground. Silk doesn't have time to think but, in that instance, she knows it's over. Awaiting the massive impact of the killer's jaws to grab her body and tear her to pieces, Silk is trembling. Out of instinct her hands go up to shield her face as if that was going to protect her from the predator's powerful jaws and wild killer instinct. With her eyes closed anticipating to be eaten by now Silk feels water dripping on her hands and arms.

When she opens her eyes, she is shocked at what is before her. There, frozen in mid-air, a mere two inches above her, is the gator with its' mouth stretched out as wide as it can go. The river water is not moving anymore. Everything is frozen and about six more gators are half way out of the swamp frozen. Everything around Silk is frozen in time. Silk looks around frantically, frozen still herself. Hers' she knows is out of fear. "Get up chile!" a woman's voice orders from behind Silk. Startled by the voice, Silk flinches and turns around to see who it is. Standing about twenty feet away from Silk is an older looking black woman dressed in what appeared to be a bunch of different dresses made into one. The woman has both arms outstretched and fingers pointed at the swamp where the gators are still frozen in place. The woman is concentrating hard on the creatures and the swamp and words are coming out of her mouth but Silk cannot decipher what the woman is saying. "Get up girly!" the mysterious looking woman barked at Silk again urging her to move away from the edge of the swamp and the alligators. Snapping out of her trance, Silk fumbles as she rushes to grab her book bag from the ground and get up out of the way of the mouths of the horrifying predators. The woman nods her head to her right-side motioning for Silk to stand beside her. Feeling desperate, Silk complies, running wobbly-legged to where the unusual looking woman stood. At this moment the woman still has her hands pointing at the alligators that almost claimed young Silk's life, and all that she is pointing to is still motionless. Standing beside the woman now gives Silk a better listening opportunity but she still cannot make out what the woman is saying. "Oyea oyea oyea, uotay uotay uotay!" the woman repeats.

The woman is speaking in a foreign tongue and to Silk's knowledge the dialect and accent both sound markedly similar to the French language. Silk is very familiar with the language because she is in a French 2 class, however, she cannot seem to make out the words that this woman was saying. "Come down now and go home now creatures of the deep," the woman says while looking at all seven of the alligators. When she drops her hands, everything begins to move again . The gators that are still in the water fall back into the water causing a loud splash, and the one that had almost gotten to Silk falls hard on the grassland causing an enormous thud. Silk jumps back terrified as the ground underneath her feet shook momentarily from the impact of the large creature. The alligator's wide mouth almost made Silk piss on herself. Afraid that the killer was going to charge at her, Silk, out of adrenaline, grabs the mystery woman's arm and hides behind her using her as a human shield. "Ha ha ha ha, girly what ju tink ya doin now?" the woman says in humor to Silk. "It's gonna eat me!" Silk answers in a trembling voice. "No he ain't girly. You gone on home now Freddie and stop scaring the heck out of this poor chile. Go on now!" the woman pushes, waving her hands in urgency at the gator. Silk peaks around the woman's wide figure at the gator in pure astonishment as it closes its mouth, pivots its huge heavy body back towards the swamp, and obeys the woman's order to return to it. "There ya see now? Everyting is alright chile," the woman says to a surprised Silk. Silk is at a complete loss for words. She is in a mixture of fright, disbelief, and curiosity. Overall, she is glad that the threat of being eaten by hungry gators is now gone. "How did you... what was tha-" Silk begins. "Oh, don't chu worry bout nun of that honey. What's your name sweetness?" the lady counters. "Silk." Silk answers. "Well Silk, you are the most precious adorable little thing I've ever seen" the woman compliments. "Thank you, but, if you don't mind me asking, who are you and how did you...how did you do that?" Silk inquires curiously. "One ting at a time chile!" the woman replies with a joyful laugh. "My name is Beatrice Victoria Devaue, and this here is my land." Silk looks at the ground feeling both complex and confused. Although she wondered about it all of the time, she didn't know that this area of the bayou, her favorite area, was actually owned by any individual. Now this was brand new news to her. "Oh... ah.. .I'm-" Silk begins, trying to find the right words to say. "No need to feel sorry baby you're alright. I've seen you come down here for the past ten to fifteen years minding your own business and not hurting nothing or nobody so don't feel sorry chile," Beatrice reassures Silk. "Oh you know I've been coming down here?" Silk asks, surprised. "Ain't that what I just said chile?" Beatrice smiles sarcastically. "It's nice to finally meet you though Silk" Beatrice adds, staring deep into Silk's glassy eyes as if she's staring into the girl's soul. "Yea... um... I'm sorry, I didn't mean to be trespassing on your property Mrs. Devaue" Silk apologized respectfully. "Call me Mama B baby. And look, I just told ju don't feel sorry," Beatrice replies. "I'm just so thankful you are here because, if you hadn't been here and did what you did, I would be dead right now." Silk admits sincerely. "What was it that you did? What did you d-" Silk begins but Beatrice cuts in with, "So you really like it down here don't you Silk?" "Yes I do, I love it down here. I love nature and everything in it. I come down here and I pick flowers, I feed the bunnies and the wild hogs, I love watching how the goldfish swim at the swamp bed, I love watching the birds in the water and in the trees, I love how it smell, I love the sounds out here, I love the freedom and peace the animals have, and I love the peace and serenity that being out here brings me", Silk passionately reveals. Beatrice listens carefully and tentatively at every word spoken by Silk and can tell that all that she is saying is real.

Chapter 5

Silk and Beatrice talk for the rest of the evening about everything from Silk's childhood, family, her infatuation with the bayou, to her social life, her dreams and goals. Beatrice takes Silk back to her home, one of the abandoned shack-looking properties that Silk was always curious about, for some tea and a band aid. When they approach the front door of the residence, Silk is initially hesitant to enter, because the outside looks so unwelcoming and unkept that she can only imagine what the inside is like. Also, she is not trusting of the unusual mysterious woman whom she had only just met in the weirdest of circumstances. With Beatrice's urging, Silk steps through the threshold of the cottage and is completely flabbergasted at what she sees. The inside of the home is nothing like the outside, nor is it anything like what Silk may have imagined looking from the outside of it. The place is very spacious despite its small outside appearance. It is immaculately clean, fully furnished with up to date couches, love seat, glass coffee table, a sixty-two - inch LED flat screen television, and various ceramics, books, knick knacks, and arts and crafts. The house is filled with items that are neat and organized. "Wow!" Silk says in complete awe. "Come in and make yourself at home, Silk." Beatrice says, welcoming Silk into her house. Silk walks in and just can't stop looking around. "Would you like some lemon tea, Silk?" Beatrice asks generously. "Yes, mam." Silk answers. "Beatrice! Call me

Mama Bok baby? I ain't old enough to be no mam and I showl ain't nobody's wife. Not yet at least. Hahaha. Ok so that's what you call me, I don't too much care for all that proper etiquette crap people down here in the south try to drill into every chile's mind growing up. Ya understand me Silk?" Beatrice quips humorously. "Yes mam... I mean, Mama B. Yea, Mama B. I like that one" Silk says with a smile. "Then it's settled then. Be right back baby. Go ahead have a look around, just don't break nothing and if you take something I'll take you right back on down there and hand feed you to Freddy myself ya heardme?" Beatrice warns. "Yes, Mama B." Silk affirms nervously. Beatrice leaves Silk in the living room area of the house as she goes to the kitchen to prepare tea. Silk's eyes wonder at all of the marvelous intriguing ornaments, jewelry, and furniture. She stops at a built-in aquarium at the back comer of the room. Upon further inspection, Silk realizes that it's not an aquarium, that it sort of looks like a window for birds. The glass partition is warm when Silk touches it. The inside of the enclosure is designed for an animal, but Silk doesn't see one inside. Beatrice walks in with a silver tray that holds a tea kettle, two glass saucers, two tea cups, sliced lemons and a bowl of ginger snap cookies. "See something you like?" Beatrice interrupts Silk out of her daydream. "Huh? Oh... yea... um. What's this for? Do you have a parrot or something like that?" Silk asks. "Chile no!" Beatrice answers. "Mama B don't fool with no feathers and poopin, and I most definitely ain't got the patience for all that hootin and hollerin them thangs be makin! Shoot, damn thangs liable to drive me crazy round here mimicking me all the time after every dang ole word I say. Like, like, "Yeeep, Mama B Mama B! Polly do want a cracker! Yeeep! Yeeep!" Beatrice says, emphasizing her point with lots of excitement causing Silk to burst into laughter. "You are so funny Mama B! I guess you is right because at the pet store in the French Quarters them parrots and African greys and cockatiels, they do be loud as heck" Silk agreed. "Yea chile I ain't foolin wit cha.

Mama B can't take all that racket them creatures make" Beatrice adds to her dislike of birds. "So, then what lives in here then?" Silk asks. "lblis", Beatrice answers. "What is an lblis?" Silk questions curiously. "You lookin right at him. What you blind chile? Yas eyes don't work to well?" Beatrice spat in a joking tone. "Well apparently not I didn't see them big ole gators huddled up ready to rip me apart" Silk replies sarcastically. Beatrice laughs, sets the tray down on the glass coffee table and walks over to the glass cage next to Silk. "Let me show you chile" Beatrice says and then she pulls out a little gold flute and blew into it three times. Confusing to Silk, no sound came out of the flute although she just clearly saw Beatrice blow into it. "There he is. You see him Silk?" Beatrice announces and points to one of the small branches of the tree inside the cage. Silk follows Beatrice's finger and spots a red and black Bearded Dragon lizard resting on the small branch. Silk is amazed because she had carefully scanned the entire habitat before Beatrice had even reentered the room but did not see a lizard. "Wow! Oh my god! Where did it? How did u?" Silk stumbles out. "Get it out baby?" Beatrice says in a soothing voice. "It was hiding from me. How did you get it to come out?" Silk inquires curiously. "I got my ways of getting people and creatures to cooperate, honey." Beatrice answered mischievously. "Well yea, I see. Like how you told those gators to get on back in the water and they listened. That was so amazing Mama B. How do you do it? I want to learn!" Silk says joyfully. Beatrice does not respond, she just stares at Silk with a loving smile on her face as if mulling an idea over in her head. "Mama B?" Silk says to get Beatrice to respond. "Say what now chile?" Beatrice says, snapping out of her trance. "Can you teach me what it is that you do to get things, animals, to listen to you?" Silk asks frankly. "Well I don't know Silk baby I... " "Please Mama B please I want to know. I'm ready to learn to do what it is that you do!" Silk persists. Beatrice looks at Silk seriously and then turns to the other side of the glass cage, opens a hidden door on the side, and in a low hymn begins singing a melody in the same sort of foreign tongue Silk had hurt her speaking in by the swamp when she had the alligators and the river frozen. "Daile... Vulle... Daile ... Daile... Vooku Vulle... " Beatrice sings. This has Silk all the more intrigued and curious. At the sound of Beatrice's voice singing, the Bearded Dragon begins moving rapidly towards the opening where Beatrice now has her hand outstretched inside of the enclosure. Silk watches in sheer awe as the lizard rests calmly in the palm of Beatrice's hand. Silk's mouth opens wide at what happens next. The lizards skin begins to illuminate brightening the red and orange, its tongue is no longer moving, and its eyes are pitch black. Beatrice holds the lizard up in the air as if it is a trophy. Silk puts her hand out indicating that she wants to hold it, but Beatrice snatched back and stops singing. "What ju tink you're doing chile? Are you mad? Crosses!" Beatrice exclaims in a scolding manner. "No I just wanted to touch it that's all," Silk explains. "Not today baby. Won't be no touching my lord today!" Beatrice replies. "Your lord?" Silk repeats out loud, but more of a question to herself. Beatrice puts the lizard, which is now back to its normal skin and eye colors, back onto the same tree branch and closes the glass door. "I like my quietness, Silk, and that's all you need to know for right now. Now come over here and sit down have some tea." Beatrice tells Silk. Silk complies, but she has more questions for Beatrice.

Chapter 6

After being saved by Beatrice, officially meeting her, and then being invited to her home for tea and cookies, Silk has become very interested in learning all that she can from the lady. The two of them have a long informative talk that day over tea and ginger snaps. Silk learns some new things about Beatrice and her upbringings and vice versa. Before Silk leaves to go home, Beatrice invites Silk to come by and talk to her anytime when she decides it is her time to be down in the bayou. Silk joyfully accepts the invitation, and from that point on, she makes it her business to go and see Beatrice every day. Silk is so excited to finally get to meet someone with the same love and infatuation with wildlife and nature as she does. She has so many questions for Beatrice, that she has to write them down on sticky notes while in her classes so that she wouldn't forget anything. Every day for the next two to three weeks, Silk makes it her business to be at Beatrice's house after school and at any other open window of free time.

Beatrice takes a liking to Silk. She adores how beautiful, patient, understanding, and non-judgmental Silk is. More so than anything, she is amazed at how brave Silk has been since the first encounter the two had. In Beatrice's eyes, any normal person, let alone a teenage girl, who would've witnessed what Silk witnessed her do to the alligators at the swamp that day would have been petrified of her and would have ran out of the woods and never returned. But Silk, Silk was not afraid, and to Beatrice this was highly unusual. That unusual quality made Silk all the more appealing to Beatrice. Silk begins visiting more, and the two of them form a strong friendship. Throughout the weeks, the two of them discover that they have so many similarities, and that they both love the great outdoors and everything it has to offer. Learning about these same passions in Silk, Beatrice begins to mentor her, showing her all around the bayou, exploring deep and wide around the entire area of the woods. She teaches Silk more about the different animals that inhabit the woods and bayous, the history of the landscape and environment, and overall teaches her some ecology about the place she called home for over three decades.

On one of her many visits to the bayou, she arrives at Beatrice's home unannounced. She knocks at the front door, but does not get an answer. Just before she is about to turn to leave, the front door opens slightly. Silk nudges at it lightly, and the door opens for her. Realizing that she really shouldn't be entering anyone's home without their permission, she starts to turn away and leave until she hears voices. She thought that by getting no answer meant that Beatrice was not at home but obviously she was wrong. "Mama B" she calls out in her small voice, but no answer. She can still hear the sound of voices but no one is in the living room. She follows the sounds to the kitchen and stops. Silk's eyes bulge open wide when she sees Beatrice bent over on the kitchen table with her house gown hiked up, exposing her large curvaceous derriere, and a man is behind her going in and out of her with enormous power with each thrust. Black spirits are circling around the entire kitchen causing whistling noises and wind to blow Silk's curly hair to the back. Mama B and this unknown man to Silk are so into having sex in the kitchen that they don't even notice that they have an observer. "Oh! Yes! Oooh... aaaaw, Right there... right there my lord....yeas fuck me my lord... fuck this pussy...." Beatrice cries out in magnificent pleasure, back and neck both arched, nose pointing to the ceiling, and her eyes rolled so far in back of her head that all you see is the whites in them. The man is fully unclothed and is putting in work on Beatrice. Silk notices that his entire body is full of muscle, not a corner or pocket of fat anywhere. The man is grunting in pleasure with each stroke. He is pounding away at Beatrice, causing her voluptuous ass cheeks to clap. He is uttering something similar to what Silk heard Beatrice uttering the day that she froze the river and the gators, but again Silk has trouble making out what he is saying, although it sounds like he is speaking in French.

"Oukay... Oukay... Okay .... Booday ....booday... oukay!" the man repeats as he loses no momentum in sexing Beatrice. The more he repeats these words, the more powerful each stroke to Beatrice's backside becomes, and the louder she moans. Beatrice is clearly enjoying every bit of this rough sex the man is giving her, because she entices him for more. "Ooow yeas my lord... harder, harder my

powerful lord. . . oow yea just like that... right there my lord ooh!"
she carries on. In the middle of the kitchen, a large clay-looking pot
sits with steam coming out of it. The entire kitchen is steamy, sort
of smokey to a certain degree, which made it kind of hard for Silk
to see everything. However, she's seen something that she knows she
shouldn't have seen, so now she knows that it's time to leave. She
turns and dashes back towards the front door, feeling both guilty and
stupid for even entering Beatrice's home without permission in the
first place. Silk trips and falls over some object on the living room
floor which causes a loud crashing noise.

Scared shitless, Silk gets up quickly and high-tails it out of the
front door. Just before Silk's feet cross Beatrice's territorial
borderline, the dirt in front of her instantly turns into mud. Silk does
not notice in time, not that she would have had time to stop herself
even if she'd've noticed, and she slides uncontrollably into it. After
feeling slightly dizzy from the abrupt fall, Silk tries to move and get
up, but finds herself sinking feet and hands first. Soon, she notices
that every time she struggles to get out of the mud she sinks even
quicker. "Is this... quicksand? Oh my god this is quicksand! Oh my
god lord Christ please save me! Please don't let me die, I'm too young
to die today!" Silk cries out as her entire body becomes submerged
up to her neck in quicksand. "HELP! HELP ME!" she screams to
the top of her lungs, just as her chin taps the base of the quicksand.
Beatrice appears as if on cue, shouts out something in the foreign
language and Silk stops sinking. Beatrice walks up to where Silk is
now stuck with her head poking out of the ground and says, "Now
how in the world did you end up down there chile?" in a sarcastic
tone. "Please Mama B, I need you to get me up out of here please!"
Silk pleads. "Fuchedda, Fuchedde, Fonsir!" Beatrice repeats three
times while waving her hands in a full circle around the area that Silk
is stuck in, and in moments, Silk is pushed out of the ground and
the spot is hardened back to its normal state. "Come on here now

nosey chile," Beatrice orders Silk to follow her back to her estate with
an accusatory expression on her face. Silk follows Beatrice silently
brushing dirt and gooey mud off of herself.

Back at Beatrice's, she unclothes Silk, takes the dirty clothes,
hands her two fresh towels, a bar of homemade soap, and instructs
her to go into the bathroom and bathe herself thoroughly. Beatrice
puts Silk's muddy clothes into her washing machine and then goes
to her wardrobe closet and fetches a flower dress that Silk could
fit. She walks into the bathroom with the dress in hand for Silk to
change into. While Silk is washing, Beatrice says, "Don't chu ever
tell another lie to me again tnissy you hear me? "Yes mam, I mean
Mama B. Im so so sorry I was just... " Silk stumbles out. "You was
just caught being nosey, that's all. Why you sneaking around here
on people anyway? Being a nosey peeping Tom? Opening doors
that ain't yours? What have ya chile?" Beatrice scolds. Silk feels
embarrassed and just wants to go home and maybe come back
another day. She doesn't know how she will explain to Mama B why
she entered her home without permission. Choking at how to justify
her actions, and still feeling quite shaky because of the magic she had
just witnessed Beatrice perform with the quicksand. The spirits she
saw in the kitchen before running out of the home had her nerves
on ten. Beatrice walks Silk to the back of the house to her bedroom,
tells her to get dressed, and leaves the room allowing Silk her privacy,
leaving the door slightly cracked.

Chapter 7: Silk

I quickly dry my entire body, fix my hair into a neat bob, and put
on the dress Mama B laid out for me to change into. I have to admit,
for an older woman Mama B has some swag and style because this
dress is right. Now that I am dressed, I have to find Mama B so that I
can get the hell up out of here before my mama goes crazy about me
not being home. Besides, after all I just witnessed, I feel awkward as

hell being in this house now. Yes, it's most definitely time for me to leave. I peek my head out of the bedroom door and I see the hallway empty. I walk towards the living room to find Mama B when I hear her voice coming from the kitchen area. I follow her voice and stop against the wall to listen . I know I should've had enough of being so nosey by now but I cannot help myself, hell it's human nature, we are all some nosey homosapiens.

Beatrice: "So what are we going to do about this, Antonio?"

Antonio: "We? You mean what are 'You' going to do about your situation? I don't know that chile and I didn't bring her here, 'you' did... now since you started this mess you finish it."

Beatrice: "But she saw too much, Antonio. I can't harm her. She is so precious and so innocent, but I can't just let her leave here with those secrets in her memory." Beatrice says to the man she called Antonio.

When I hear that name, I ponder on it for a moment, then I run his face through the mental rolodex and then it hits me like a ton of bricks: Antonio; the tattoo shop owner from downtown New Orleans. I knew I had recognized him from somewhere, but it didn't dawn on me until Mama B just said his name. I didn't know that the two of them messed around though. Not that it's any of my business, but still, why are they so fearful about me knowing that they are screwing? Nobody cares. I know I sure don't. But what if it's something else? What if Antonio is married to someone else and Mama B is his mistress or just his little piece of ass on the side? Hmmm? I listen more to see if I can find the answer.

Beatrice: "I need your help with a solution, Antonio. What are we going to do?"

Antonio: "I tell you what we should do. Say we bury her out there in the swamp bed. Nobody will know where to find her because no one would think to look down here, because no one knows she comes down here if what you say about her is true? Besides, even if they do somehow find her someday, it wouldn't be very hard to assume that the heifer somehow fell into the river and got eaten alive by the gators."

Beatrice: "Are you out of your damn mind Antonio Bernard Devaue?" I hear Mama B shout followed by a hard smack.

Antonio: "Well, I don't see you coming up with any suggestions Ms. Victoria Devaue."

"Wait a minute... Did they just call each other by the same last name?" I say out loud to myself.

Beatrice: "I'll just put a forgetful spell on her... " Mama B begins and then pauses. "Silk! Get in here chile I see you round that wall. Come on around that corner."

Mama B calls out to me. "Shoot! Me and my big ole mouth", I say to myself as I round the corner and walk into the kitchen head low and feeling hopeless about what this outcome will be. All I know is I got to convince Mama B and this man not to hurt me. "Pick your chin up girl," Mama B says to me, and I do as I am told.

Silk: "Mama B I am so sorry for coming unannounced and walking into your home without your welcoming. And I am so sorry for what I saw, but I promise that if y'all let me go home and don't hurt me I will not tell a soul. I promise Mama B, I promise, please believe me!" I plead with solid sincerity.

Beatrice: "Chile, nobody gone lay a finger on you now hush up with that type of talk." Mama B assures me.

Antonio: "Shhiiet! Hell if I ain't!"

Beatrice: "Shut up damn fool! Like I said, ain't nobody gonna lay a finger on this poor chile" Mama B asserts in my defense.

Antonio: "Always the loving mother."

Beatrice: "Shut!" Mama B shouts in frustration clearly annoyed by Antonio's threats. "You know, if you were not my cousin, I would've skinned you alive a long, long time ago," Mama B says to Antonio.

I am now shocked to the core, but I dare not say anything.
I cannot believe what I just heard Mama B say. The man I just
witnessed her throwing that ass in a circle on, having porn star sex
with is her cousin. Wow, talk about crazy. But, then again, this is
the south, and down here in these parts, kissing cousins is not
uncommon. Not saying I agree that it is ok, I'm just saying because
of all the stories and folk tales I've heard growing up. Deep down in
the gulf, that's how a lot of people been getting down for years and
years, generation after generation. So now I've learned something
new about Mama B... Awkward to say the least, but still, I'm not
judging.

Silk: "Mama B, you got to trust me! I won't tell anybody. I put
that on my soul!" I plead some more.

In all honesty, I am telling the truth. Obviously, Mama B feels
the same, because she takes a deep breath and calmly says,

Beatrice: "I believe you sugar. And like I said, no one is going to
harm a hair on your little body ya hear me? Now come on here, your
clothes should be done drying. Yous needs to be getting home now.
Cherrin out walking after dark in these parts ain't too bright."

I nod my head in agreement and follow Mama B to the adjoining
room where her laundry area is. As we leave the kitchen, I glance
nervously at Antonio who is hawking me down with an unpleasant
mean mug on his grill. I instantly turn my head and look at the
ground, not wanting any type of confrontation with the huge scary
looking man. Mama B hands me my clothes and we head back to her
bedroom so that I can change again.

Beatrice: "You'd be wise not to tell a soul about what happened
today, Silky."

Silk: "I swear on it I won't tell nobody!" I declare pointing at my
heart for emphasis. Beatrice: "Good. Everything will be good."

I get dressed quickly and let Mama B know how ready I am to go.
She ushers me out of her room and to the front door. As I reach for

the door knob, Mama B's hands clasps around mine tightly. Staring me hard in my eyes, almost causing me to piss myself, she says,

Beatrice: "Only warning chile. Don't ju tell a soul lest you surely die!"

Her last words come out with so much confidence and conviction that I feel condemned in a tomb. I swallow spit hard and nod my head.

Beatrice: "Alright Silky, get on home now and don't make no stops ya hear? And remember. .. not a soul!" She says, too calm for my nerves, and puts a finger up to her full lips, emphasizing for me to keep quiet.

She doesn't have to worry about that, Silk's lips are sealed shut like a mummy. Quivering, I walk out into the warm night air and jet home. I am so anxious to get home and so happy to have made it out of this situation untouched tonight. God must really be looking out for me.

Chapter 8: Silk

I make it home way later than usual, so I know that I am in deep crap. My dinner plate is sitting cold on the kitchen counter, my three sisters Roberta, Essance, and Zayonna are done eating and are preparing for bed already. I don't know where daddy is, but I'm glad he doesn't see me coming in this late. "Where is mommy at though?" I must've spoken her up, because as I stuff a cold chicken leg in my mouth, here she comes around the comer. "Well how nice of you to come home in time for dinner, Silk. I break my back in the damn kitchen for an hour to make sure my babies get their proper nutrition and don't go to bed hungry, and you don't even show up to enjoy it with the family or tell me thank you or nothing," she scolds me. What am I to say to combat that? I feel so bad now. I know how passionate my mommy is about her cooking. Yes, I still call her mommy. Lol.

Silk: "I'm sorry mommy but I-"

Lashunda: "Where have you been Silk? And what happened to your arm? I know you ain't call ya-self running round here with some young boy now tryna act like you grown now?" she scolds, throwing questions at me a hundred miles an hour.

I don't even have an opportunity, and I know better than to interrupt her while she's talking so I just sit calmly and patiently for her to let all of her frustrations and anger out on me and then she will let me go to bed. I am used to this. Mommy stays on me and my siblings' backs while daddy will let us get away with murder because to him we are all pure as angels. After about a minute or two more of her ranting, mommy finally gives me a chance to answer, but I don't know what to say. I'm sitting here like a deer in headlights with my mouth open but no words come out.

DeAngelo: "What's all this noise about Shunda baby?" my daddy says to mommy as he enters the kitchen.

Whoooh I am saved by the bell. Thank ya Lord, daddy is here to save the day. I shut my mouth again and put on my innocent puppy-dog face that gets daddy every time.

Lashunda: "Hey baby. Naw Silk just now waltzing in here and I'm getting to the bottom of this mess. Ain't called, texted, or did nothing." My mommy goes on for a minute venting out her concerns to daddy.

Initially he looks pissed at what mommy tells him, but his entire demeanor changes when he looks at me.

DeAngelo: "Silk baby next time, call before you decide not to come straight home after school ok baby?" Daddy says.

Silk: "Yes, daddy." I answer sincerely. Mommy knows all too well what I am doing and she cuts in.

Lashunda: "Uh uh, look at her arm and legs, scratches and bruises and whatnot. Now where she get those from!" She points to my injuries from my earlier fall.

DeAngelo: "Let me see, hold ya arm up baby" Daddy says to me with a concerned expression on his face.

I start to feel nervous and I look at my Mommy and she can feel it in me. Daddy asks me how I got the bruise on my arm and I feel so weak. I cannot lie to this man. He will surely spot my lie lest I try to. I don't know how my daddy does that shit. It's like he can see right through me.

Silk: "These are weeks old daddy , Barrika-"

DeAngelo: "So why you getting in so late tonight baby? Where you been?"

The truth about what happened today threatens to spill off of my lips. I can feel it coming.

Silk: "Daddy I":..., but as soon as I begin to respond I'm suddenly interrupted.

"Aaaaahhhh!!!" We hear Zay Zay's piercing scream coming from her bedroom and race to see what's going on. I get in the doorway of my baby sister's room.

Lashunda: "Baby what's wrong?" mommy says.

Zay Zay is up on her bed and is still screaming at the top of her little lungs. She looks terrified and continues screaming as me, mommy, and daddy all call her name. Still screaming, Zay Zay points towards the corner by the window. When we all look down and see what she's pointing at, my heart drops. There in the corner is Beatrice's pet lizard, Iblis. Mommy jumps back and nearly falls, but the wall in the hallway catches her. She and Zay Zay are scared to death of every kind of insect, rodent, and anything that crawls.

DeAngelo: "What the hell...Lord Jesus", my daddy yells as he raises his right foot and takes off his size thirteen steel toed work boots.

Zayonna: "Dadday, dadday help please, kill it dadday, kill it dadday!" poor Zay Zay screams out helplessly, tears running down her puffy frightened little face.

DeAngelo: "Hold on baby, Daddy got it, hold up!" Daddy yells as he finally gets his big boot off of his foot.

Silk: "Daddy no wait!" I try to yell over mommy and Zay Zay's screams but daddy doesn't hear me.

DeAngelo: "I rebuke you Satan in the name of beloved Jesus!" Daddy announces as he readies the boot in the air to smash the little lizard.

Zayonna: "Get em dadday get em please!" Zay Zay cries out some more, giving daddy even more momentum.

I doubt I can stop this because daddy can't hear a word I'm trying to say due to all of the hootin and hollering him, mommy, and Zay Zay are doing, so before daddy can smash him I run to the corner and grab the lizard from off of the floor. Daddy stops in his tracks as I cradle the critter, however, I can still see it in his eyes that he wants to kill it.

Silk: "Don't kill him daddy, look I got 'em alright?" I say calmly.

Zay Zay calms down a little bit but she's still crying and appears very afraid.

Silk: "It's ok Zay Zay. It ain't gonna hurt you baby, sissy got em!" I say in a soft voice trying to coo my baby sister.

Zayonna: "No sissy, it's not good. I a'scared!" baby Zay Zay replies through sniffles. Deangelo: "Baby put that nasty thing down so I can kill it!" Daddy orders.

Silk: "Kill it? Why daddy, it's harmless." I rebut.

Zayonna: "No, it tries to eats me when I fall asleep. Kill it dadday!" Zay Zay urges.

Silk: "It ain't gonna eat you baby Zay Zay. Look how little he is." I say to my baby sister.

Zayonna: "No. It gon try eat me." Zay Zay responds, pointing accusingly at the lizard in my hands.

Silk: "No he won't I promise he won't. He nice lizard, see?" I reply.

I make the mistake of raising my hands with the lizard in it in the air so that Zay Zay can see it's harmless, but what in the heck did I do that for. Zay Zay is immediately startled and goes berserk, screaming so high and loud that I thought the bedroom windows would break, and she jumps back on her bed hitting her head on the wall.

Lashunda: "Silk! Get that nasty ass thing out of my house right now and stop scaring my baby!" my mommy yells at me desperately.

She has not moved from her position in the hallway with her back glued against the wall. Low key, I can see it in her eyes that she is just as afraid, if not more afraid, of the lizard than baby Zay Zay. Funny, this strong strict black woman is afraid of something so small and harmless. I laugh about it on the inside but I dare not crack a smile. Instead, I hurry running out of Zay Zay's bedroom with the lizard safe in my hands. As I run down the hallway to me and my twin's bedroom, I brush pass my older sister Roberta and my twin Essence. The two look at me both in bewilderment and surprise and they both ask what's going on, simultaneously. I do not answer. I keep it moving, getting the lizard as far away from mommy, Zay Zay, and especially away from daddy. I go into me and my twin's room and shut the door behind me. Underneath my bed, I find a plastic container I got from my fifth grade science teacher and put the lizard inside it. The container which I kept was originally used for our class project where we got to care for caterpillars and watch them go through the stages of metamorphosis and become monarch butterflies. I don't have to worry about the little guy not being able to breathe because there are dozens of air holes in the top of the container.

Once I have the lizard situated and safe, I undress and slip into my silk pajama outfit. I lay in my bed holding the container up, marveling at the beautiful bearded dragon. "You are a cool looking dragon, you know that? Bet you can't blow fire out of that mouth of yours?" I chuckle as I say to the lizard in the container as if it could talk back. My daddy comes through and opens the door. He stops and looks back and forth at me then the container skeptically for a minute. Then he walks in, shutting the door lightly behind him and says,

DeAngelo: "Sugabear, what did your mother tell you to do? To get that reptile out of this house, not take it in your room and make it a pet. You don't know where that nasty thang done been."

Silk: "But daddy it's not nasty. And it's so cool, come here look at it!" I say, sitting up with the container in my lap motioning for daddy to sit next to me. He sits and looks down at the lizard.

DeAngelo: "Do you know what it is?"

Silk: "Yea, it's a red bearded dragon lizard. Look, you can tell cus he got a beard just like Papa!" I reply, causing daddy to laugh.

What he does next surprises the heck out of me. Daddy opens the lid to the container, reaches in, and picks up the lizard. I ain't gonna lie, my heart is beating like a kick drum is in my chest right now, because I don't know what daddy's intentions are. What if he still wants to kill it? If he does, I can't stop him now because he has the lizard in his hands. But he doesn't do anything to harm it. He holds it up and examines the lizard's whole body in amusement.

DeAngelo: "Yea, you right Sugabear. It is kind of cool. I like the patterns of red, orange, yellow, and green it has." Daddy opines.

Silk: "Really? Cool? Wow daddy didn't know you liked animals like that." I respond sounding a little confused, which I am at this moment.

DeAngelo: "Where do you think you get it from Sugabear?" Daddy replies.

Silk: "Huh?" I add.

DeAngelo: "I don't hate animals, that's your momma. She is terrified of anything that runs, waddles, leaps, crawls, swims, or flies, you name it, she scared of it." I laugh. "Not me. I always loved animals err since a youngin. I used to be just like you baby." Daddy explains.

Silk: "Wow daddy. I never knew that. Does mommy know?" I ask.

DeAngelo: "Of course Sugarbear. But out of my true love for her I don't tarry into that side of me. But yea, I like him though, he very extraordinary." Daddy remarks about the lizard.

Silk: "So what chu sayin daddy, I can keep em?" I ask at the right time. Or so I believe.

DeAngelo: "No Suga. That's not what I'm sayin at all." Daddy declares.

Silk: "But daddy you said yourself that he is cool and that you like him. I never had any pets befo and you know how bad I been wanting one. Please dadday!" I beg using my purposeful little charm voice and my puppy dog eyes which gets daddy every time.

With a pressured expression on his face, daddy begins,

DeAngelo: "Look Sugabear. Now I know what I said, and you know I love you more than anything, but what your mother says goes and she won't go for it."

Silk: "But daddy can't you talk to mommy?" I plead desperately.

DeAngelo: "I'll see what I can do, but don't count on getting a yes. Not about this one." Daddy answers in an unconfident tone.

As the words leave his lips the bedroom door swings open and there mommy is holding Zay Zay in her arms.

Lashunda: "The answer is no and you know it is Silk! And what did I tell you, D!?" Mommy grills and turning her attention to daddy she says, "D! What are you doing? I told her to get that thing out of here!"

DeAngelo: "I know baby, I was just telling Sugabear that-" daddy begins but mommy cuts him off.

Lashunda: "But nothing, D! Why are you holding that nasty thing in your hands then if you told her what I said then huh?" Daddy looks down at his hands dumbfoundedly, I guess forgetting he had the lizard in his hands still. Instantly he puts the lizard back in the container and I put the lid back on top.

DeAngelo: "Look baby, it's late. I told Sugabear she gotta get rid of the thing. Right Suga?" Daddy looks to me for confirmation. I affirm him and he continues.

DeAngelo: "She will take care of it in the morning first thing. For now, let's go to bed alright?" Daddy ends.

He gets up, kisses me on my forehead and heads toward the door where mommy is still standing holding Zay Zay. He reaches out to put his arm around mommy but she instantly jerks out of his way to avoid any physical contact.

Zayonna: "Eww. Eww dadday, you hands icky, no touch us no touch us!" Zay Zay yells at daddy in an authoritative tone.

We all can't help but laugh at how cute Zay Zay is when she call herself getting serious. I love my baby sister, she is too funny.

Lashunda: "Like she said. Go wash yo filthy hands now before you touch anything, and I'm not playing!" Mommy demands daddy.

Daddy doesn't say anything in his defense he just walks out speechless, which I find super funny, seeing as though daddy is as dominant and bold as a leader of the Taliban in Afghanistan.

However, mommy is just as strict, so I guess they'd make great leaders. He toys with her, though, and leans in and steals a kiss on her neck, but also receives a smack to the ear from baby Zay Zay.

Zayonna: "Gon! Get back! No touch us Dadday you nathy" Zay Zay yells some more.

DeAngelo: "What? What chu say to me lil pumpkin cheeks? Huh, what chu say?" Daddy responds playfully to Zay Zay acting as if he's gonna touch her with his hands, but mommy moves further back into the hallway so he can't.

Zayonna: "No touchy Dadday! You icky you touched da monster! Go watch you hands!" Zay Zay orders daddy again.

Lashunda: "That's right, tell him again, pumpkin!" Mommy encourages.

Zayonna: "Go watch yo hands dadday you icky!" Zay Zay repeats.

Lashunda: "Go wash your hands with your nasty animal loving butt. And you too Silk, wash them disgusting hands of yours after touching that thing, and I want it out of here in the morning do you understand me?" Mommy demands, full of power and authority.

Silk: "Yes, mam." I answer. As they all disappear down the hallway my twin comes in our room already in her pjs and looks at me and the lizard all weirded out.

Silk: "What chu lookin at heifer!" I say breaking the silent stare off.

Essance: "How you just gone put that thing in there and you don't know where it's been? It could be carrying infections, diseases, whatever, and you just got it all on your bed, touching on it and whatnot," She complains, with her face twisted up in a look of pure disgust.

Silk: "Look trick, mind ya own bizness ok?" I say in response.

Initially, Essance says nothing. She rolls her eyes and climbs into her bed opposite of mine. Then she says,

Essance: "Like mommy said, bitch, wash yo nasty ass hands before you get to touching anything around here bitch, ok?"

Silk: "Shut the fuck up hoe I know." I say in defense.

Essance: "Yea aight, you better, bitch!", she replies before lying down to go to bed.

I begin talking to the dragon in the container letting him know that he will be alright and that I am going to return him safely to where he came from. I ended by calling him handsome. I feel eyes on me, so I look up and there Roberta is in the doorway staring hard at me with a sly grin etched on her face. "What?" I ask, feeling kind of embarrassed.

Roberta: "You in here talking to that thing now. Really, bitch? You a Dr. Doolittle child or something?" She says and begins laughing.

Silk: "Shut up Berta." I shoot back as she leaves down the hallway talking to someone on her cell phone.

I get up and wash my hands like mommy told me to do. I lay back down in my bed and marvel again at the lizard in the container on my nightstand. Despite how bizarre tonight's happenings seem to me, I can't help but to be glad that the lizard was spotted when it was by Zay Zay, and glad that her screams got all of my parent's attention off of me the way it did. "Woo! You are a lifesaver, you know that?" I say out loud looking at the lizard once more before closing my tired eyes and falling asleep.

Chapter 9: Silk

The next day I wake up at 6:30 a.m. like any normal school day, despite how little sleep I got last night after coming in late and then the whole fiasco with the lizard scaring the bugeebeez out of mommy and Zay Zay. Not to mention I couldn't sleep much thinking about all the weird shit that had happened to me yesterday at Mama B's place. I'm not gonna lie, Mama B is cool peeps and all, she's my heart, but her and her cousin creep the hell out of me. I ain't lying to ya.

So I wake up, wake my twin up, who does not hear her alarm clock buzzing because she is dead to the world. Let me tell you this girl knows she can sleep her butt off woe ya heard me. Anyway, I shake her until she's awake and then I make my way to the bathroom to get myself straight for the day. After I shower and put my clothes on, I notice that both of my parents' presence is missing. Zay Zay is gone too. 'Hmm, must've had to get up outta here early' I think to myself.

So, instead of me doing what my mommy told me to do last night 'first thing in the morning', which is get rid of the lizard, I take it out of the container and put it in my little gold fanny pack that daddy bought me for Christmas. I just hope this lizard don't poop in here though, cus' I love my fanny.

The school day flies by, and before you know it, everyone is leaving the school. I tell my twin and Lilli that I will catch up to them later and I proceed to Mama B's place so I can return her pet lizard to her. At lunch time I got a bag of carrots and some lettuce out of the salad bar to see if the lizard would eat, but I guess he ain't no vegetarian because he ain't budge. I knock on the door to Mama B's place, she opens the door with a warm welcoming smile and lets me in. I sit down on the couch trying to act all normal and nonchalant. I want to surprise Mama B with what I have to return to her, but I don't know how much longer I can hold it in. Mama B asks me how my day went today and I tell her all went well. Then I bust out and tell her, "I got a surprise for you. Look at who I found snooping around my house last night?" I reach into my fanny, grab the lizard and hand it to her. I wait on some type of surprise or excitement to appear on Mama B's face, but it never comes. I sit feeling flabbergasted at how Mama B starts kissing on the lizard and cooing it like it's a human baby. What really blows my mind is when she calls the lizard by the name, "Iblis." I say nothing for the moment, I just sit and watch. "Dang this woman really loves her bearded dragon lizards. And I thought I was crazy about animals. Shoot, I can't touch this woman. Mama B takes the cake!" I say inside my head. Mama B then gets up and opens the glass partition towards the back of the living room and gently places the lizard into the habitat.

Then she turns around and thanks me for returning her 'baby' to her and claims to had been searching all night for it. I don't find this last statement too convincing, because she said it in such a nonchalant way and in kind of a mumble, so it sounds like a fib to me.

Silk: "Oh yea, no problem Mama B. I kind of figured you would be looking for him and would want him back. But what I'm still trying to figure out is how on earth did he even get to my place?" I ask curiously.

Beatrice: "Not a clue my dear." Mama B answers with a pondering sort of gaze on her face. "But tank you sweetness for keeping me darling safe and for the safe return."

Silk: "Oh no problem Mama B. Yea, he just scared the crap out of my folks last night that's all."

Beatrice: "Oh really?"

Silk: "Yea my baby sister Zay Zay and my mommy."

Beatrice: "Ohhh. Poor little darling! I'm deeply sorry for that, sweetness!" she says sympathetically.

Silk: "It's alright. It was no harm done to anybody, just a scare that's all."

Beatrice: "Well good. I'm glad to hear that my dear. But you remember the promise you made last night about keeping quiet 'bout what went on here now don't cha dear? You ain't go off and run ya lil trap to ya folks now did ya?" she asks me sternly.

Silk: "Yes I remember Mama B, and like I told y'all last night my lips are sealed. I have not and I will not tell a soul." I answer her sincerely.

Mama B makes us some tea and we begin having a normal girl chat. Well, I wouldn't say a 'normal' girl chat, because I don't think normal girls would understand, let alone be interested at all in the conversations that me and Mama B have. My curiosity gets the best of me and I ask her why she stays so close to the swamps, why is her place like a sanctuary for amphibians, and most importantly, I want to know about the magic that I'd seen her do on the two separate occasions. I ask her about what she and her cousin Antonio were doing in the kitchen yesterday, with the big pot of whatever that was cooking in the center of the kitchen; the spirits or ghosts, or whatever they were, that were soaring all over the house; and the language that the two of them speak whenever those type of magical things are happening. Mama B stares into my soul long and hard for a few minutes before responding to my questions. I feel the nervous sweat forming on my brow as I wait for her to stop sizing me up and give me an answer.

Finally, after five anxious minutes, Mama B opens up and lets me know that she trusts me with her secrets and will tell me all I would like to know. She begins with giving me a brief rundown of her family history. Come to find out her mother was a Haitian immigrant and her father migrated from French Guyana to New Orleans in August of 1875. Her father was a voodoo priest and her mother was a voodoo Queen back home in Haiti. The two met in Biloxi, Mississippi when they were still teens and eventually settled down here in the N.O. and had her along with her two younger brothers, one of which had passed away due to a poisonous snake bite. Antonio's mother, Mama B's mother's sister, was also a voodoo priestess, but she never came to the United States. She then begins telling me all about the history of voodoo and where it originated from back in Africa centuries ago and how that was the religion of majority of the African tribes before 1776. Mama B goes into grave details about the core principles of voodoo and sorcery and witchcraft, which raise the small hairs on the back of my neck. Now ya average teenage black girl would be scared shitless right about now, running out of this woman's house getting as far as hell away from Mama B as possible, but see now, I ain't cha average teenage black girl, ya heard me! I find these stories interesting and I am intrigued to be discovering the history and traditions of my African ancestors before they were kidnapped and transported to America to be forced into slavery to the Europeans.

After talking, well I was mostly listening and asking questions about certain things she was telling me, but after discussing voodoo, witchcraft, and sorcery for three long hours, I let Mama B know that I am fascinated by what she has taught me and that I am eager to learn more. My heart is telling me that I should stay away from this and never come back, but my mind is telling me to learn what Mama B knows and start practicing voodoo myself and become a voodoo Queen like her and her mother. I can't help but wonder if I did excel to the level of becoming a voodoo queen, would I be the first in my bloodline to be a queen? Hmm, probably not seeing how far back this stuff goes. Mama B obliges my request and agrees to be my voodoo teacher.

She pulls out a book and teaches me the basic language of voodoo and magic. I learn a quick spell that she explains is used to keep any negative energy away from me and to be more prosperous in my everyday endeavors. I know my parents will kill me if they were to ever find out what I am over here learning. Since I was a child, they've tried to push Christianity on me and my siblings by forcing us to read scriptures out of the Bible every night and making us dress up and go to church faithfully every Sunday, Wednesday night Bible Study, Friday night prayer groups, and Easter Sundays. This is a secret that I will make sure never reaches them for sure.

Chapter 10

Silk's visits to Beatrice's become more and more frequent, and longer durations. She shows up every evening after school and stays till it gets dark outside, on weekends, designated family days, and even skips out on going to church a couple Sundays which has both of her parents hot at her. Zela, Beatrice's closest neighbor who also resides in the swamp, and also a voodoo queen, notices Silk's frequent visits to Beatrice's. So she stops her one day to expose her knowledge of Silk's secrets, and forewarns her to stay away from

Beatrice, lest trouble seize her from all around. Silk is frightened by the warning, but more so at how creepy this old lady looks. She calls Beatrice an evil witch but her appearance was more evil looking, Silk thought. With a nervous thank you, Silk trails off, fast pacing to get to Beatrice's estate. When she reaches her destination, she is let in warmly as usual, and begins to inform Beatrice about the encounter with Zela and about the warning she'd given her to stay away from her and her cousin Antonio lest she have great troubles. Beatrice throws back the insults at Zela, referring to her as 'The Bird Lady', calling her nuts, and reversing the warning back on Zela. Hearing the name The Bird Lady shocked Silk, because growing up, she and her sisters and neighborhood friends had all heard many tales about the mysterious 'Bird Lady' who stayed in the swamp and used to kidnap and kill young boy children then turn them into stuffed dolls that decorated her house. When she was young, Silk and her playmates actually believed this tale, but it still never deterred Silk from going down to the bayou to enjoy nature. She figured that she was lucky to be a girl because then that meant she was not a target for the Bird Lady, since the legend had it she snatched young boys to make into dolls. Still, no other little girl would ever dare go anywhere near the wilderness that led to the swamps and bayous, only Silk.

The next day, Silk arrives for her voodoo lessons. She knocks on the front door and on the fourth knock the door props open. "Mama B, I'm here!" Silk announces as she walks through the threshold and into the house shutting the door behind her. She gets no response, so she calls out for Beatrice some more, but still no response. She sits her book bag on the couch and makes her way to the kitchen then to the back room to find Beatrice and still comes up empty. Silk figures Beatrice maybe went into town to grab some things from the market to cook tonight for their lessons. She decides she'll just sit and wait for Beatrice to return. She opens Iblis's cage and picks him up. After holding him and petting him for a few minutes then returns the dragon to its tree branch and closes the partition. Next, she picks out one of the love spell books that she spots on Beatrice's massive bookshelf, thinking of a spell to use on Lorenzo, the star quarterback for her highschool's football team, and also her boy crush. She closes her eyes and fantasizes about the two of them hugging, kissing, and making love for the first time, losing her virginity. These lustful thoughts cause her to sweat, her nipples harden in her bra, and her panties get soaked. Thinking about Lorenzo, Silk is hot and horny.

Antonio arrives at his cousin's home, walks in and creeps up behind Silk, startling her out of her lustful daydreaming. He asks Silk what is she doing there while Beatrice is gone. He observes the spell book that Silk is still holding in her hands and falsely accuses her of attempting to burglarize and steal from his cousin. Silk immediately denies his accusation and tries to explain her presence for being there in the house and that she was just waiting on Beatrice to return.

Before Silk can finish with her explanation, Antonio grabs her by the wrist. Silk protests and tries to make a run for it, but he tackles her down to the floor, pins her down on her back with both of her hands above her head, straddles her, rips her skirt away, and cups her breast through her shirt with his free hand. Silk is horrified because she knows this man is going to attempt to rape her there on the floor. She is so afraid of the big man she can't even scream so she tries to fight him off but it is useless because he is so powerful. For some reason she cannot speak, she is powerless, and Antonio is mumbling some sort of chant or spell inaudibly. He sticks his finger into Silk's pocket book and licks her juices from fantasizing about Lorenzo off of it. He then swipes his pants down and flicks his manhood against her pelvis. Silk braces herself for the dreadful act that is about to be done to her. He inserts his manhood into her and begins to take her innocence and her virginity. Silk lies on the floor defenseless, bleeding profusely, and begging him to stop, but he ignores her pleas and continues thrusting himself inside of her even harder as if enjoying her innocent cries. Silk eventually passes out from the pain, the heat, and exhaustion from rustling trying to fight him off. Her body can't take anymore and goes into shock.

Chapter 11

Silk wakes up lying on Beatrice's couch with a cold rag on her forehead, a thick blanket covering her now naked body. She looks around and spots her ripped skirt and soaked blouse sitting in a dining room chair. Beatrice walks in with presumably some tea in a tea cup. She gives the cup to Silk and asks her if she is alright. "Where is Antonio?" Silk whispers with an apprehensive expression. Suddenly he appears from the bathroom with a damp blood-stained towel over his shoulder, mean-mugging Silk. Beatrice frowns at him and he leaves the room chuckling. Silk begins speaking to Beatrice frantically, explaining that Antonio had just raped her but Beatrice, to her surprise, shuts her down which shocks Silk to her core.

Beatrice tries to convince Silk that what Antonio did to her was a part of a voodoo ritual called, "sex magic", proven one of the most effective ways to raise the power required to perform magic, which she explained was exactly what they were doing the day that Silk caught the two of them making love in her kitchen. Beatrice tells Silk to forget about what happened and just accept what she told her. Silk argues that it wasn't right for Antonio to do what he did to her because she did not want to do it, nor did she want to be forced to lose her virginity to him.

Annoyed at Silk and not wanting to hear any more of it, Beatrice starts insulting Silk, calling her a whore and accusing her of trying to purposely entice and seduce men by her attire and referring to her as 'hot pussy.' Silk gets angry in return and starts cursing Beatrice out.

Beatrice shuts her up with a spell and then tells her to leave. Silk puts on her clothes and leaves only after Beatrice reminds her again to remain silent. This time her threat weighs heavier on Silk's heart and she leaves without another word. For safe measures, Beatrice places a spell on Silk to ensure that she returns to her within 24-hours.

Chapter 12: Silk

I rush home crying and soak myself in the bathtub. I feel sick and cannot eat. I wash myself thoroughly and go to sleep ignoring everyone's attempts to interact with me. I tell myself that I am never going back to Mama B's house again and contemplate on whether I should tell my parents about me being violated tonight. I can't do that though, because knowing daddy he will blow a gasket. Mommy will lose it too and call the police immediately. There will be a manhunt for Antonio's ass all over N.O. and everything will be put on front-street, and I do mean everything. I cannot risk people finding out that I have been friends with Mama B the voodoo Queen, or that I have been learning to practice myself or I am dead too. As I think I've mustered up the strength to go and tell mommy what just happened to me, Mama B's voice rings through my head, her threats sending chills down my spine, causing the hairs on the back of my neck to raise. No. I know I can't tell anybody. I just have to deal with this shit on my own. I will get Antonio back. I will make him pay for violating me. But how? Frustrated by not being able to think of a way to get revenge on him, I fall asleep soaking my pillow with tears of rage and frustration.

Chapter 13

Silk's frustration stays with her the next day in school. She is highly irritable, talking crazy to people including her teachers and other staff members, something that is so out of character for Silk. She even gets overly aggressive with her bestie Lilli, who she is always nice to. Lilli tries to see what's bothering Silk but she gets dismissed. When Silk and Lorenzo cross paths, he smiles and says "hi", but she can't even speak, she takes off running to the girls' restroom in tears. Lilli follows her best friend to the restroom after sensing something very weird about Silk's demeanor today. Again, Lilli tries to see what's going on with Silk and tries to comfort her, but again Silk is very dismissive towards her, blaming her unusual attitude on her monthly menstrual cycle.Lilli is not persuaded by Silk's explanation and knows something isn't adding up so she tells herself that she will keep a close eye on her friend.

At lunchtime, Silk and Essance wind up both fighting Barrika in the cafeteria after Barrika attempts to steal Silk's seat at a table, and her bottle of apple juice, and for snatching Essence's gummy worms out of her hands, causing the bag to rip and the candy to go flying, spilling on the cafeteria floor. The two sisters both go in rage swinging wildly at the big bully, backing her into a cement pillar in the dining hall. Spectators spectate in awe of how the twins put the works on Barrika whom many feared in the school for her aggression and viciousness. One-on-one neither Silk nor Essance were any match for the huge powerful teen who is bigger than the two sisters combined, but fighting together the twins are highly effective in taking her down. Silk is normally the one fighting Barrika alone and every time taking a beating. Today, with the help of her twin, she gains a victory underneath her belt. However, she still gets a fresh shiner underneath her right eye which is highly visible on her light caramel skin. She is pissed but she brushes it off, satisfied with finally getting the best of Barrika; about leaving the bully with a bloody lip and a couple mountains on her forehead.

Silk, Essance, and Lilli all leave the school together heading home for the day when out of nowhere an angry vengeful Barrika comes storming out of a Chevy Blazer followed by two teenage boys. The angry group rapidly approach the girls and immediately commence beating them like they stole something. Felix and a few of his comrades, including Lorenzo, all witness the vicious attack on Silk, Essance, and Lilli and jump in helping them fight Barrika and the two dudes. Both Felix, Lorenzo, and their friends all land several punishing punches to the two dudes who had punched Silk and Essance in their faces, causing one of the boys to fall to the ground and fold and the other to duck and flee like a coward yelling for his comrades to follow, which they do. After helping fight their attackers off, Felix and Lorenzo simultaneously offer the three girls rides home safely. Seeing that the girls grew up with Felix and knew him most of their young lives, Essance and Lilli agree to let him drive them home. They didn't know Lorenzo very well being that he was new to New Orleans and to their school. They felt safer riding with Felix because they knew he was more hood and savage, but Silk of course wants to ride with her boycrush. With a shy, puzzled look on her face Silk looks at her group of friends then back at Lorenzo and then accepts Lorenzo's offer for a ride. Essance and Lilli both giggle at Silk's dilemma, the two of them already knowing the feelings going through Silk's mental. Silk apologizes to a disappointed-looking Felix as her and Lorenzo strode off to his two-door 1999 Chevy Tahoe. Essance and Lilli both wave good-bye to Lorenzo and the rest of the gang after thanking them all for helping them fight Barrika's crew off, and with mischievous grins on their faces, they both let Silk know that they'd see her in a bit.

During the short ride home, Silk and Lorenzo talk the entire way, getting to know each other more personally. When they arrive at Silk's residence, Essance, Lilli, and Felix are already standing waiting on the walk-way. As she exits Lorenzo's truck, he offers to give her rides to and from school every day. Silk smiles meekly and accepts his offer. She blows him a kiss before shutting the door and walking up to her house. As soon as Silk gets within arms' reach, Essance and Lilli bombard her with one hundred and one questions about what her and Lorenzo talked about: Did he say that he was attracted to her? Did she tell him that she was crushing on him? Does he want to go out with her, and so on and so on. Without answering, Silk simply smiles with a look on her face which lets the girls know that she was concealing what they knew was the true answer, and that everything had worked out perfectly on the little ride. The girls all giggle and continue having girl-talk. Meanwhile, Felix is off to the side with a jealous scowl on his face, clearly annoyed at the fact that all the girls want to talk about is Lorenzo, worst -—Silk and Lorenzo. Fed up with them not getting his hints when he tries to interject and change the subject, Felix tells the girls he'll see them later and storms off in frustration. Essance and Lilli are too into their conversation about Silk and Lorenzo that they don't hear Felix tell them he is leaving. Silk breaks out of the conversation to acknowledge Felix and tell him bye and she'll see him later, but he just storms off to his car mumbling profanities. He gets in his car, slams the door, and skirts off, leaving the smell of burnt rubber and a trail of gray smoke from his screeching tires. All three girls now look at Felix's car as it speeds away loudly.

"What the hell is wrong with him?" Essance says with a confused look on her face. Lilli looks to Silk with a sly grin on her face indicating that her and Silk both knew the answer to that question. Silk is dismissive of Lilli's accusatory stare. "I don't know, but he's tripping hard" Silk replies. "For real though" Essance adds. "I can guess. That boy mad about that lil stunt chu just pulled on him with ya lil boycrush. You know boys hate rejection, especially FeFe." Lilli remarks in a matter-of-fact way. They all share a hearty laugh and then Essance invites Lilli inside to chill and talk some more, but Lilli declines, opting to go home and study for a calculus exam she has tomorrow. Essance hugs her friend and then she goes into the house, leaving Silk and Lilli in the front. Silk offers to walk Lilli halfway home, but she declines again and insists that she call her mom for a ride. When Lilli calls and doesn't get an answer, she gives in to Silk's offer, and the two begin walking in the direction of Lilli's house. On the walk they talk some more and Silk almost slips up and lets her new routines be known, until Beatrice's voice booms through her ears.

She stops walking and talking abruptly with a dazed facial expression, which baffles Lilli. She urgently tells Lilli that she has to go, even though they had not even made it halfway to Lilli's house. Before Lilli can even respond Silk is gone, running off in the opposite direction, leaving Lilli stuck and even more confused, because the direction in which Silk was running was not where she lived.

Chapter 14

When Silk is sure she has lost Lilli, she treks her way towards the bayou. Zela, the Bird Lady, stops Silk again as she passes her property line. Because she could tell that Silk was clearly trying to avoid contact with her, Zela quickly re-warns her about associating with the voodoo queen, Beatrice, and recites a short chant for her to use to fight her desire to return to the voodoo queen. Silk thanks Zela before she walks away. A huge part of Silk believes the Bird Lady, and she wants to take her advice and not see Mama B anymore, especially after being raped by her warlock cousin, but something else in her could not resist her desire to return to Mama B.

Silk arrives at Beatrice's and finds her relaxing on the same sofa that she'd awoken on the previous evening, drinking something hot while petting her Iblis. Beatrice greets Silk and welcomes her to join her on the sofa. Silk complies and begins asking Beatrice about Antonio and the ritual, about her lizard Iblis and why she refers to him as her Lord, and finally she asks her to explain to her what the true meaning of love is? As Silk spills out all of her questions,

Beatrice studies her face intensely and notices the discoloration and swelling forming underneath Silk's right eye, which makes her very suspicious. Before answering any of Silk's questions, Beatrice begins interrogating her about if she's told anyone about the rape, the voodoo, the magic, etc. When Silk confirms that she has told no one concerning any of those things, Beatrice asks Silk about the mark underneath her eye. Silk touches the spot under her eye and tells her about the two fights she had gotten into earlier in the day. Upon hearing the news of Silk being attacked, Beatrice becomes enraged like a protective mother, and gently grabs Silk's face by the cheeks for a closer inspection. Silk tells Beatrice that Barrika has been a problem for her for a significant part of her young life. She asks Beatrice for a spell that she could teach her to use to defend herself against the bully; one that could cause great bodily harm to Barrika, to completely embarrass and humiliate her in front of everyone. Beatrice jumps at the mention of a defense spell and goes to her large bookshelf, retrieves a large hardcover book, returns to her spot next to Silk, and begins flipping pages until she finds exactly what she needs to teach Silk. She recites the short spell to Silk until she is sure she has it down-packed. She also reminds Silk of the magical power in the written word and the magical power in the spoken word, telling her, "the foundation of successful spell casting lies in the power and mystery of, "the word". In magic, to have said is to have done, and to affirm and will what ought be done is to create. The necessary ingredients for magic to work effectively is the strong belief or desire, willing that it be so, and the right words at the right time". At the end of the voodoo lesson, she warns Silk of the danger behind the magic spell and behind magic as a whole and warns her not to let anyone know about her knowledge or magic practices, lest she be compromised and sentenced to death.

After installing significant fear in her with that last warning, Beatrice changes the subject in an effort to reduce Silk's fears. She goes back to the questions Silk asked initially, starting with her questions about the sex-magic ritual, about Iblis and his significance to her voodoo. Well, she tells 'her' watered down version of why she calls Iblis "her Lord." She reassures Silk that what Antonio did wasn't actually a rape, that it was a common part of voodoo practice, and continued to attempt Silk to believe that she actually consented to the rape. Also, she told Silk that she enticed men by the way she dressed. Then she goes into the question about love and asks Silk if she has feelings for someone. That is when Silk confesses about her boy-crush Lorenzo. Beatrice smiles gleefully and asks Silk to tell her all about him. Silk reveals all of her inner emotions and feelings, admitting that she is infatuated with Lorenzo, and laying out everything she adores about him. Beatrice approves of Silk's feelings, and describes what love is to her. Then she tells Silk about her second love, a man named Randy. A surprised Silk asks all about the man Beatrice claims to be the love of her life, yet she never once saw him there at her residence. They talk for about an hour about love and men. Before Silk leaves to go home, they repeat the defense spell for reassurance that she has it properly memorized. On the way out of the door, Silk is given one last warning to keep herself conservative and to not be compromised.

Chapter 15

The next morning, Silk, Essance, and Lilli all ride to school in Lorenzo's Tahoe together. When they arrive at the high school, Essance and Lilli both thank Lorenzo for the ride before quickly departing to the school cafeteria for breakfast, purposely leaving Silk alone with her boy-crush. Her and Lorenzo talk in his truck and she asks him if he believes in love; loving a person you don't know? He is surprised by the question, but agrees that it's possible. Silk confesses to him how she really feels about him, and in the moment, he leans in and kisses her right on her glossy lips. Silk receives the kiss and returns it even more passionately, grabbing the back of his braids, while their tongues dance to a melody created by the two of them. The kiss is definitely intense, with the two of them feeling and grabbing each other, and in the moment, he grabs her breast and squeezes a little too rough. This causes Silk to go into a trance-like state for a few seconds, and in this time a vivid vision of the horrible incident that occurred at Beatrice's home of her being raped by the warlock, Antonio, envelopes her mind. In this vision she hears Antonio's heavy breaths and his grunting in pleasure as he thrusts violently into her tight opening, not showing any type of remorse or sympathy and her young virgin vagina, and also feels him grabbing her big but firm breast so hard she thought they would bust and cause her to bleed to death. In her mind now, she relives the entire scene, showing the same terrified and helpless facial expressions. A loud, horrifying scream escapes her, the one she'd tried to let out while Antonio was raping her but she couldn't. Her scream is so loud that, although the windows in the truck were only slightly cracked, nearly everyone in the entire school parking lot turned in the direction of the Tahoe. Seeing how horrified Silk looked scrambling out of Lorenzo's truck in a panic, you'd think that Lorenzo had actually attempted to violate her in some sort of way. Felix and a parking lot security officer see this and they both intervene, the officer rushing to Silk, grabbing her in a protective fatherly way, as Felix rushes to the driver's door of the Tahoe, forcefully pulls Lorenzo out of his seat, and starts punching him all in his face and body. Two more parking lot security officers approach and stop Felix from beating on Lorenzo and all three of the teens are escorted into the administrative office.

Silk is taken into the principal's office where the school's head nurse is there to examine her. After a preliminary examination and a few routine questions following a sexual behavioral incident in the school, the nurse leaves Silk for the principal to deal with. By this time Silk is completely back to normal and realizes that things had gone completely wrong. Lorenzo is being detained in the school liaison's office, a New Orleans police officer. From where Silk is seated in the principal's office, she can see clearly into the liaison's office out of the glass partition separating the rooms, and she locks eyes with Lorenzo. He is being questioned by the police officer and also being scolded by the school's dean. Silk feels completely embarrassed and apologetic. She tries to explain to the principal, the extra nurse who is still in the office taking notes of the incident, and the parking lot security officer who brought her into the office, that it is all a big misunderstanding and trys to make a stupid excuse as to why she freaked out without disclosing any of her secrets, Beatrice's threats ringing in her head as she speaks carefully. The staff try hard to fish information out of her, asking leading questions regarding her home and personal affairs. Silk is very intelligent and knows that these types of questions are to find any indications of a history of physical or sexual abuse by family members but she insists none of that was going on in her life.

After a grilling hour and a half spent in the administration office, Silk and Lorenzo are released with passes to their second-hour classes, both with stern warnings about sexual acts on school premises. As she and Lorenzo both walk out of the office, she apologizes to him. With a weirded-out expression on his face, he accepts her apology and returns one of his own. When he attempts to ask her why she freaked out the way she did, the principal comes out and yells at them both to hurry to class. As they comply with Principal Jackson's order, Silk promises Lorenzo that she will tell him about it soon, when the time is right. Lorenzo doesn't respond. He looks at Silk skeptically and turns to walk to his history class. As she is about to follow behind him, Essance, Lilli, and Felix pop up all at the same time from the side of the administration office.

Immediately, all three of them begin bombarding her with one hundred and one questions about what happened. Silk has no desire to tell them what had happened, not at the moment at least, although she was sure Felix had already opened his big ass mouth and spilled the beans to her girls. She tells them that she couldn't talk at the moment, that she had to get to her class, and that they would talk about it at lunch. Reluctantly, Essance agrees and the trio departs. Silk is worried and feeling paranoid like she just knew she had just screwed up her chances of becoming Lorenzo's girlfriend. Beatrice's spell comes to her mind. She takes a shortcut to her chemistry class so that she can see Lorenzo when she passes by his history class. It works perfectly, she spots him but he doesn't notice her. In a low but audible voice, she recites the love spell with much desire and conviction just as Beatrice had taught it to her. Once the spell is complete, and he enters his class, Silk hurries down the hall to her own class.

Chapter 16

At lunch, as promised, Silk tells Essance, Lilli, and Felix all about what really went down in the parking lot, in Lorenzo's Tahoe that morning. The girls find her story rather funny and fascinating while Felix is the less humorous one. After lunch, Silk, Essance, and Lilli are in the girl's restroom, each taking care of their business and then occupying a mirror, checking their lip gloss, and adjusting their hair styles, when the restroom door comes bursting open wildly, scaring all three of them nearly to death. In walks Barrika with the same menacing scowl on her face as the day before, but this time with a swollen lip and apparent scratches on her face which she'd received from the big throw-down yesterday. She'd watched the girls as they ate lunch, chatting away having girl talks, and followed them all the way to the restroom. Now she has them just where she wants them. She wastes no time. As soon as the door bangs shut behind her, she brandishes a chrome and black swiss army knife and rushes the girls swinging it viciously while calling them all sorts of profanities. She first attempts to stab Silk with the knife, but she misses, slicing Essance on the forearm instead, causing her to scream in pain as blood starts pouring out of her arm.

With the three girls backed into the comer afraid, Essance crying and bleeding profusely, Barrika closing in on them with the bloody knife in her hand and murder on her mind, Silk feels a mixture of fear, anger, panic, and helplessness. Although she is outnumbered, Barrika still is big as hell and now she has a knife that she apparently knows how to use well. Feeling these mixed emotions and desperate for help, the words from Beatrice's chants suddenly ring through Silk's ears and in effect come out of her own mouth rhythmically as if she had known spells all of her life. As Silk recites the spell, suddenly Barrika is stopped in her tracks, by an unseen force, as if she was frozen in time. Next, the knife flies out of her tightly gripped hand as if someone or something has snatched it away from her. Now the knife is in the air floating. Silk is no longer terrified, instead she is in a trance-like state again as she continues reciting the spell. Essance isn't crying anymore, and her and Lilli's terrified desperate expressions have now turned to shock as they observe Silk as she speaks in a foreign tongue. Barrika is confused and now fear creeps up into her. After a minute's pause, the knife idling in the air by an unknown force, is turned to where now the blade is pointing right at Barrika. Her eyes grow as wide as saucers, but before she can make a sound her own knife drives down at her neck with enormous force, and begins slicing and dicing away at her. Silk is still stuck in a trance as she continues reciting the spell. The more she recites the harder and faster Barrika is stabbed. Essance and Lilli cannot believe what they are witnessing Barrika gets butchered like a pig right before their eyes.

Silk stops speaking and falls back into Essance's and Lilli's arms as if all the energy has been sucked out of her body. When all is said and done, and the spell is over, Barrika lies on the restroom floor, now drenched in a pool of her own blood, diced up like a lamb all throughout her midsection. Silk, now out of the trance, is lost in shock from what lies before her and the girls. Essance and Lilli are both shocked as well and at a loss for words as they also look at the heinous scene. The two of them turn and gaze at Silk in pure bewilderment. Instantly, all three girls take off, grabbing their bags and things, racing to get out of the restroom as quickly as possible, Essance and Lilli screaming in horror. Before exiting the restroom, Silk takes one last look down at her childhood bully who lay on the tiles choking on blood from her slit throat, then she runs out following her girls.

The three of them run full speed out of the school building. Felix sees them dash out of the restroom screaming. He goes and opens the restroom door, and sees Barrika lying on the floor gargling on blood, with blood surrounding her entire body, and a swiss army knife lodged in her chest near the breast bone. He pulls the knife out of her body, causing her to let out an agonizing grunt, then the choking on blood ceases, and her eyes roll all the way to the back of her head.

After quickly wrapping the knife in a red rag he always carries, Felix runs out of the restroom and after the girls. He catches up to them as they are running through the school parking lot with a ton of spectators all gazing curiously at them. He yells the girls' names and signals for them to get into his car. They all get in and he speeds out of the school parking lot.

As Felix drives further away from the high school, they see 9-1-1 emergency vehicles with their sirens blaring, speeding in the

direction of the school. Silk is riding shotgun while Essance and Lilli
are in the back-passenger seats, their bodies shaking in pure fear. The
car stops in the projects of the 17th Ward of New Orleans. Felix tells
the girls to stay put and jumps out of the parked car to dispose of
the bloody knife he'd taken out of a lifeless Barrika. The girls sit in
the car shaking scared, not of the area, but about the events that had
taken place at the school. Within minutes, Felix returns, ordering the
girls out of the car and to follow him into apartment 65A on the
ground floor of the building. The girls follow quickly without asking
any questions. Once inside apartment 65A, Felix offers the girls seats
on the couch and something to drink.

Essance and Lilli each find a spot on the dingy couch, but shake
their quivering heads no to the drink offer, but Silk asks for a cold
soda. Felix goes to the kitchen to get Silk's drink. When he arrives
with a can of Sprite, Silk drinks without spilling a drop. All was silent
until Silk spoke "Dead ain't she?" she asks Felix, which sounded like
more of a statement than a question. After Felix confirms what they
all knew was true, he asks what happened. Essance and Lilli both
speak at the same time, not answering Felix, but instead asking Silk
what the hell was it that she'd done in the restroom?

"So... are you a witch?" Essance asks straight-forwardly. Lilli's
questioning gaze said that she was consciously asking the same
question. Felix is completely confused as he looks from mouth to
mouth wondering what the hell Essance and Lilli are talking about.
He then asks who actually stabbed Barrika? Were they wearing
gloves when they did it? Did they touch anything in the restroom
without gloves on? And, was anyone else in the restroom before,
during, or after it happened? All three girls answered the same to the
last question: "No one." But when Essance and Lilli begin explaining
to him what happened, even he becomes a little nervous and
skeptical of Silk. He for sure wants answers from Silk too, his
childhood friend. Silk knows she cannot tell them about her,

Beatrice, Antonio, the voodoo lessons, witchcraft practices, the sex; none of this can she reveal to her twin and lifelong friends. In an effort to provide some information to satisfy their curiosities, Silk diverts them by telling them that she met Zela and began talking to her, and that she taught her the defense spell; "The Bird Lady." She denies practicing voodoo and witchcraft but admits to asking the Bird Lady for a spell to use against Barrika's continuous attacks.

The girls stay at Felix's trap spot for the remainder of the evening talking about the Bird Lady and the spell, then they get into planning out their next move, with Felix helping them to come up with an alibi for the police and school officials regarding Barrika, and for their disappearance from the school after lunch hour. Felix provides Essance with a clean rag, a bottle of hydrogen peroxide, and some band aids to treat her arm wound that Barrika caused. At some point Silk and Felix wind up alone in the bedroom that he said was his. There she gives him thanks for being there to save the day for the second day in a row. Felix tells Silk that she doesn't have to thank him and to not worry, that he would be there for her and the girls all the way. Felix's assurance and protectiveness throws Silk into a mixture of emotions, and what was supposed to be a simple thanks turns intimate between the two. She brings her head forward and their lips lock for a few minutes. This surprises the hell out of Felix. However, he returns the kiss with a lot more passion than Silk expected. He slips his tongue into her mouth and now they are hugged up, French kissing, and feeling on each other's bodies like lovers do. Silk stops Felix after he squeezes her butt cheeks and then tries to slide his hand down into her backside, underneath her jeans, in places his hands don't belong. She knew she had to stop him before things went too far. She had to admit though, he was a good kisser; actually, a great kisser, however, she cannot see herself going that far with her childhood friend. She stops kissing him, pushes him off of her, and tells him they have to stop. Felix tries to persist that they continue, but Silk reaches her hand out, stopping his advance, stating that they couldn't do it because she didn't want to ruin their friendship with intimacy, and she also added in the fact that she has feelings for Lorenzo.

Hearing Lorenzo's name sends Felix off the mountain. He gets angry and becomes loud and aggressive with Silk causing her to become nervous and a bit afraid of him now. He backs her into a corner of the room, approaching her with a predatory expression on his face. Flashbacks of Antonio, the rape, the alligators lunging out of the swamp water at her, and Barrika's bloody butchered body lying on the floor, causes Silk to become engulfed in apprehension. Just as she is about to let out a terrifying scream, one of Felix's homeboys bursts thru the door, startling the two, and asks about the two young cute girls sitting on his living room couch, Essance and Lilli, with lust on his mind. Silk comes back to normal, the flashbacks now gone, and asks Felix to take her and her girls home. Felix calms down, now feeling foolish after sensing that he had just installed fear into his best friend, and calmly apologizes and agrees to take them home.

Chapter 17

Felix drives towards the Seventh Ward to drop the girls off at home in silence, he and Silk, all except for the 21 Savage songs that are playing through the car speakers. Both Essance and Lilli sense that something had went on between those two, because when the two of them were in the bathroom of Felix's trap tending to Essance's arm wound, Silk and Felix were no longer in the living room where they'd left them, and had ducked off into one of the rooms. They both witnessed the nervous look on Silk's face when she and Felix exited the room after Felix's homeboy rudely burst in on them. Now, with the awkward silence and them two not making eye contact is a sheer indicator that something foul happened in that room, they just didn't know what exactly.

As they get closer to their Ward, Felix turns the music down, breaks the silence by reminding all of the girls not to mention a word to anyone about the stabbing incident and to say to the school officials and police that they left school early to go purchase the brand new Air Jordan sneakers that had actually been released that day, which he'd have a pair for each of them in their sizes when he arrived in the morning to pick them up and ride them to school with him. Felix arrives at the twins' house first. Essance gets out of the car still trembling, and thanks Felix again for helping them and farewells him goodnight until morning. Silk does not get out with her twin, instead she stays in the car, stating that she wants to see Lilli home. Essance doesn't question, she just turns and goes inside their house. Felix pulls off and drives around the corner to Lilli's house. There, Silk and Lilli both exit, Silk thanks him again with a weak smile on her face, not wanting to come off as being rude. Felix accepts the gratitude from both girls, and then asks Silk if she needs him to swing her back around the corner to her house now that Lilli was home safely, but Silk rejects the offer and tells him that she will see him in the morning. When Felix pulls off, presumably heading back to his neighborhood in the Seventeenth, Lilli and Silk talk briefly. Lilli assumes that Silk is going to come inside for a second but Silk has other plans. She says her good-byes and departs quickly before Lilli can protest, heading for the bayou.

Chapter 18

By it being late in the evening and dark outside, Lilli senses something very unusual about Silk's decision not to go straight home after what all occurred today and to come this way. The fact that she admitted to using a voodoo spell from 'the Bird Lady' and was now heading in the direction of the bayous without so much as a word of where she is going has Lilli very suspicious. She throws her book bag into the doorway, just enough so that her mother can see that

she has made it home from school, and quickly begins trailing the
way Silk had just taken off to in a hurry. Being that Lilli is the #1
long-distance runner on the school's track team, she catches up to
Silk in record timing, but Silk has no clue at all that she is being
followed.

Silk passes by Zela's house which is unusually black and quiet,
no bird noises at all. She makes it to Beatrice's house and knocks.
The door opens slightly, so she lets herself in. She smells something
funny in the air, which only means one thing - it is potion cooking
time. She walks in, greets Iblis as she passes his enclosure, through
the dining room and into the kitchen, but still there is no one. She
goes to the back of the house heading to Beatrice's bedroom. As she
approaches the bedroom door she notices it is cracked slightly and
a glistening light is protruding out of the cracks. When she gets up
to the door is when she can hear funny sounds coming from inside.
She gently puts her fingers on the door, slowly eases it open and she
sees Beatrice on her knees, with barely anything covering her skin,
her vagina facing the doorway, her butt swaying in a circular rhythm,
giving Antonio a blow job as he's sitting back comfortably in a chair.
He looks as though he is meditating with his eyes rolling to the back
of his head and his toes curled up, and is reciting a spell in a low
tone. Silk notices that there is a huge iron link chain tied around
Beatrice's waist that is connected to a fixture in the bedroom. Silk
watches for a moment, shocked at first, again at how they could be
doing something like this being as they are blood first cousins. But
this time what surprises her most is how into it Beatrice is, how
passionate she is in sucking on Antonio's dick as if he were Randy,
her so-called lover, instead of her own cousin. Antonio takes the
shocked expression off of Silk's face with a lustful gaze and then
says, "the voodoo princess has arrived," with the most devilish grin
plastered on his mug.

This causes Beatrice to jump up, turn to face Silk, and say "Silk, don't ju know how to knock girl?" She gets up on her feet, and now Silk sees that her sundress is pulled down to her stomach and big brown hard nipples point in her direction. Beatrice grabs a towel from her bed and begins wiping the dripping saliva off of her lips, cheeks, and breasts from the sloppy toppy she was giving Antonio. She then pulls her sundress back up and adjusts her big titties inside of it. Once decent, Beatrice instantly becomes worried as she observes the troubled look on Silk's face, and this leads her to wonder why Silk is there so late at night. She ushers Silk into the living room area and they both sit on the couch. She asks Silk what was wrong and about what had happened at school. Silk explains what happened at school, her using the spell, and what wound up happening to Barrika as a result of the spell. Beatrice becomes the worried mom and grabs Silk, hugging her in a comforting manner as she thinks up a plan to help her now. All Silk can smell is sweat, saliva, and ball juice which grosses her out, but she is too nervous to say anything, so she lets Beatrice hug her. Silk, clearly worried for Essance, Lilli, and herself, pleads with Beatrice for a resolution to their problems, which they all know are sure to follow. Beatrice assures Silk that she will take care of everything, but warns her against her best friend Lilli -—telling her that Lilli is bad news, and to stay away from her.

Antonio, who was eavesdropping, comes into the living room from the kitchen holding onto a cup with steam coming from it. He hands the steaming cup to Silk. "Drink it while it's hot" he tells her. Silk does as she is told and drinks hoping to feel relaxed, but more so hoping that whatever is inside the cup will remove all of her problems. Antonio watches her predatorily as she gulps down the drink, licking his lips and cutting his eyes over at Beatrice who is quietly lulling over both him and Silk with a lustful gaze. Within thirty seconds after Silk has consumed the final drop of hot liquid from the cup, the potion starts to kick in and does its work. Silk's head begins to spin, demonic voices reciting spells and chants fills her ears, she begins hallucinating seeing beautiful people and creatures that she has never laid eyes on, and then out of nowhere a surge of ecstasy courses through her body making her feel as horny as a rabbit.

Eyes low and hazy, she looks at Beatrice then at Antonio, who both stare at her smiling mischievously, and then she lunges forward at Beatrice, yanks her sundress down and starts sucking on her large breasts like a hungry newborn. Next thing you know, Antonio joins in, removing Silk's clothes from her body as she sucks on Beatrice's hard nipples. While reciting the same chants as Antonio, Beatrice gently guides Silk's head further down south until she reaches her precious jewel. Unbeknownst to Silk she has just officially sold her soul. Beatrice and Antonio have Silk right where they want her and have fulfilled their goal.

Chapter 19

Lilli watches from one of the far back windows of the old cottage looking house. She'd followed Silk throughout the woods, past Zela's home, and to the Voodoo Queen's home. She is extremely baffled as to why Silk had come to Beatrice's house, and why she had lied to them earlier about learning the spell that killed Barrika from the Bird Lady? She saw when Silk walked in looking for Beatrice but did not find her, and when she walked towards the back of the house to a room that Lilli couldn't see from the front window. Minutes later, Silk appeared again, coming back into the living room area of the house, with the voodoo queen and her warlock cousin both in tow. She heard Silk rehash the day's events to Beatrice, and saw the look of worry on Beatrice's face to the news. Lastly, she heard Beatrice tell Silk not to worry about anything, that she'd take care of everything, and to stay away from her.

After hearing Beatrice tell Silk to stay away from her, and Silk didn't defend her or protest against what Beatrice just said about her, Lilli feels a mixture of let-down, betrayed, and disgusted by her childhood best friend. Lilli hears crackling sounds coming from the woods behind her and turns her head just as Antonio enters the living room with the hot cup of potion. Zela appears out of the woods and approaches Lilli. She hugs her tightly then turns her in the opposite direction, and says to her, "You've seen enough chile. You can't save her. She is gone. Let's go." Lilli complies, walking away from Beatrice's house with her shoulders slouched and head hung low feeling defeated. As they walk away, Zela looks over her shoulder back through the window one last time at Silk in pity as she consumes the last bit of the sex potion and starts getting loose. Zela shakes her head before escorting Lilli away so that she doesn't bear witness to what her best friend is about to do next with Beatrice and Antonio. Zela looks up from Silk and there Antonio and Beatrice both are smiling back at her through the window with sinister grins on their faces as she walks away with Lilli.

Chapter 20

Silk wakes up around 5 a.m., in Beatrice's bed, feeling refreshed and rejuvenated. Antonio is gone, but Beatrice still lay asleep naked under her silk sheets. Silk gets up out of the bed, wondering what happened the night before, why she felt so good but also so filthy, and more importantly, why was she naked? She quickly erases all of those thoughts out of her mind, because she knows she has to hurry up and make it home so that her and Essance can get to school on time. She finds her clothes on the floor and gets dressed. Before making an exit out of the bedroom, she goes and gives Beatrice a good-bye kiss on the cheek. After kissing Beatrice, Silk feels her own vagina, and it still feels hot in a good way. The cup that she'd drank the potion out of from the night before lay on the floor, and the sight of it sends a jolt of ecstasy through Silk again, but she objects to it. She says bye to Beatrice and turns to leave, but Beatrice stops her and tells her to give her another kiss this time flipping the sheets off of her naked body and patting her furry wet box. Silk does as she is told and gives Beatrice's pussy a peck on the clitoris.

Beatrice stops her from leaving again and says, "uh uh! What ju tink ya doing girl? No... French it!" Again, Silk complies and goes down on Beatrice French-kissing her pussy for a minute.

"Ahh... Good girl." Beatrice says as her eyes roll back in pleasure. "Ju have a nice day now Silky ok" she says in a pleased manner as Silk gets up from the bed again to leave.

Zela spots Silk cutting through her territory sort of wobbly in the legs as if intoxicated, and reeking of sex, sweat, and magic potions. She scares Silk when she speaks abruptly, stopping her in her tracks. "Why did you not listen to me? I warned you didn't I? Now you got yourself in too deep chile. I told you them people are bad... bad people, now you gone see what happens to bad-spirited people, girl. Just like Barrika Barnes saw." The mention of Barrika frightens Silk to the core causing her to bolt off running away as fast as she can.

Silk makes it home, opens her bedroom window from the outside and climbs in. She tip-toes in and changes out of her yesterday clothes into clean pj's. She wanted to take a shower badly to wash off the funk of last night, but she doesn't want to wake the house with running the water. "Girl you stank! What is that smell? Where you been at? Back with FeFe getting nasty again?" Essance says, awoken by Silk's movements around their bedroom. Silk laughs and then denies her twin's accusation sternly and lays down in her adjoining bed. Her mind is racing with thoughts, visions of everything that went down at Beatrice's the night before, the stabbing at the school, Beatrice's threats and warnings to her, and then she drifts off to sleep fantasizing about Lorenzo.

Chapter 21

Silk only got about an hour of sleep when her alarm clock sounds off, waking her for the school day. She gets up and heads to the bathroom to brush her teeth and shower. When she looks at herself in the mirror she notices teeth marks on the back of her neck, just above her shoulder blade. This was odd to her, because for some reason, she had no clue how teeth marks could've gotten there. She doesn't remember being bitten. She soothes her hand over the area just to feel if it was really a bite mark and to see if it hurts to the touch, because she was not feeling any pain or burning. As her fingers run across the marks, immediately her body begins trembling with ecstasy and complete bliss. Her nipples harden, her clitoris begins throbbing, wanting some attention, a puddle forms in her panties. Voices ring through her head singing chants and spells, visions of sexual encounters, her legs go weak and her knees buckle underneath her from the sexual sensation, causing her to fall over onto the face bowl, catching herself. She regains her composure, finishes brushing her teeth, and gets in the shower.

Silk is out of the shower and fully dressed in exactly fifty-five minutes. Essance is already set to go and waiting for Silk. She'd already texted Felix to pick them up while Silk was still in the bathroom dressing up her hairdo for today. "He said that he would be to them in five minutes. Say he at Lilli's house picking her up." Essance announces. Hearing Lilli's name put Silk on the defense. "Why Felix go to her and pick her up first? And why she even gotta ride with us school anyway?" Silk protests. This only confuses the hell out of Essance. Hearing Silk and Essance talking, their mother,

Lashunda, pokes her head in their room and jumps into the conversation.

Lashunda: "Who is Felix, baby? And why y'all both keep talking about him? Which one of y'all like him?"

Essance looks at Silk with an accusatory grin on her face -—a dead giveaway to the answer to Lashunda's last question. Silk denies having any feelings for Felix, but admits to her mother that there is a new boy at the school that she is checking for.

Lashunda: "So why are you throwing so much shade on Lillianna then baby? That girl been like a sister to y'all since pre-school."

Silk: "Ain't nobody throwing shade on that heifer... I just heard through the grapevine yesterday that Lilli had been sneak-dissing me behind back to people."

With an unconvinced expression, Lashunda throws back:

Lashunda: "Well, I just want to tell you that you shouldn't ever let a boy come between your good friendships. When you have a good friend like Lilli, you keep 'em. Shouldn't anything come between y'all unless it's something serious, and trust me honey, he ain't serious. Y'all clean up this room before you leave ya heard me?" she says before exiting the twins' bedroom.

Silk is glad that her mother left out of the room before getting a response, because something might have been said that shouldn't be said, something like her real reason behind her new ill feelings towards Lilli. Hearing Silk lie to their mother about hearing a rumor that Lilli had been back-biting her has Essance even more confused now than she was before. Just when she is about to call Silk on her bullshit, her iPhone chimes. She looks at it -—a text from Felix, letting her know that he is waiting outside. "Come on, they outside." she announces to her twin. The two grab their school bags and leave the house to get in Felix's car.

The car ride to school is stale and awkward. Neither Silk nor Lilli speak two words to each other. Lilli speaks to Essance, who returns the greeting back to her and to Felix as well with her usual enthusiasm. Silk got in the car and speaks to Felix first and rolls her eyes at Lilli. There is silence and eye-contact is avoided between the two best friends. Felix and Essance are both very confused about Silk's and Lilli's behavior and demeanor towards each other -—especially Felix, because when he'd dropped Silk and Lilli off together, they both seemed fine and were getting along. He wondered if maybe something bad had taken place between the two after he'd pulled off from them. Felix breaks the silence by brandishing each girl their new pair of Air Jordans, as promised, in each one's correct shoe size. All except for Lilli get excited by the brand new sneakers. "Am I missing something here?" Felix asks, looking back and forth at Lilli and Silk, waiting for either one to respond. Both girls remain silent and play dumb as if they didn't know that how rude and snobbish they are both acting towards each other is noticed. "Yea, forreal like, what the hell is goin on wit chall ... like?" Essance joins in with a puzzled expression on her face.

"I'm good!" Silk and Lilli both answer simultaneously, dismissively and with a whole lot of attitude. Essance and Felix look to each other and both say "What the fuck?"

They arrive in the school parking lot and Felix finds an open parking spot very close to the cafeteria entrance. The group gets out and separates into twos, the twins going one way, Lilli and Felix heading the opposite way. Before separating though, Essance says goodbye to both Felix and Lilli, however Silk only farewells Felix and thanks him for the ride and the J's. This raises Essance's and Felix's suspicions even higher. As soon as both parties get out of earshot from the other, Essance and Felix both stop to investigate. Lilli tells Felix about how after he'd left she'd followed Silk and explained to him all that she witnessed and heard. Essance doesn't get the same acquiescence from her twin -—Silk simply blows her off and proceeds to the school cafeteria to get her breakfast.

While sitting down and eating their breakfast, it is still the same thing when Essance tries to ask Silk why she and Lilli were both acting shady towards each other all of a sudden. After seeing that she isn't getting anywhere, Essance changes the subject to talking about her paranoia about what the school knows regarding Barrika. Silk reminds her not to appear nervous and to just let her do all of the talking when they do get called down to the administration office. She also reminds her of their alibi that Felix helped them concoct just in case they were called down and questioned separately. As they talk, Lorenzo walks past their table so smoothly it appears as though he is floating as he walks. Silk calls out his name and gets his attention. He approaches and she greets him with a super seductive 'good morning.' He returns the greeting to both twins and Silk waves lustfully at him as he passes by. Lorenzo did not wave back, still feeling kind of weirded-out and confused about Silk's intentions. His response makes Silk look and feel kind of stupid. People standing and sitting around laugh at Lorenzo's player move -—how he just curved Silk to a certain degree.

Felix enters the cafeteria and catches Silk drooling over Lorenzo, who is now in the breakfast line filling his meal tray. Seeing Silk gawking over Lorenzo pisses him off, but he corrects himself before approaching the girls for the important news he'd come to deliver. The inevitable was occurring -—Principal Jackson, the school's dean, and N.O. PD are looking for the girls -—to question them about the incident with Barrika. Silk notices the envious look on Felix's face as he approaches, which re-boosts her confidence level, at the same time turning her on. Her nipples get hard and her little pussy gets hot and wet for some reason. The sensation is short-lived when Felix discloses the news about their real problem.

Felix: "Lilli already got snatched up at her locker by security and took to the administration's office. I suggest y'all go down to the office too on ya own so it don't look suspicious."

Reluctantly, Silk and Essance both rise from their seats without bothering to take their breakfast and head for the administration office with Felix right behind them reassuring.

Felix: "Don' t even trip... y'all a be alright. .. Remember what I said... to stay calm, and remember the alibi we came up with."

When they arrive in the administration office, they are immediately escorted into Principal Jackson's office and told to take seats beside Lilli. Principal Jackson's demeanor is very genuine and concerning in a sympathetic sort of way, unlike the school's dean and the two police officers who are also present in Jackson's office. One police officer is in full S.W.A.T. gear, looking like a G.I. Joe, with his K-9 partner lying beside him. The K-9 is trained to detect everything from narcotics, ammunition, explosives, and fear. Silk is not afraid of animals so she is least intimidated by the K-9 officer being in the room, yet she still is very cautious about how close she gets to it. Essance and Lilli on the other hand are petrified of dogs and they let it show, moving their chairs far off to the right of the small office room. Principal Jackson began the interrogation of the trio, beginning with Silk, by acknowledging her frequent presence in his office over the past week. Jackson seems to be singling Silk out of the group, because he directs most of his questions towards her: What was she wearing the day before? Where did she go after the ordeal that led to her and Lorenzo being in his office the day before? About her altercations with Barrika on and off of school property which he had been notified of; the situation that Mr. Easley had brought to his attention regarding Barrika slamming her into the locker in the hallway, and about the fight in the cafeteria earlier in the week, with her and Essance jumping Barrika?

Principal Jackson laid it all out, even telling the girls that he heard rumors that Barrika had been a bully to them ever since grade school and even throughout junior high school.

Silk: "Dayumn... Jackson know everything " she says to herself mentally, feeling perplexed. His last question is directed to all three girls:

Principal Jackson: "Why were you all absent for the remaining half of school after lunch? After Barrika's body had been discovered?"

This last question makes everything go silent in the room as the school's dean and the police officers' eyes stay glued on the girls, searching for any sign of deceit or guilt.

Principal Jackson then switches gears with his questions without even getting answers to the former. Next, he asks the twins about their parents and their familial affairs. He asked if their father possessed any knives, guns, or any other sort of weapons? He asks about how their upbringing was. Did they see a lot of violence within their home? Did their parents argue and scream a lot? Did they ever witness their parents getting physical in their arguments with each other or anyone else for that matter? None of the three girls had ever been interrogated like this before. Well, at least not by anyone besides their parents. When the questions first began Silk was nervous as hell because she hadn't anticipated what would be asked of her, however, she held her composure like Felix instructed her and followed the script verbatim he'd given to them and to a 'T'. Principal Jackson seems to accept her alibi, however, not the police officers; they smell something fishy about Silk's explanation. Essance and Lilli both back up Silk's version of events. Principal Jackson's questions come to an end, but now the police officers want their turn. As the one without the K-9 begins his methods of interrogating suspects, the begins describing the medical examiner's report of Barrika's autopsy. He opens a manila folder, removes a stack of papers, and spreads them out on Jackson's desk. They are crime scene photos of the gruesome remains of Barrika Barnes. The photos cause Essance and Lilli to cringe in horror and begin crying, but not Silk.

Her expressionless reaction sends all sorts of red flags to all of the officials in Jackson's office.

The officer handling the K-9 whispers something to the Belgian Malinois to get him to pick up on any fear Silk might be concealing. The K-9 stands up on alert, looking very aggressive and intimidating, but when it makes eye contact with Silk it immediately tucks its tail and begins bitching up; crying behind the officer. When Silk stares into the dog's eyes it immediately springs up, trying to run and hide underneath Principal Jackson's mahogany desk -—the sudden jolt of the chain and rope leash causes the handling officer to fall to the floor, knocking items off of Jackson's desk on his way down. This move shocks everyone in the room. Essence and Lilli jump out of their seats out of fear. The officer gets back up on his feet and shouts repeated commands for the K-9 officer to resume its position beside him, but the dog would not obey.

The Malinois stays underneath the desk whimpering and crying out a horrible cry, and begins pissing itself. The girls are all dismissed with stern warnings from all of the officials in attendance. The girls talk outside of the office and they all vow to never use the restroom that Barrika was killed in again, although technically no one could use it right now because it has been boarded up.

Chapter 22

Felix meets the girls by their lockers and asks if they are good and how the meeting went. Essance and Lilli both shrug their shoulders with confused expressions and turn to Silk. "Yea, we good. Thanks to you, handsome." Silk says with a warm smile and a sultry wink which causes Felix to blush on the inside, which he tries hard not to let show. "Anything for my besties" he replies, licking his lips and sizing Silk up and down lustfully as he'd done the day before, only this time Silk returns the stare indicating that she enjoyed the little flirting game the two of them are playing.

Lilli notices their flirting and rolls her eyes, annoyed at the gaming the two are doing, so she walks away without a word, heading to her 1st hour class. Lilli and Essance have chemistry together for first period, so they routinely walk to class together every morning -—they sit close to each other in class, and they partner up for every class project or group assignment. But today, Lilli just storms off leaving Essance with Silk and Felix. Essance is surprised yet again this morning. To her, it seems as though the surprises just keep on coming. She waves good-bye to Felix and to her twin, and races off to catch up to Lilli. She succeeds and stops Lilli just inches before she embarks the classroom doorway.

Essance: "What's really going on between you and Silk?"

Lilli: "What do you mean?"

Essance: "Y'all acting weird as hell, that's what I mean. Now tell me what is all this bull-crap about, girl?"

Lilli: "Nothing... look, just let it go Stink, okay?"

When she sees that Essance isn't going to, she gives in and reveals every detail to Essance about where she followed Silk to last night, just as she'd done for Felix about a half an hour ago. Upon receiving this news, Essance is even more confused and now vows to find out what is really going on with her twin, and to get behind this suspicion that Silk might be into some kind of evil cult.

By lunch time, rumors were going around the entire high school that Silk, Essance, and Lilli all had jumped and stabbed Barrika to death repeatedly in the girls' restroom. Felix, being the word on-the-streets king that he is, is the one to deliver the news to Essance first in their third-period gym class. Afraid to death of what might come of the rumors, she hurries to the girls' locker room to shower and change back into her regular attire, and then rushes with Felix to the cafeteria to find Silk and Lilli.

As Silk leaves out of her third-period French class waving good-bye to Mrs. Floedboe, her French teacher, she feels all eyes on her as soon as she ascends down the hallway heading to lunch. All of the fellow students she passes appear to be whispering about her, moving out of her path, and trying to avoid direct eye-contact. Even the most popular teens and the gangbangers in the school look nervous as Silk walks past them. She overhears one of the school's cheerleaders trying to whisper, but too loudly. "Yup that's her girl. I heard she cut that girl's eyeballs out the socket and flushed them right on down the stool!" Silk had no clue what the girl was talking about, and wondered how in the hell did the story get out in the first place. Moreso, she wondered how in the hell did the story get twisted into what this stuck-up ass little cheerleader was saying. She has a funny feeling that with all of the rumors floating around the school, and so rapidly, that something serious is about to go down. By the time she arrives to the lunch table where her group usually eats in the cafeteria, the story is out.

As Silk approaches, Essance and Felix are already seated at the lunch table with their food, Essance's untouched, picking at her slice of cheese pizza.

Silk: "Felix, can you please tell me what-the-fuck is going on around her and why-in-the-fuck are all these people jabbing at what happened? They don't even know what-the-fuck they talking about Fee"

Essance: "I think we should wait until Lilli get here."

Not answering Silk's questions, Felix looks down dumbfoundedly and nods his head, agreeing with Essance. Silk eye-balls her twin quizzically but doesn't protest. She goes to the lunch window, grabs her own slice of cheese pizza and an apple Snapple and returns to the table, coating the slice of pizza with ranch salad dressing and then dipping it over in a small cup of Louisiana hot sauce. Essance observes her twin's nonchalant demeanor as people in the cafeteria walk by their table whispering and with nervous expressions on their faces. However, none of this seems to bother Silk. She chews away at her delicious slice of pizza as if having not a care in the world about how others around her feel or what any of them thought. Essance stares baffled at her calmness because she feels the total opposite of her twin; she is a nervous wreck, scared shitless. Seeing her twin like this low-key frightens Essance. "Do I really know my sister?" she thinks to herself.

Lilli approaches, sits her tray down on the table, and searches everyone's faces for any signs or answers to any of the thousands of questions that she knows her and basically the entire school has about Silk. When she looks at Silk, Silk rolls her eyes and continues eating her pizza.

Silk: "So Felix, please begin to tell us what-in-thee-fuck got all these mafuckin doe does all googly eyed and whispering about dead bitches and me?"

Silk's words shock all of them. Gatorade spurts out of Felix's mouth as he chokes off of Silk's blunt words.

Felix: "Well damn, um. Rumor has it that y'all stomped a mud hole up in ole girl's ass and then butchered her like a hog in dat ther bathroom" he answers meekly.

Silk and Lilli both gasp simultaneously.

Lilli: "Y'all??? What-the-hell do you mean 'y'all'? Lillianna didn't touch that girl not one time. People need to get their facts straight for real woeday. That shit ain't cool woe. That's one thang I don't do. I might cheat on a test or on my lil boyfriend or something like dat, but I don't kill people, uh uh not Lillianna!" Lilli vents.

As Lilli talks, Silk sees red through her eyes, she is so pissed. She goes nuts on Lilli for indirectly pointing the finger at her, which in all reality they all knew that she was the cause of Barrika's gruesome death, only that she did not actually stab her herself. Still though, Silk feels it is not fair for Lilli to be acting as if she, Silk, and Essance weren't all in the bathroom at the same time and witnessed the same thing. That just doesn't sit well with Silk at all.

Silk: "You a real no-good back-stabbing lil bitch forreal, ya heard me!?" she states.

Essance jumps into the argument in an attempt to mediate, but it's too late. They are already going at it, yelling, throwing curse words and insults at each other like they haven't been best friends for the majority of their young lives. All this occurs right in the middle of the school cafeteria.

Felix reminds them of the situation and of the fact that they are being watched closely, using only his eyes to signal towards the school liaison officer standing against the wall, hawking the girls down. Noticing the officer surveying them, they immediately calm themselves. Essance throws her lunch in the trash uneaten, and the group heads out to the school's courtyard.

As the group of four walk out of the cafeteria, nearly all of the other students that they pass by look at the three girls cautiously, some avoiding eye contact completely. The entire school is now spooked of Silk and her clique to say the least. Essance looks timid, Lilli looking as innocent as can be, as though people have her all wrong, and Silk appears to be the only one unfazed out of the clique. With her chin up and nose pointing high to the sky, her confident stride let Felix know that she is enjoying the fear that has been instilled into people following what happened to Barrika. He walks casually, observing everything around him like he normally does, and shakes a few hands of guys he deals with in passing.

On the way through the door to the courtyard, Silk sees Lorenzo approaching from the courtyard to come into the building and into the cafeteria. He is walking and talking to the leader of the cheerleader squad. The girl is clearly choosing up on Lorenzo. Silk can tell by the googly eyes the girl is giving him and that wide smile on her face. The cheerleader looks away from Lorenzo for a second, and spots Silk and her clique exiting the cafeteria and coming out on the courtyard. The girl's eyes get wide as saucers. She stops abruptly after noticing Silk's appetizing stare at Lorenzo, so she hesitantly hands Lorenzo a slip of paper with her name and cell phone number written down on it before rushing away in the opposite direction. Silk observes this as an opportunity, so as Lorenzo is telling the cheerleader good-bye, she purposely bumps into him.

Lorenzo jumps back, startled at first by the impact. When he looks and sees that it's Silk, a lump forms in his throat, and he too becomes wide-eyed. Silk picks up on his nervous reaction and tries to calm him by relaxing her expression and talking slowly. She compliments him on his sneakers. That is when he looks down and realizes that he and Silk have on the same new pair of Air Jordans and he returns the compliment. Just as Silk is about to offer Lorenzo her cell phone number, Felix boldly jumps in between them, mean-mugging his once-homeboy:

Felix: "Why you even talking to this clown dawg?"

She tries to answer, but Felix cuts her off, putting a hand on her shoulder ushering her into the courtyard and away from Lorenzo. After feeling offended by Felix's rude intervention, Lorenzo gets defensive.

Lorenzo: "What is yo issue with me, my dude? Do you got something you wanna take care of?" he says as he raises his arms out, challenging Felix to a fight.

Felix: "Holl... up... what is you saying woe?" he replies, pulling up his pants, getting into his fighting posture.

Lorenzo: "You betta watch ya self dude and stay out my way!" Lorenzo warns.

Felix: "Nah, you betta watch it playboy ya herd me?" Felix replies over his shoulder with a no backing-down attitude as he walks off with Silk.

She stops briefly and tells the both of them to stop the fighting over her. She then tells Lorenzo that she'll see him later and proceeds to walk away with Felix's arm still around her shoulder. Lorenzo is left by himself still standing there on the courtyard with a mug on his grill while Felix walks away with Silk on his arm. This is the perfect scene in her eyes; two attractive boys about to fight over her in front of everyone in the school, and then she walks away with the one whom she doesn't have intimate feelings for, to let the one she is truly checking for sulk in jealousy for a moment. She walks away with Felix feeling satisfied in a big way.

Silk: "I am so petty!" She prides herself silently.

Now in the·center of the courtyard, Felix takes his arm from around Silk's shoulders and begins scorning her like he is her boyfriend. To Silk, this is kind of cute. She lets him rant on and remains silent, just staring at him blankly as if she is listening to him, although her mind is completely somewhere else at the moment, on a completely different person; Lorenzo. All she can think about is how fine Lorenzo just looked when angry. That was her first time ever seeing him get angry and aggressive, and the image of his angry face, the bravado in his threats to Felix, has her moist in between the legs. The fantasy of Felix and Lorenzo, two young attractive athletes, throwing down over her is driving her completely wild. Subconsciously she puts her fingernail to her lips and bites down seductively as she looks on at Felix talking, in a mesmerized state. Felix, seeing Silk lost in her trance, snaps his fingers in her face and when that doesn't snap her out of it, he puts a hand onto her shoulders and shakes her a little bit. His fingers touch right on the spot where the bite mark is. The finger snapping was useless, however, as soon as his fingers come into contact with the teeth marks on her shoulder, he gets an immediate reaction out of her, although nothing like he was expecting, let alone ready for. The touch brings an immediate erotic sensation to Silk, causing her sexual arousal. Her eyes roll to the back of her head as her body becomes filled with ecstasy. Flashbacks of being raped by Antonio course through her mind -—demonic, sort of angelic voices singing the chants and spells ring through her ears, the visions of people and creatures in dark places she'd never seen nor been before appear in her head, playing like a snippet video. Her nipples are hard as rocks, her panties are soaking wet underneath her jeans, and her clitoris is throbbing, begging for some attention.

When she opens her eyes, the look she gives Felix says, "Take me down right here, right now!" She rolls her neck back and puts a hand on his, feeling an orgasm approaching. Her soft moans become louder and louder. Felix is half shocked and freaked out but also turned on by how sexy she looks and sounds.

Silk's sexual escapade is ended when Essance walks up and grabs her by the elbow, forcing her to the side of a pillar blocking them from everyone's view. Lilli approaches also, followed by Felix. Essance goes right in on Silk:

Essance: "What has gotten into you lately?... Be honest with me and tell me what's been going on?... Where have you been going all of them nights?... And why you been coming home so late at night?..."

When Silk doesn't answer Essance opens up and asks her:

Essance: "What was you doing at Beatrice the voodoo queen's house last night, huh Silk?... And why would you lie to me about learning the spell that killed Barrika from Zela, the Bird Lady?... Why Silk? Why are you trying to learn voodoo anyway when our entire family is good Christian folk?... I can't even understand why you even likes the swamps and bayous and why you even choose to go down there? Please make this shit make sense to me cus' I'm lost and confused and shocked, all that shit!"

Essance's rapid questions and the revealing of her secret activities catches Silk completely off guard and the surprise is etched on her face. Silk questions to herself:

Silk: "What the hell? How does she know all of this shit? Has this lil sneaky bitch been following me low-key woe? No, she couldn't have followed you, Silk... Felix dropped her off at the house first. Did I say something out loud in my sleep? Maybe I was sleep talking, damnit!"

For a brief moment Silk stood there shocked; mouth open in the O shape, in bewilderment about all that Essance knew. Silk cannot find the answer fast enough at the moment. Essance spills the beans that she learned about all of Silk's late happenings from Lilli who is standing right there quietly and also waiting tentatively to get some answers out of Silk.

Essance: "We need answers and explanations as to it all, Silk." She demands.

The stares of anticipation that the group is giving her causes Silk to sweat profusely. Her mouth gets dry and her palms sweat also. "Well?" Essance says as she, Lilli, and Felix all stare at Silk, desperately awaiting answers. Silk doesn't answer any of Essance's questions, instead she has questions of her own to deflect:

Silk: "What makes you think that's true? Who told you that? I mean, how did you find out?"

Lilli becomes irritated because she knows what Silk is trying to do; she is playing little mind games with her twin, so Lilli rudely bursts in:

Lilli: "She got it from me. I told her and FeFe about how I followed you last night and saw you go into that witch's house, walking in unannounced like you live there or something... Now answer me this, what business you got with that witch lady Silk, huh?"

Silk feels shocked, confused and foolish to not have known she'd been followed all the way to Beatrice's last night. She starts to ask Lilli why she followed her but Essance cut her off:

Essance: "It doesn't matter why she followed you... the question is why are you kicking it with a voodoo queen? A known witch? Why Silk? Are you tryna become one of them evil witch thangs now or wassup? You been to just as many Bible studies as I have so I know you know that all evil people are gone burn in hell come Judgment Day right? Is that what you want?" she asks.

Silk chuckles, staring Lilli point blank in her eyes. She tries to turn the focus away from her and starts to ridicule Lilli about not allowing her her personal space and invading her privacy. She then tells Lilli that because she did those things to her that she is not a loyal friend and that she has changed up on her. "You not the Lilli you used to be at all" Silk asserts. Lilli responds with a hysterical laugh and then:

Lilli: "You are a pathetic liar... Did Mama B tell you all that stuff about me when she told you to stay away from me? Huh? Did she say that I'm a no-good friend and that I'm trouble? And that I need to be left alone? Is that what got chu walking around here with yo nose up yo ass and ya legs as wide as a field-goal pole? Huh Silk? Is it Mama B that got you acting like this Silk?... Oh, and the reason why I followed you is because I was afraid that you may be headed to somewhere to find trouble which I was absolutely right about now wasn't I?" she asserts matter-of-factly.

Silk cannot believe that Lilli knew all of this about her secret rendezvous as of lately. "How does she know her name is Mama B? How could I have been so obvious and so careless in how I move?" Silk ponders over in her mind. She looks from Lilli, to Essance, then to Felix with a perplexed facial expression, as they all return her looks with curious expressions of their own. Silk's emotions change to now feeling angry, so she, out of nowhere, bucks up toward Lilli, rushing to swing on her, but Essance steps in between and stops her.

Essance: "Why Silk?" she asks, looking at her twin with pleading eyes. Silk does not answer. "Did The Bird Lady really teach you that spell or did that other lady, the voodoo queen tell you it?" she persists in a pleading tone of voice. Again, all eyes are on Silk anticipating answers, making her feel trapped. She wants to tell a lie but she can't come up with one quick enough. Low-key she really wants to confess all that has happened to her for the past couple of months -—how it all started with almost being eaten alive by hungry alligators down at the swamp; to Beatrice casting the spell on the gators to save her life -—that being the reason why she felt indebted to Beatrice so she befriended her -—the mentorship Beatrice started giving her; all the things that she discovered about both Beatrice and Antonio and their weird incest relations; the voodoo lessons and practicing she's been learning from the two; her being raped by Antonio, the potions and the magic. She really wants to reveal everything she has been hiding to the closest people in her life, standing face front of her right now, but she knows she can't. She is too afraid of the consequences. She knows that these three people standing in front of her are the only ones she can truly confide in and she feels like now is the time to finally get it all off of her chest and then deal with whatever came next when it got there. So, she internally musters up enough confidence to lay everything out on the table to her twin and besties.

Chapter 23

Just as she is about to open up completely, a loud scream booms over the courtyard coming from a freshman female who is sitting down eating at the wooden bench table a few feet away from Silk and her clique. A large circle of students quickly gathers around to see what all of the commotion is about, including Silk and her group. When the four of them get to the center of the audience, where the freshman girl is still screaming hysterically, Silk follows the girl's terrified eyes to where her finger is pointing to, it is aimed at the tray she was eating her lunch off of on the table. "Ah" Silk gasps, surprised at what she sees. Sitting dead smack in the middle of the poor freshman girl's pizza is an exotic looking lizard. Out of sheer curiosity, Silk pushes her way through the tight crowd of onlookers to get a closer look at the creature that has the freshman frightened so. Just as she closes in on the lizard, here comes the school's janitor running towards the table with a broom in hand. Everything happens so fast Silk doesn't have time to react. The janitor swings his broom wildly, knocking the lizard onto the courtyard ground. Silk screams at the janitor in an effort to get him to stop, but he continues to swing his broom at the lizard as it is now on the ground trying to flee. The janitor looks at Silk like she's retarded for a split second, and then continues his task of trying to kill the small creature. The whole crowd gasps and screams as the little lizard makes its run for it in their direction, instilling fear in them all. One of the linebackers from the football team lifts his large Timberland boot in an attempt to smash the lizard as it crawls in his direction with the janitor in hot pursuit, broom still swinging crazily. The linebacker lifts his big leg in the air, ready to stomp on the lizard. Silk reacts quickly and pushes the linebacker's leg, causing him to fall to the ground hard, missing the lizard completely. She then bends down and retrieves the lizard, who stops all movement the moment it reaches her hands. Silk is in utter disbelief when she realizes that the lizard she'd just saved is indeed Iblis.

Beatrice's threats ring through her ears and she realizes that Iblis' presence just caused her from breaking her oath to Beatrice and Antonio. "Is she watching me too? Am I being followed some more?" Silk thinks to herself. She shakes the thoughts out of her head and carefully puts Iblis into a small compartment inside of her book bag. "You're ok, I got you." she whispers to the lizard as she tucks it away. Now all of the onlookers are observing Silk with weird-looking grossed-out expressions.

Essance: "Yuck! That is so nasty. That thing looks dangerous and you're just grabbing it with bare hands and stuffing it into our bag. What if it's poisonous and it explodes in there or what if you smash it?" she protests.

Lilli, clearly unbothered by the lizard incident, rudely goes in again:

Lilli: "Uh... I think we were in the middle of a confession that is still of the utmost importance ... Not the time to be catching new pets ya herd me?"

Silk responds to Lilli's insults with the evil eyes, but before she can rebut, Essance consigns with Lilli.

Essance: "Ya Silk, now what were you about to tell us before that dumb mess?" she asks, rolling her eyes away from the screaming crowd of onlookers.

Silk looks at the both of them with the same panicky expression as before. She's lost for words again and can feel the sweat forming on her hair line, causing her layed baby hairs to puff up, sweating out her flat iron treatment. Before she can speak, Beatrice's voice rings off in her brain. At that moment the bell rings signaling the end of the lunch hour. Silk shakes her head and snaps:

Silk: "It's none of y'allz damn business what I do in my free time, ya herd me? I'ma grown ass woman and the last time I checked I don't have to answer to either one of you huzzies. Now if ya'll will excuse me, I gots ta go, can't be late for Bio Chem. And Stink, tell yo friend if she ever snoop on me again she gone get dealt wit!" Silk ends, mean-mugging Lilli up and down.

"Bye, Felix!" Silk says, giving Felix a friendly hug, and then she takes off. Essance doesn't have a clue what has gotten into Silk but her gut tells her it isn't good. She believes Lilli isn't lying about Silk, and her strange reactions only support Lilli's accusations. Essance feels helpless, because she only wants what's best for her twin. Silk is literally the closest person to her. She has to know what is going on with Silk and the voodoo queen. Everyone in New Orleans, and hell, all of Louisiana for that matter, had heard the stories about Beatrice. Some even believed she was five-hundred years old.

Essance: "Are you sure you saw her go in that woman's house?" She turns and asks Lilli with pleading eyes, praying on the inside that Lilli will have doubts herself as to the accuracy of what she witnessed.

Lilli: "I'm one-hundred and one percent positive Stink!" she answers in a stern but sincere tone.

Essance: "So this means that my twin is becoming a witch?"

Lilli: "If she ain't one already." Lilli answers, nodding her head in confirmation.

Essance: "She really told her to stay away from you Lilli?"

Lilli: "Straight like that, Stink"

Essance: "How does she even know you though, I mean?" Essance questions more.

Lilli: "She practices voodoo and sorcery and what not, Stink. She's a witch" Lilli points out matter-of-factly.

Essance: "Damn... " she replies, looking at the ground with a defeated expression on her face, which tells it all.

Lilli: "She must've done put one of them spells on her, because that most definitely ain't our Silk. Nope, not anymore."

This scares Essance to death, but she knows that she has to be there and try to help her twin if it is the last thing she does. Essance and Lilli walk out of the courtyard together with Felix behind them not saying much.

Felix: "Y'all think it's true? Y'all think Silk killed ole girl with that voodoo shit?" Essance looks at Felix in confusion.

Lilli: "That's exactly what happened, because none of us touched that girl nor that knife" Lilli answers him. "It's like a ghost was there and did it. Well, that's what I thought at least. Now I know though.

A witch did it: Silk." she adds with much conviction, looking at Essance and Felix.

Felix: "Shit! I might need best friend to teach me some of that voodoo shit too, shoot... How she fucked ole girl up with that shit, shit I on't even need to carry my heat no mo, I could just say... " he states, looking up at the sky star-gazed and fantasizing about killing people with voodoo.

"Shut the fuck up damn fool!" Essance and Lilli both turn and yell at Felix simultaneously. He shuts up and they all walk back through the school cafeteria wearing troubled expressions as they think about Silk.

Felix: "So what chall wanna do bout it? Go holla at the old witch and be like, "Aye bitch, leave Silk the fuck alone foe we come burn these mafuckin woods to da ground ya her me!" he suggests.

Essance and Lilli both turn and look at him like he is a complete damn idiot, which he is for suggesting such a stupid course of action.

Essance: "What? Excuse me? Did you just say what I think you said?... Uh uh... I ain't goin down there, hell naw!" she responds, shaking her head no frantically.

Lilli: "Mane, you must be smoking crack rock if you think you finna go down there into them woods and make any type of threat, or even the slightest notion of a threat, to that witch. Is you dumb nigga? That whole damn family is wicked! -—the mommas, daddies, uncles, aunties, cousins, grandbabies, you name it."

Felix: "Well, all I know is that if Silk is really a witch... I mean, if what you sayin is true and all Lilli, then 12 can't get wind that Silk's magic spell and whatnot is what got Barrika her issue, otherwise she toast, and y'all is too, ya herd me?" he points out.

Lilli: "I'm not lying Fe... and I for damn sure ain't crazy. Well, I may be a lil crazy, just a tad bit... but I know what I saw, ya herd me? Silk is most definitely on one. She is with that voodoo mess y'all" she positively asserts.

Felix: "Well, just remember, y'all can't say nothing to nobody! I mean zip, nada!" he warns in a stern whisper, motioning as if pulling a zipper closed across his lips for emphasis.

Both girls nod their heads in agreement that they know to remain silent about everything. Felix goes on about his way, Essance and Lilli go to their lockers and grab their books for their next classes, and then go their separate ways also before the bell rings for the start of 4th hour.

Chapter 24

Everyone is either in their 4th hour class or on their way to class as the bell rings, all except Silk. She is in the girl's locker room with Iblis in her hand, petting and nursing him with water from one of the showers. She is talking to him quietly, the same way Beatrice often did, when the locker room door opens and someone enters. She frantically tries to put Iblis back into her bag, but she is not quick enough. The same janitor that had just tried to kill Iblis in the courtyard walks in to clean up, with Sony headphones on, loudly singing some type of blues song that he is playing on his MP3 player. He opens his eyes and spots Silk trying to stuff the lizard back into her bag and screams out.

Janitor: "Hey! What chu derrin in her girl? Ain't no P.E. dis hour... What n' the hell you derrin in her!? What's dat cha got right ther? Lemme see" the janitor demands, looking at Silk's hand with Iblis in it.

Silk looks at his MP3 player and comes up with a quick lie;

Silk: "I came back to get my iPod that I left in here after third hour, sir."

The janitor isn't listening as Silk speaks, his focus is on the red, orange, and black figure in her hand that she is obviously trying to conceal from his view. Without warning, he rushes her, grabbing at her book bag, trying to yank it off of her shoulder, and in the process, rips a piece of her blouse which causes her bra to come down and one of her plump breasts to become exposed. She screams and pleads with him to stop, to let her go, and tells him that he is hurting her, but to no avail. He yanks the bag with more force and causes Iblis, her school books, and her homework to go flying in the air, landing on the wet shower floor. He sees the lizard land and it begins crawling frantically.

Janitor: "What the? You again huh! Well I'll take care of ya, ya little nuisance!" he shouts out to the top of his lungs.

He stomps towards Iblis and lifts his boot to smash him, when Silk pushes him from behind, causing him to slip and fall hard onto the wet floor, cracking his head and denting the floor tiles. For a moment, he is shaking as if he's having a seizure, but then he slowly lifts his head off of the floor, still lying down dazed. The back of his melon now has a bloody gash and he is barely conscious. Silk tries to save Iblis who is now running away from the janitor, heading toward the shower drain hole in the middle of the shower floor area. The janitor suddenly regains his strength, rises up to his feet grabbing his mop stick from off of the floor, and swings it wildly at Iblis and connects, sending the little lizard crashing into the shower wall. Silk scowls and screams angrily at him to stop. When Iblis bounces off of the wall and hits the floor his red, yellow, and orange colors start glowing super bright. Its tongue is no longer moving in and out its mouth.

It is still as a statue. Its greenish eyes have turned pitch black. All of a sudden, the janitor's wooden mop stick turns towards him, then goes through his chest like a sword. He dies instantly while still standing up on his two feet. Silk is scared to death as the man's lifeless body falls onto the shower floor tiles and blood rushes out of him. She picks up Iblis who is no longer illuminated, fixes her bra and straightens out her now torn blouse, then quickly gathers her books and what homework papers she can manage, and runs out of the locker room full speed.

She doesn't bother going to class, she's too shaken up. She leaves the school, book bag dripping wet, gets on the bus, and heads to Beatrice's house. She arrives at her destination and knocks on the door. Beatrice answers and, noting the worried look in Silk's eyes, quickly ushers her in. Silk rehashes everything that had just happened at the school and gives Iblis back to her, which Beatrice places back into its habitat safely. Beatrice chastises Silk about her still associating with Lilli even after being warned to stay away from her.

Beatrice: "See ther Silky, I told ju dat lil heifer would bring you only grief. Now look at cha, not one but two folk dead. Two bodies in one week" she adds.

Silk is confused and afraid and doesn't know what to do. She asks Beatrice,

Silk: "What should I do?"

Beatrice: "Wait... "

Silk and Beatrice sit and talk for a while. They do a couple of voodoo rituals and readings, study some voodoo history, and then they make some new potions, all in an effort to distract Silk and to calm her nerves.

Silk: "What is with him?"

Beatrice: "With who baby?"

Silk: "Iblis... "

Beatrice: "I don't know what cha mean chile... say what chu want to know... "

Silk: "Like... how does he possess the power to kill the janitor the way he did?"

That is when Beatrice introduces Silk to the once guardian of hell, Ludiah, and the Queen of the damned Amineelia, both evil jinns. The stories she tells Silk about the two ancient demons sends both chills and thrills down her spine. Again, in her watered-down version, Beatrice explains the history of the two jinns and lblis' significance to Ludiah. She explains to Silk that she prays to the evil entities to receive powers and to transform earthly forms, and about how she uses the reptiles as a means for the jinns to survive the elements of earth. Beatrice convinces Silk to crash at her place for the night, which doesn't take much convincing being that she is scared shitless to leave due to the latest news she'd received from Felix and Essance. They had been calling and sending her text messages all evening, asking about her whereabouts, and informing her about the janitor being found dead in the girls' locker room. A group of girls had walked into the locker room to prepare for their 5th hour gym class and discovered the janitor lying in a pool of his own blood with his wooden mop stick stuck right in his heart. The school went on lockdown early and the police were on the scene investigating. Word had spread that they had already recovered lip gloss and a piece of paper with Silk's name on it in the crime scene. Silk didn't feel safe anywhere else at this moment. Essance also informs Silk that the police had questioned her while still at the school, asking where Silk was and that she is a number one suspect in the homicide case of the school janitor. Essance tells Silk that she has an active felony warrant out for her arrest. Silk faints at this news.

Chapter 25

When Silk awakes Antonio is there drinking something at the table with Beatrice braiding his long hair. Silk's phone buzzes, but when she tries to answer, the call drops, which is strange because she'd just been on it talking to Essance and Felix when she fainted. She gets up to move to a different area of the house to get better reception. As she passes Iblis' habitat she looks at him and is startled as the lizard stares deep into her soul with the same pitch-black eyes that she saw when she witnessed the janitor's gruesome demise earlier in the girl's locker room. Now she knows for a fact that those aren't Iblis' normal eyes, and she instantly is terrified at what it could mean now. She runs towards the front door knocking a cup off of the coffee table which causes Beatrice to frown and scowl at Silk.

Beatrice: "Slow your ass down heifer and quit breaking shit in here. Where ju tink ya run off ta anyway gul?"

Silk: "I'm sorry... I ain't getting a good signal in the house... I need to find a spot where I can get a good signal to see who keep calling me... The call could be important, Mama B."

Reluctant to let her leave at first, Beatrice agrees to send Silk off with a warning not to speak to anyone nor identify herself to any stranger. Silk acknowledges her warnings and is off in search for an area with a good signal.

As Silk heads through the woods, getting nearer and nearer to the city area, she passes by Zela's place. Zela is outside in a brown worn-looking wooden rocking chair petting three white doves in her lap. The old woman spots Silk moving fast on the path to civilization and calls for her to come over to her. Silk shyly complies, walking over to Zela with her head hung low to hide her emotions.

Zela: "What have you been doing lately chile? Why do you look so worried? What type of evil them devils done put on you now my dear?"

Zela knows exactly what is happening with Silk, every bit and piece of what has gone down since the first instance of her meeting Beatrice down at the bayou, to her dark secrets involving Beatrice and Antonio, to her now being the number one suspect in not one but two homicides, but Silk is clueless to her knowledge of these things. Zela knows everything but she doesn't let Silk know this. She plays clueless while attempting to fish the truth out of Silk. However,

Silk thinks she can outsmart Zela by misleading her but the bird lady is all-the-wise to her games. Silk tries to move on and change subjects.

Zela: "Where ya going dear?"

Silk: "I need to find an area where I can get good reception so I can answer a call on my phone mam."

Silk tries to walk away in a hurry but Zela halts her urgently.

Zela: "Do not go back to the city area... turn that cell phone off."

Silk looks at Zela with a baffled expression on her face as if the woman is crazy. For a minute she feels as though the bird lady may truly be nutso and contemplates jetting off on her, leaving her standing where she is. She thinks about it for a second but decides against her intuition. Zela grabs Silk by the arm and frantically ushers her into her home, closing the door and locking it behind them and shuts the front windows, just as a K-9 police cruiser passes by on the city street only one-hundred feet away from her residence. Silk is continuously trying to work her iPhone 10 Plus, when Zela snatches it right out of her hands, then opens a large bird cage and throws it inside. The birds immediately begin attacking the phone, destroying it and its contents completely. Silk immediately becomes pissed at Zela for destroying her expensive phone. Zela instructs Silk to take a seat at the table and starts explaining to her the real danger that is headed her way. She pulls out some cards, begins doing palm readings on Silk, and finally pulls out a round crystal ball. She uses the crystal ball to show Silk exactly what is happening in the world, in Silk's world, outside of the woods. Silk sees what looks like hundreds of police fully equipped in tactical and combat gear going door-to-door all throughout the city of New Orleans in search for her, asking people if they knew Silk and about her whereabouts. Silk sees her family being questioned at their home, with dozens of S.W.A.T. officers guarding the premises, and more police officers ransacking their home. She lets Silk see that it was actually the police that were calling her phone, trying to ping her cell phone's location which is why she'd told her to turn the phone off.

Now Silk feels grateful, because she realizes why Zela took it upon herself to destroy her phone. "That's why I hate technology," Zela says. She then shows Silk a glimpse of the future. Silk is beyond frightened and feels as though she will faint again when she sees an image of her in a dirty, tom up jail scrub outfit, shackled and handcuffed, while being ushered from a small cold jail cell into a federal courtroom to be tried for capital murder. The part that causes her heart to skip a beat is when the judge sentences her to the death penalty. The vision then goes on to her living in prison on death row getting beaten, raped, and tortured by other inmates and prison guards as she awaits her death date by lethal injection. Silk begins to cry, pleading with Zela for some kind of help. She feels hopeless and like she is already dead. A knock on the door nearly causes Silk' s heart to bust out of her chest. Zela shushes Silk from crying out loud and goes to see who it was. Billy Ray, Beatrice's younger brother, has come over to get a palm reading from Zela.

Zela allows Billy Ray inside. He instantly recognizes Silk.

Billy Ray: "Do you know that your name and face is all over the news about a double homicide at the high school?"

Silk begins crying hysterically and begs for help. Billy Ray is very remorseful as he sees her weeping and begging for help, but he knows that there is not much that he can do to help her.

Billy Ray: "Take you away from ... can get cha the hell out of Louisiana her is bout all I can do baby... Drive ya far away from her... Maybe take ya North... Illinois... Missouri? Maybe Minnesota or Michigan ... Somewhere far from here."

At that moment, Zela has a vision of Silk being apprehended by highway patrol in Missouri.

Zela: "No... that's not an option... "

Billy Ray looks at her quizzically while Silk has a frightened expression on her.

Billy Ray: "What did you just see?"

Zela: "Trouble ... "

Silk: "What do you mean trouble? What... what? Tell me please!"

Zela: "Same kind of trouble you saw in the ball chile... I'm sorry baby."

Silk: "Oh my god... What have I gotten myself into... My life is ruined now, thanks to those fucked up ass people... "

Billy Ray: "Calm down now sugar. .. everybody makes mistakes ... it's gonna be alright... What people?"

Zela: "Your sister Beatrice and your cousin Antonio. Silk been fooling with them folks, after I warned her not to go there, but she didn't wanna listen to me. I'm the 'crazy' one though, right?"

Zela finishes explaining to Billy Ray his family members' involvement, and how it is largely their fault that all of these things were happening to Silk. Billy Ray becomes angry and disgusted when hearing about the perverted diabolical things his family members had done to a young Silk. He storms out of Zela's front door in rage, mumbling profanities about Beatrice and Antonio, with Zela in lieu of him pleading for him not to go over to his sister's house. She tries to get in front of him to block his path but Billy Ray is too powerful. He climbs into his Ford F250 and smashes down the dirt trail, into the woods, heading towards Beatrice's estate, leaving a cloud of dust behind him. Zela, having feelings for Billy Ray, fears that things could get dangerous for him. She quickly grabs her hat, a rod, and a hawk.

Zela: "Stay put here. Do not leave or go outside, and do not open the door for anyone ya hear?"

Silk nods her head nervously in compliance, shaking like crazy out of fear. Zela palms her cheeks, eying her sympathetically, and then races off after Billy Ray. She gets to the entrance of her estate, stretches her arms out like bird wings while she says a short chant, then two huge bald eagles fly up and clutch each one of the shoulder pads of her jacket, then whisks her into the air flying towards Beatrice's house. Silk stands gazing out of Zela's living room window in sheer awe as she witnesses the phenomena.

Chapter 26

The Magical Battle Royal

Billy Ray's truck tires screech to a halt in front of Beatrice's home. She already is expecting him to arrive because she and Antonio were performing one of her meditation rituals and observed everything as it were happening at Zela's place. Beatrice smiles wickedly at her angry younger brother as he exits his F250 in fury.

Beatrice: "Sa pa se mi love... how aren't ya? Good seeing ya again, won't cha come inside, have a drink wit cha big sissy and let's catch up, shall we!" she greets him pleasantly and welcomes him into her abode.

He walks in fuming in rage cursing and screaming insults at his sibling in their native Haitian/Creole tongue. "WHACK!" Beatrice backhands him, shutting him up for a moment. Antonio puts on his shirt laughing at his little cousin. He begins mocking Billy Ray for being different from the two of them.

Antonio: "You always have been weak ... and a coward."

Billy Ray talks back and is lifted into the air by his throat, being choked by Antonio.

Zela bursts through the front door, a hawk on her shoulder, points her rod at Antonio which causes his body to go limp, and he drops Billy Ray on the floor. Beatrice looks to Zela with a wicked grin on her face, then to her little brother who is holding his neck gasping for air, and snickers while shaking her head in pity.

Beatrice: "Why have you and this pathetic disgrace of a sibling of mine come and disturbing da peace round here aye? And where is my little princess Silky at aye?" she asks, in a teasing manner.

Zela and Beatrice argue about Silk, Zela defending Silk, Billy Ray chiming in scolding Beatrice about how wrong she and Antonio are for taking Silk's innocence. He turns around mean-mugging his older cousin, who in turn jumps in defending Beatrice, and making belittling comments to Billy Ray about his masculinity.

Billy Ray: "Y'all got-damn incest babies... y'all are the abominations of the gulf!"

This enrages Antonio. He attempts to strike Billy Ray, but Zela points her rod again, says a few magical words, and hits him with a powerful blast that sends him flying across the room, crashing into and shattering a glass tank filled with reptiles in Beatrice's living room.

Chapter 27

Silk is sitting in Zela's porch area, mind racing. She looks up and spots Lilli fast-pacing it towards Zela's house. After her discovery at the school courtyard earlier, Silk presumes Lilli knew that she was there and was coming looking for her to talk about something important.

Silk: "How would she know I'm at The Bird Lady's if she followed me to Beatrice's place last night," she says, thinking out loud.

She suspects that Lilli must've stalked her again, but she can't fathom how it was possible. She gets up out of the chair she is seated in and tries to hide within the entryway of the house. Lilli walks up and opens the front screen door as if she lived there, or like she was a welcome guest, and surprises Silk when she calls out:

Lilli: "Mrs. Z!... Mrs. Z! Are you home, it's me Lillianna."

She walks through the porch and through the entryway too fast for Silk to try to hide anywhere.

They both flinch and look at each other for a moment in shock. Silk is shaking nervous, and Lilli looks at her completely stunned.

Lilli: "Oh my God, what are you doing here Silk? Where is Mrs. Z? Are you okay?" she asks Silk in succession.

Silk: "I'm fine girl" she answers, shaking her head pitifully.

Lilli: "What happened at school today after the courtyard Silk? Do you know that 12 got a statewide manhunt out for you right now? They're charging you with murder. Two. Barrika and the janitor", she informs.

Silk feels flustered and becomes light-headed as if she is going to faint again. She falls back onto Zela's couch, lays her head back and facing up, looking to the ceiling as if searching for some type of resolve. She feels helpless and hopeless. Felix gave them an alibi for Barrika's murder and it seemed to have worked to a certain degree, but she didn't know what she would say pertaining to the new murder case.

Silk: "I am screwed Lilli. I don't know what to do..."

Still feeling kind of betrayed, yet also very sensitive to her best friend's current dilemma, Lilli eases closer to Silk and begins trying to figure out how all of this came about.

Lilli: "Why would you choose to start chilling with Mama B and her wicked ass cousin, and learning voodoo anyway, that ain't you at all? Like why would you just go and change yo life 360 degrees like that out of nowhere?... You were doing so good. What did them people do to you huh Silk?"

Lilli also is curious to know how Silk really feels about their friendship, wondering if it was just Beatrice brainwashing her or if it is really how she felt about her. Silk is so overwhelmed she doesn't know how to answer any of her friend's questions. She feels so overwhelmed and exasperated from holding everything in and knows she needs to let it all out. She lets her guard down because she knows she needs all the help she can get right now, so she confides in her lifetime friend, breaking her oath to Beatrice and Antonio against her better judgment.

Confessions of everything from her falling in love with the bayou and nature at a very young age, to how she almost met her fate and was rescued by Beatrice, to how she felt indebted and befriended her, then to how Beatrice became her mentor over time and began teaching her the secrets of voodoo, about catching Beatrice and Antonio performing sex magic rituals, about being raped by Antonio, all of the potion making and magic spell lessons, the night she drank the potion and wound up involuntarily bedding Beatrice and Antonio, the spell she was taught to defend against Barrika that wound up killing her, about Iblis and him causing the death of the school janitor earlier after the courtyard incident. Silk tells Lilli everything.

Lilli soaks in everything Silk says and has mixed feelings. She sits down next to Silk and puts her arm around her to comfort her. Silk rests her head on Lilli's chest. As she is finishing revealing all of her secrets, the voices, chanting spells, and visions play their role on her mind.

Lilli: "So what about the repeated warnings you said that Zela tried giving you before all of this happened?... Why didn't you take heed to the woman's warnings?"

Silk does not have any answers. She is lost in a trance-like state. She sits up and tries to explain the kind of powers Beatrice, Antonio, and Iblis all possess, even telling Lilli about what she'd just learned earlier in the day from Beatrice regarding the evil jinns Ludiah and Amineelia. Silk then explains more about what happened earlier on the courtyard with Iblis, the lizard, and the freshman girl's scream, which interrupted her from revealing to them all what she'd just told.

Lilli nods her head in understanding. Silk finishes telling her about what happened with the janitor in the girls' locker room after she left the courtyard, her discovering that the lizard that caused the panic was actually Beatrice's pet, Iblis, and that this was the second time she had to save him from being squashed to death in the past three days. She explains about the janitor barging in, assaulting her, and attempting to kill Iblis. She tells her about how the entire ordeal transpired with Iblis glowing and killing him, and then how she left the school. She explains that she went to Beatrice's afterward and fainted upon hearing from her twin and Felix that she is now a fugitive from the law, and finally how she lost her signal and wound up there at Zela's place. After laying all of this on the table to Lilli, Silk breaks down crying on her best friend, soaking the top of her blouse shirt in tears. Lilli feels extremely sorry for her best friend, for her vulnerability and because she was robbed of her innocence. She places a hand in the middle of Silk's back and begins rubbing it, trying to soothe her as she lets all of her emotions pour out through her tears.

Lilli: "Everything gonna be alright Silk, ok? Don't worry it's gone be okay... "

Silk: "No it won't Lilli. Will it?" she states, tears rolling down her cheeks.

Lilli continues rubbing Silk's back while letting her cry out in her arms. Her hand finds its way up Silk's back, across the shoulder blades, and lands on the spot where Antonio left the bite marks on Silk. Flashes of their voodoo sessions, the rape, the heated sex session, various reptiles, and the voices chanting spells instantly ring and cloud Silk's mind. A sudden wave of ecstasy shoots through her entire body, and she opens her mouth and lets out a soft moan. A drippy puddle quickly forms in between her legs soaking her panties.

Her nipples turn rock hard and she is full of bliss and lustful desires. With tears still falling down her face, and the sexual sensation building more rapidly by the second, her moans become louder. Lilli doesn't notice the change in her emotions. She thinks that Silk is just very afraid at the moment so her sobbing is intensified, which she is correct to a certain degree, so she continues rubbing on the area where the bite marks are, unconsciously and unintentionally causing Silk's sexual arousal to escalate.

Silk has reached her peak and is hungry for some sex, and her best friend Lilli is fresh meat.

Chapter 28

After a couple harder, much louder moans, Silk goes in, opening her mouth and wraps her lips over the top of Lilli's perky right titty, and sucks on it hard, leaving a wet hickey on Lilli's bosom. Lilli is completely caught off guard. She jumps backwards on the couch, away from Silk. "Girl, what chu doin?" Lilli yells, staring at Silk in utter confusion while cupping her right breast. The voices and chanting are still going off in Silk's head so she is still in a trance and feeling hot and homier than ever, lusting over her best friend desirably.

Silk: "Lilli. I love you so much. I don't want us to stop being friends. I'm so sorry for what I was saying and how I was acting earlier. I don't want to lose you. What if I go to jail and never... we never see each other again? Or what if they stick me with that needle and kill me, Lilli? Then I won't ever get to say goodbye!" she cries out sincerely.

The scared look in Silk's eyes and the sincerity in her trembling voice when she speaks causes Lilli to break down now, because she knows everything Silk said could be a very accurate outcome in this situation. She never knew that things would ever come to this point, especially with someone whom she loved dearly like Silk. Neither of them knew. They both stare silently at each other for a few minutes. Silk then leans in and kisses Lilli right on her full lips. This time Lilli doesn't jump nor flinch, she accepts it and even returns it. This is something completely new to Lilli, so she is not as into it and adamant as Silk is, however, she no longer rejects Silk's sexual advances. She actually has thought about what sex with another girl would feel like for a while now, she just never acted on her curiosity. Now she was kind of feeling it. They begin making out passionately on Zela's couch. Silk grabs Lilli's medium-large breasts while their tongues dance and do tricks in one another's mouths. Silk eases her kisses down to Lilli's neck. Lilli arches her back from the blissful feelings.

Lilli: "Damn, I never knew this shit felt so good. I see why girls become lesbians" she thinks to herself.

They both take turns flipping each other over, taking one another's breasts out and sucking on them, rubbing their nipples together, kissing each other's entire upper body, both of their eyes rolling back in pure ecstasy. Lilli bends over first in the doggy-style position, arching her back like a cat in heat, elbows planted on the arm of the couch, with her plump, petite butt in the air. Silk makes a trail of kisses all the way down her back, all the way down, till she reaches the start of her cinnamon brown butt crack. She unbuttons Lilli's skirt and pulls it down, revealing her pink and black Victoria Secrets thong.

Silk: "Oow girl" she cheers, admiring the set.

Lilli: "Michael bought me the set for my birthday girl" she responds, looking back and snickering.

Silk gets to kissing and then sucking on both of Lilli's ass cheeks, going back and forth from one to the other, soaking her butt cheeks down, nearly letting her tongue slide down in between, in Lilli's asshole. She then slides the thong off of Lilli, revealing her gorgeous, fat, dark, clean shaved vagina. She positions her mouth right in front of Lilli's pussy, sticks her tongue out, and just as she is about to start devouring Lilli's wet box from the back, the birds in the house start going crazy -—flying in from all different areas of the house, screaming and squawking frantically above them, as if they're going to attack them. The storm of angry birds causes the girls to stop immediately, scurrying to get back dressed. As they dress, they look at each other, both appearing sort of embarrassed. Once they have stopped, and all sexual energy between them are gone, all of the birds seem to vanish and the room is back calm again, although now filled with different feathers. One mysterious looking bird stood out in particular. Silk guessed it could be a young raven by its appearance. It has goldish-silver colored eyes and is perched straight up adjacent from Silk, staring directly in her eyes with its beak open making noises as if talking to her. The bird's behavior causes Silk's nervousness to return.

Lilli: "How long has it been since Zela left after Billy Ray?" she asks, picking up on Silk's fear.

Silk: "Almost an hour ago" she answers. Lilli pauses to think for a second.

Lilli: "We should go over to Beatrice's to make sure that Zela and Billy Ray aren't in any kind of trouble!"

This confuses Silk a lot and causes her to wonder why Lilli seemed to care so much about the bird lady or Billy Ray for that matter? She's still wondering what even brought Lilli here to Zela's house? And why did she walk in so casually and comfortably when she first arrived? Those are all the questions going through Silk's mind that she would need her best friend to answer for her at a later time, but right now she protests leaving Zela's place. She repeats Zela's instructions not to leave to Lilli.

Silk: "Don't leave and don't open her door, lest 12 get they paws on me. That's what she said Lilli."

Silk is trembling after repeating the part about being apprehended by law enforcement.

Lilli: "I think that you will be fine as long as we stay in the woods... But naw forreal though... I just got this funny feeling that... like... Zela may be in some sort of grave danger dealing with Beatrice and her cousin Antonio." Silk looks at Lilli with a puzzled gaze.

Silk: "Why, what would make you think such a thing like that?" she asks, fishing for some information out of Lilli.

Lilli dismisses the question, brushes off her blouse and skirt, and tells Silk that she is going to go alone to find Zela and make sure that she is safe. Silk, refusing to let her best friend go out at something like that, straightens her bra and runs out of the door after Lilli. Before departing the living room, Silk notices the mysterious majestic looking Raven still in the same spot staring at her intensely. Silk pauses, returning the stare, but looking puzzled at the bird. It begins flapping its wings violently and screaming as if telling Silk to hurry up and go, "Leave". She dashes out after Lilli, a nervous wreck. At a glimpse she spots a piece of her damaged cell phone in the Raven's talon which makes her think.

Chapter 29

Two NOPD detectives from the homicide division had already started investigating the case that involved Barrika being murdered at the high school, and now they are assigned to the new case with the janitor as well. Detective Billy Bob, a twenty-five-year veteran of the New Orleans Police Department, detective for fifteen years, and was a Sergeant in the Marine Corps. Detective Valorie Santos, New Orleans Police Officer for seven years now, one and a half of those years she's spent as detective, starting in the street crimes division and transferring to homicide just six months ago, and is a Navy Seal reserve. One old-fashioned, trying to fit in with modern day swag, Billy Bob, while the other, Valorie, is very classy, sophisticated, driven to solve her cases and rid society of the bad guys, as she'd refer to the criminals she arrested, not to mention an extremely attractive young Latina. The two detectives started out at the school where both murders had occurred, today, in the girl's locker room where the janitor's dead body was discovered. Now that they had a suspect, Silk, they headed the statewide manhunt, starting at the Greenes' residence. They instructed a few officers they'd brought with them for extra help to search the perimeter of the Greenes' property with a S.W.A.T. team at the end of the block on standby.

Entering the Greenes' with just a few police officers and using the S.W.A.T. team only for security purposes was entirely Detective Valorie's call. Billy Bob's first choice was to order the S.W.A.T. unit to go and crash through the front door locked and loaded, and to tear the place up until they either found their suspect or someone told where they could find and apprehend her. Detective Valorie won that argument. Both detectives talk to Lashunda, since she is the only parent present in the house when they arrived with a search warrant for Silk. Deangelo arrives home from work moments later, tired from a long day on the construction site. He walks in the house very suspicious about the heavy presence of police vehicles parked in front of his home, and the ones all around the neighborhood as he drives through. He has a worried expression on his face as he drops his lunch box and jacket on the floor and approaches his wife, who clearly appears to be overwhelmed by what the two detectives are telling her. Zay Zay is in her bedroom with her television on Nickelodeon watching cartoons and playing with her Barbie Doll Dreamhouse. Roberta is in the living room on her cell phone talking to her fiance, but hangs up when the police enter the house asking about Silk. The police never disturb Zay Zay once they see her playing so innocently. When they went door-to-door searching in bedrooms, Zay Zay was so into her cartoon that she didn't even hear or notice that the officers had opened her bedroom door and shut it back. This kind of annoyed Detective Valorie, and she made a note to self that she'd go back and check the toddler's room again much more thoroughly than her subordinate officers had. Now both detectives are explaining to both parents and to Roberta why they are there looking for Silk and the extremity of the situation at hand. The Greenes are completely flabbergasted at what they hear from the detectives. Lashunda, Deangelo and Roberta all become filled with shock and disbelief, and Lashunda's anxiety immediately starts to kick into overdrive. They tell the detective that Silk hadn't been acting differently lately, she didn't tell them about Barrika bullying her or Essance. Ultimately, Silk's family is really no help to the detectives when it comes to figuring out a motive for murdering Barrika and the school's janitor. Detective Valorie decides to go to Zay Zay's room now. She kindly asks the Greenes for permission to speak to her, which Lashunda permits through a face filled with fearful tears.

Detective Valorie gently opens the bedroom door and kindly introduces herself to Zay Zay. Lashunda and Deangelo both stand in the doorway of Zay Zay's room while Detective Valorie speaks to their child. Detective Valorie sits down across from Zay Zay, although not directly in front of her so she doesn't block her view of the television, smiling pleasantly at her. Zay Zay smiles back as the show goes on commercial break, and tells the detective her name. Detective Valorie compliments Zay Zay on her having a cute name and then she tells Zay Zay her own name. Detective Valorie muses over the huge Barbie doll dreamhouse set and all of the Barbie accessories Zay Zay owned, being that she was infatuated with Barbie when she was a little girl, and Zay Zay had things she wanted badly but never had growing up, which has her in awe as she views Zay Zay's massive Barbie collection. She then begins to ask indirect questions about Silk.

Zay Zay tells Detective Valorie that she loves Silk and that she hadn't saw her today. Not wanting to pry too deep and cause the child to worry much, Detective Valorie only asks a few more questions pertaining to Silk's role as Zay Zay's big sister, which she finds out from Zay Zay that Silk is a wonderful loving sister to her. Detective Valorie ends the question there and resumes talking about the Barbie doll collection, which Zay Zay was overly excited to discuss. Detective Valorie decides that her time spent in the Greenes' home has concluded, and readies the unit to leave. As the police are leaving their cards with the family, in walks Essance and Felix. Essance, in complete shock, gets questioned immediately by her parents and the detectives.

Chapter 30

Silk catches up to Lilli who is walking so fast one would say she is jogging to get to Beatrice's estate. Silk asks Lilli if she had her phone on her and asks to use it. Lilli looks at her quizzically for a moment not knowing why Silk wants her phone at this moment. Lilli reluctantly hands Silk her cell phone. When she looks at the screen a call comes in from an unknown number. Silk hits the answer button, puts a finger up to Lilli's lips for her to be silent, presses the speaker phone button, and listens. A woman's voice comes over the phone speaker:

Detective Valorie: "Hello. Lillianna? Hello? Lillianna if you can hear me my name is Detective Valorie Santos from the NOPD. Are you there? Can you hear me? I am trying to find your friend Silk Greene and I was wondering if you could help me out a bit? Lillianna

I really need to find Silk so that we can talk, because I feel she may be in deep trouble and it can get really dangerous for her to be walking the streets, so I need your help in finding her and making sure no harm comes to her" she continues speaking through the phone even though she hasn't even gotten a response.

Lilli reaches for her phone while the detective is speaking but Silk chucks it into the swamp water. The iPhone 10 sinks in the swamp, however, because it is waterproof, it doesn't shut off. Detective Valorie shakes her head and hangs up at the disconnection sound. She radios into the police command center RV parked a few blocks away from the Greenes' home to give the IT team Lilli's cell phone number so that they could attempt to ping the phone's location. Essance had reluctantly given the detectives Lilli's cell phone number. Felix protested and advised Essance not to give the police the number, but both of her parents and her older sister Roberta demanded that she cooperate and give up Lilli's number so that Silk could be found. Detective Valorie informed the Greenes that they would be leaving some officers there to survey the perimeter for Silk's arrival. Deangelo and Lashunda both plead desperately with the detective and officers not to shoot Silk when they do locate her and move to arrest her. Detective Valorie sympathetically and sincerely assured the Greenes that she would see to it that Silk will be apprehended with the most care and compassion. Detective Valorie's promise put just a slight ease on the Greenes' fear of their daughter and sister being harmed by overly aggressive police officers, but Felix is not convinced. He is from the streets so he knows better than to believe anything a police officer promises you. All of the warrant posting on the media reads that Silk is "a suspect in a double homicide" and that she may be "armed and dangerous." Felix knows how the police will proceed and approach his best friend. What Detective Valorie just sold the Greenes is a line of bullshit to him. He must find Silk before the police do.

Chapter 31

The Throw-Down

Lilli: "Why you throw my phone in the swamp for, bitch, instead of just hanging the phone up... Now jump yo ass in that damn water and get it bitch!" she demands in pure frustration.

Silk: "You smoking crack, bitch?" she counters, looking at her as if she has lost her damn mind.

Lilli: "Maaan, my mama gone be pissed at me for this shit woe! She just put me on my plan when I got fired from the Hut."

Silk: "Be forreal bitch... you know 12 got all of the advanced technology that can track yo ass down and me too... Come on now I know you remember all that shit we used to see growing up from watching all of the CSI and forensic evidence crime shows on TV girl... come on now, you playin crazy!"

Lilli: "Yea, you right woe. I ain't even think about that one. Luckily, she got insurance on dem phones", she agrees and they keep it moving.

They continue tracking their way through the bayou towards Beatrice's property. Silk looks around at the vegetated woods because she hears movements coming from the long grass. Her and Lilli already knew that the likely source was moccasins, frogs, toads, maybe a squirrel or a gopher. The sound of water splashing diverts their attention to the swamp waters where they see a gang of alligators, rapidly scouring through the waters, heading in the same direction that they are headed, towards Beatrice's estate. The creatures in the grass all seem to be heading in the same direction as well at a rapid pace also. Darkness covers them, and when they look up to the sky, they see hundreds if not thousands of birds speeding through the air, making the ground shake from all of the different sounds and calls they are making, heading in the same direction. Silk and Lilli look at each other for a moment, both feeling really nervous. Lilli jumps when she feels snakes and lizards running and qawling over her feet as they make their ways through the grass heading towards Beatrice's. She screams and moves closer to Silk, who doesn't seem to be fazed by the reptiles. Lilli is frozen for a moment in fear. Silk grabs her arm, pulling her forward with her so that she can keep up the pace.

Silk: "You was right bitch... Something is most definitely going down over there at Mama B's. We gotta get over there!"

Lilli: "See hoe I told yo ass... I be right about shit all the time... my gut, my heart... they never lie... come on let's go!"

They are nearly within eyesight of the voodoo queen's estate. Lilli shakes her head nervously and regains her pace.

An older white fisherman who had just casted his boat into the swamp river only moments ago to do some crawfishing witnessed the entire exchange between Silk and Lilli. He saw Silk throw Lilli's iPhone into the water. When the girls walk off, he moves his boat to the area where the phone sank, casts his crawfishing net over the area and successfully retrieves it. Before arriving to the bayou, he'd seen newsfeeds on his smartphone and had heard on FM radio about NOPD looking for a black teenage girl who is a suspect in a double homicide investigation at a high school in the area, and immediately recognizes Silk's face from the pictures shown in the newsfeeds. Moreover, during his eavesdropping, he overheard Silk say that the police were trying to track the phone right after she threw it into the swamp. This fisherman also remembers that the newsfeed had mentioned that there has been issued a fifty thousand dollar reward for anyone with information leading to the arrest of Silk Greene. He snatches the discarded phone out of the net and then fetches his own phone in an attempt to call 911. Suddenly, a powerful wave rocks the boat causing both phones to go flying into the swamp waters. The fisherman, a native of the swamps and bayous in this area, is startled because he knows that the type of wave that just hit his boat is extremely unusual in these types of waters. He stands still, hands and legs trembling as he waits for something to happen. Next thing you know two enormous alligators rock the hull of the boat, sending him flying overboard and into the water to be torn to shreds.

Chapter 32

Silk and Lilli make it to Beatrice's house to find it heavily surrounded by all of the creatures they'd saw heading that way plus many more, on both sides of the property as if about to have a faceoff. The birds' feathers are all ruffled up, flapping their wings, and squawking defensively at the reptiles, while the reptiles all are in their defensive modes, hissing, showing razor sharp teeth, and some spitting venom at the other side. Silk and Lilli both pause, star-struck and afraid to go any further. A window in the front of the house shatters, taking their attention to Beatrice's home. Screams can be heard coming from the inside of the house and Silk recognized one coming from Beatrice and Lilli recognized the opposite's being Zela. Little did the girls know, although not expecting anything to be civil when they arrived, but they have just walked into a magical battle between lifelong rivals.

After sending Antonio crashing into the tank, Beatrice becomes enraged and starts casting spell after spell in an effort to defeat Zela, who uses her magic also to fight back, defeating every spell or magical weapon used against her. Beatrice throws a zap of magic which misses its intended target, bounces off of a steel fixture, ricochets off a cast iron pot, and lands right on Billy Ray's chest just as he is regaining his strength from being nearly choked out by his warlock cousin.

The magic in the spell begins working instantly, coursing through his torso, up his neck, along his arms, causing his skin to bump up like a toad. Zela quickly throws a blast of magic at him, hitting him in the exact same spot on his chest, which reverses Beatrice's spell and destroys the lepers. Beatrice and Zela continue to battle against each other with their voodoo and witchcraft. Antonio recovers and moves to assist his cousin and also his lover, throwing his own spells at the bird lady, but Zela is too quick, too powerful, and also more experienced in their craft than the both of them. Her counter attacks come and go too quickly for the warlock, making her untouched. Antonio tries to hit her with a super powerful blast of energy but as he prepares to release it Billy Ray clubs him in his temple with the back of an axe, sending him crashing to the floor with a bloody gash on his right temple. Beatrice moves in on Zela and tries to overpower her using her own body weight, but the bird lady's magic powers are too strong. She sweeps Beatrice right off of her feet with one swipe, sending her falling down on her plump wide ass, smashing through the glass coffee table in the center of the living room. Antonio slowly gets up on his feet, staggering from the blow to the temple, and is seeping with anger at his little cousin for his treacherous acts. With his strength coming back to him, he throws a powerful blast of magic at Billy Ray. This time Zela is so busy containing Beatrice that she is not fast enough to stop Antonio's blast. It hits Billy Ray and sends him crashing right through the living room wall. He lands in the kitchen, directly into the big pot of boiling potion, causing some of the magic potions to spill out onto the kitchen floor and on his back. Some of the burning pieces of wood that were cooking the potion are knocked out of place due to the crash, and send a mixture of ashes and fire pellets all over the kitchen, catching onto the drapes, the wooden countertops, and the tablecloth.

Silk opens the front door. She and Lilly observe the chaos going on inside of the house in shock. Beatrice is on her big ass, laid out on top of a glass coffee table that is now shattered into tiny pieces. Zela is poised over her in a defensive posture, ready to fight off Beatrice's anticipated reaction. Antonio lay on the ground with a gash and blood running profusely down his face. The front of the house is completely destroyed from the battle with broken furniture everywhere, one of the reptile tanks completely busted with the reptiles crawling all over the room, and everyone is screaming some sort of profanity mixed with a spell or chant in French. "Nooo! Stop!" Silk yells out over the chaos. Zela jumps and looks towards the doorway behind her at Silk. Surprised to see Silk and Lilli in the doorway, both clearly horrified, Zela quickly transforms her energy into a calmer state and momentarily stops using her magic on Beatrice. This split second of opportunity is all the time Beatrice needs. She sends a blast of magic at Zela's backside which hits her, throwing her through the open front door, over the girls' heads, to the outside. Silk and Lilli duck as Zela came flying uncontrollably in their direction, and what happens next has Silk in total disbelief; Before Zela can hit the ground outside, Lilli stretches out her arms, points at Zela, yells out a spell that catches the bird lady in mid-air, and allows her to land upright on her feet, unfazed. Before Silk can say anything, the girls jump to the side as Beatrice gets up off of her butt and comes storming their way in pursuit of Zela. Antonio follows behind the voodoo queen, with an army of the loose reptiles behind him. Shortly after, Billy Ray also comes racing out of the home that is now engulfed in flames from all sides. Beatrice and Antonio aren't ready for the fight to be over, and seeing her house in flames enrages Beatrice even more. The two resume casting their spells and throwing blasts of magical energy at Zela, but by her being

an older witch than the both of them, she is alone more powerful
and more knowledgeable than the two of their experience combined.
Although Zela is powerful enough and wise enough to combat the
two relative oppositions on her own, she now has the help of Lilli,
her young apprentice, on her side to go to battle with. Lilli stands on
Zela's right side, in front of the large crowd of angry birds that are
still flapping and making all sorts of eardrum busting noise, and joins
in the magical battle, throwing spells she'd learned from the bird lady
at Beatrice and Antonio. They fight her and Zela relentlessly, using
the reptiles also as ponds to help them curve their attention so that
they can get a cheap shot in, to no avail. Beatrice becomes more
and more angry at how calm and contempt both Zela and Lilli are
as they block and counter every weapon of magic thrown their way
by the queen and the warlock. She is screaming wildly, hair frizzed,
eyes bulging, and spit flying out of her mouth as she yells wicked
obscenities at young Lilli.

Beatrice "You see, you see now? Didn't I tell you this little bitch
is trouble? She is not your friend, and if she is you see the Iil bitch
is a no-good friend, now don't cha? Look at her!" she yells to Silk
through her episode.

Hearing Beatrice talk down on her to Silk right in front of her
face strikes a nerve in Lilli, so she fires back at the mouth, cursing
and swearing back at the voodoo queen, feeding her emotions. This
is one thing her mentor, the bird lady, always warned her against.
Lilli begins advancing towards Beatrice, throwing blow after blow
of magic and spells. Zela yells in a desperate attempt to stop her
but Lilli hears nada. Beatrice, far more experienced in magic, returns
with a vicious spell that Lilli is totally unaware of and smacks her
body violently, her flying into the crowd of birds. A huge bald eagle
expands its wings and catches her fall.

Seeing her friend get hurt in the battle, Silk starts screaming and
swinging closed fists at Beatrice and then Antonio grabs her up from

behind in a bear hug, restraining her. As Silk kicks and screams for Antonio to let her go, Beatrice walks up and smacks fire out her. Lilli, a little dazed feeling is being helped up to her feet by Zela. She regains her focus when she catches Beatrice smacking Silk so viciously in her mouth, causing blood to pour out profusely. Lilli becomes enraged and instantly Zela whispers into her ear, "Don't mix emotions with magic baby. Be calm. Control your emotions." Lilli straightens herself up, recites a few help anecdotes in her head and nods to her mentor in understanding. They both turn and resume throwing blasts of magic spells at Beatrice. Antonio drops Silk quick enough to block the ball of energy from hitting his queen. Silk falls to the ground near the front door of Beatrice's home. She looks inside of the burning house and notices something appears to be illuminating behind a glass wall.

She soon realizes that it is Iblis that is glowing and that he is trapped inside of his habitat amongst the smoky, blazing house. She quickly leaps off of the ground, and without a split thought, makes a daring race inside of the house, through the thick black smoke and raging growing flames, risking her own life to save the lizard. Lilli and Zela both scream for Silk not to go into the burning house but their screams are useless because she's already inside. Beatrice and Antonio both look at each other with confused, nervous expressions on their faces, unsure of what to do in response to Silk's move. For a brief moment the magical battle ceases as the four try to decipher why Silk would run into a burning house instead of running the other way, perhaps out of the woods. They all ponder what is happening as they watch the flames rise and fully consume the house.

Chapter 33

Billy Ray makes it back to his pickup while the witches and warlock battle it out in the front yard. He starts the ignition and as he is about to shift the F250 into gear he hears a hissing sound. Then he feels a wet, slimy-like tongue hit the back of his neck. He turns to face the noise and as soon as he does he is swiftly struck right below his right eye by a snake. He screams in pain and instinctively ducks, shielding his eye. He then grabs a can of bug repellant off of the floor, points it and sprays towards the snake until the can is empty. The repellant disables the snake by momentarily blinding it. While he has the chance, Billy Ray grabs the snake, then grabs his Bic lighter and puts it up to the snake's open mouth. Venom is shooting out of the snake's fangs wildly as Billy Ray aligns it to his lighter. He then strikes the lighter igniting the snake and then tosses it out the door. He puts his pickup in drive and guns the gas pedal, steering straight toward Beatrice and Antonio. With the raise of one hand, Beatrice turns the dirt road he is driving on into thick mud, stopping the truck about ten yards away from where her and Antonio stand. Lilli reverses the magic, hardening the dirt road again and allowing Billy Ray's pickup to continue smashing their way. Beatrice and Antonio both dodge the truck abruptly, and the pickup goes crashing through the front of Beatrice's house.

Silk is blinded by the thick black smoke, and her lungs quickly start to fill with it. She reaches Iblis' habitat, opens the glass partition, retrieves him, and stuffs him into her bra. To her, the lizard feels a little weird nestling inside her bosoms, only the flicking of its tongue to breathe tickled her, but she is far too occupied with the task at hand to even think about it. She needs to get out of this burning house quick. She turns to go back the way she'd came in, when all of a sudden, the entire front wall of the house comes crashing in on her, sending burning pieces of the wooden house, furniture, and glass from the front windows spraying all the way to the back of the house where Beatrice's bathroom and bedroom is. A fiery, smoking piece of lumber falls from above and hits Silk in her forehead, knocking her to the ground.

She is able to open only one eye just barely before passing out. Through fuzzy vision, she sees the front grill of Billy Ray's Ford pickup truck just inches away from her face. She observes the driver's door open up and, through blurry vision, a figure gets out, and then everything goes black. Silk is out cold.

Billy Ray sees a female figure in the debris of the burning house he'd just driven his pickup through. He gets out of the truck coughing and wheezing horribly from the thick smoke, and approaches Silk to find her unresponsive and bleeding from her forehead. He picks her up and rushes her to his four-door pickup, opens the rear passenger door and lays her gently across the back seat. He hops into the driver's seat, throws the truck in reverse, and guns it out of the burning house before the fire can catch his truck completely. He expertly fishtails the truck as soon as the front grill makes it out of the house, and then he pulls up to Zela and Lilli, reaches over and opens the passenger door, and yells for them both to get inside, which they quickly do in one quick swift motion, too fast for the naked eye to catch. Billy Ray races off, away from the wreckage, with all of the hundreds of birds in tow.

Beatrice nor Antonio are aware that Silk is in the backseat of Billy Ray's pickup truck. They both think that she is still inside of the burning house. Together they use their magic, casting a spell over the house that sucks all of the smoke and flames out and douses the fire completely. Beatrice steps through the big hole in the wall that Billy Ray's truck left, stepping over debris and wreckage. She looks around intensely at the destruction, Antonio on her ass literally, gazing in shock as well, but young Silk is nowhere to be found. She looks up and observes Iblis's cage, sees that the glass door is wide open, and rushes over to it, eyes as wide as saucers and looking around frantically, but no Iblis. Beatrice lets out a screeching scream that forces Antonio to cover his ears, a huge gust of wind blowing stuff around, causing the reptiles to go running back to where they'd come from. Antonio looks at his cousin in terror and assures her that they will get their dark Lord back safely. Beatrice stares devilishly off into space, hair frizzling wildly and her big breast heaving from her deep breathing.

Billy Ray guns the pickup through the wooded swampland road to get back to Zela's property where they'd all be safe. The effect of the King Cobra's deadly venom is settling in and starting to work on him. His blood begins to clot in his nearly closed eye, near the bite wound is changing colors, and his heartbeat slows down drastically. He is becoming dazed and begins to drift causing the truck to swerve. One of the truck's front tires hits a huge log sending the truck airborne and to its' side. Lilli is in the back with Silk trying to get her to wake up, soaking Silk's face up with tears of worry and fear. Billy Ray faints, losing total control of the wheel, and the truck takes a nosedive into the ground. The hit causes everyone in the truck to bounce around.

Zela says a spell but is stopped when her head hits the top of the truck. Lilli and Silk are rolling in the back seat, when suddenly Lilli sees something glowing remarkably down in Silk's bra, between her breasts.

Upon further inspection, Lilli meets Iblis's pitch-black eyes and tongue as he is snuggled comfortably between Silk's titties. Lilli jumps back and pushes Silk off of her, which causes an unconscious Silk to drop to the floor like a doll. Suddenly the truck is no longer rolling nor skidding, but just feels like it is lifted into the air. Lilli looks out the front windshield and is stunned when she sees two enormous bald eagles on each side of the truck's hood, talons clamped on, lifting and flying the truck with what appears like very little effort. As she turns and looks out the rear window, she spots two more huge eagles on the end of the cab assisting in flying the pickup through the woods. The majestic eagles airlift the truck to Zela's place peacefully. Lilli is in awe at these spectacular birds during the entire ride, thankful to have been saved from the near-fatal crash. Initially, she believed the eagles were there by Zela's doing, being that she is the Bird Lady and all. However, she looks in the front passenger seat and sees that Zela herself is barely conscious, painfully holding her forehead after being knocked around by the rumble and tumble. Lilli asks Zela if she was ok. Zela let her know she was fine. Lilli then asks her if it was her who cast the spell that put the eagles on life-saving mode. Zela answered no, it wasn't her. Lilli looks back down in between Silk's bosoms and it was in the same spot, and Iblis is still there with pitch-black eyes, staring back at Lilli. Her hands trembling unconsciously, she taps Zela and points to the lizard. Zela looks, then her eyes get wide, and covers her mouth with both hands, looks out at the eagles flying with the pickup, then back to Iblis in a complete terror. Was this her lucky day, or her last day? Zela thought to herself.

Honestly, Zela could not believe her eyes, and now she knew why Silk had went storming back into the burning house; Iblis. She did not interrupt nor try to harm the majestic lizard in any way, instead she let his evil powers control their safe arrival to her place. She'd deal with Iblis once everything was under control. That is, once Iblis decided to relinquish control to the Bird Lady. Right now, Silk and Billy Ray both need serious medical attention.

The eagles land the truck full of passengers safely on Zela's estate. Lilli's eyes stay glued on to Iblis from the moment she discovered him hiding in Silk's bosom. When all four of the truck's tires hit the ground, the lizard returns back to its normal state, no longer illuminating, and its eyeballs are no longer pitch black. Lilli is frozen in fear and astonishment. The eagles walk off peacefully into the sanctuary of birds. Lilli is taken out of the trance-like state she was in from Iblis when Zela thrusts the driver door with worry sketched all over her face, looking at Billy Ray slumped over the wheel, bleeding profusely from his head and his left eye swollen shut. His head had banged against the driver's side window, cracking the glass. Zela orders Lilli to get Silk out of the truck as she struggles with getting Billy Ray out. Lilli complies and drags Silk into Zela's house and lays her on one of the couches before running back outside to assist Zela with lugging a muscular built Billy Ray into the house. Zela really needed help after losing much of her energy during the magical battle with Beatrice and Antonio. The two manage to get Billy Ray into the center of Zela's living room, laying him flat on his back.

Chapter 34

Lilli: "What happened to Billy Ray?"

Zela: "I'm not one hundred percent sure baby."

Zela then points at the only visibly logical explanation she could see: the bleeding, swollen closed eye, and two tiny holes -—a snake bite. Lilli goes back to the couch and tends to Silk as Zela races to a cabinet in the kitchen and fetches some elixir and medicines in an effort to bring Billy Ray back. He's still alive, however, his pulse is extremely faint, he's unresponsive even to touching, and his entire body is starting to turn a pale light bluish. Zela, in a low calm voice, fumbles with her words while trying to cast up the right spell to fight the venom as she pours the liquids onto the bite area, and injects him with some type of antivenom she'd invented herself. Her remedies stop him from dying, buying him some time, but he needs real snake antivenom, and the right kind fast. With these facts in mind, Zela thinks of the only person she knows that would have what they need and know most definitely how to save her lover from death. That person is her long-time friend, snake specialist, Hernando. She hurries and finds a piece of note paper and pen and begins writing a brief S.O.S. message to Hernando. She then summons one of her messenger pigeons with a distinct call, and attaches the note to its ankle device.

Zela: "Go get Hernando. Hurry! Hurry!" she commands, and the pigeon takes off flying at lightning speed.

Zela looks down at Billy Ray sympathetically and whispers, "You will live, my love, just hold on. You will be alright. Do you hear me, handsome young man?" She places a bowl of water with freshly diced onions and garlic on the floor, dips a white washcloth in it, and places the rag on his exposed chest. Lilli startles Zela when she comes to where Lilli is standing over the couch where Silk is laid out on and looks at what Lilli is pointing at. Atop of Silk's forehead, Iblis is sitting there facing the opposite direction, tail rested in between Silk's eyes. With its head cocked, Iblis is looking directly at Zela and Lilli, although not facing them. Zela calmly approaches, not wanting to startle nor intimidate the creature. She slowly reaches in an attempt to cradle the lizard when Silk suddenly wakes up, sees Zela's hands in her face, and flinches, causing Iblis to go rolling onto the floor. Lilli jumps back frightened to death, while Zela remains still. Silk realizes Iblis had fell, and looks at Zela and Lilli for a reaction to her now exposed secret, then slowly gets off of the couch, although still woozy feeling and body screaming in pain, and gently scoops Iblis up off of the floor.

Zela: "Just what do you think you doing now chile?" she asks Silk, eyeballing Iblis curiously. "Do you realize the great amount of power that reptile you holding there possesses? Or the evil significance within that little creature? You have put not only yourself, but us all in grave danger my dear. What, you don't think the voodoo Queen and all of her evil beings ain't gonna come hunting you down to find their Lord? You do know that it is their Lord don't you chile?" she snaps.

Silk: "Yes mam... Yes I do", nodding her head with confidence and rubbing Iblis's back for emphasis. "And, I also know how special he is to Beatrice, and he is special to me as well. Very special", she states with conviction.

Lilli is in utter confusion at this point about what powers, significance, or evil Zela and Silk are referring to, but judging by Zela's reaction she knows it cannot mean anything good.

Zela's eyes shoot daggers through a naive Silk after what she stated.

Zela: "Chile, have you lost your rabbit ass mind? Do you mean to tell me you have gotten accustomed to the evil jinn within him? Ludiah?"

Silk looks directly at Zela but no answer comes out. There is no need for her to answer with words, because the guilt is sketched on her face.

Zela: "Well chile, I don't know what you thinkin when you took that demon, but it gotta go and it gotta go now!" she commands forcefully.

She then tries to grab Iblis from Silk, but Silk is too quick and sidesteps, dodging the old woman. Zela looks at Silk in shock. Disgusted and confused all at the same time.

Zela: "Chile have you lost your mind? That evil really does got chu don't it?"

She reaches for Iblis again but this time Silk catches Zela by her wrist and is glaring angrily into her eyes. Zela realizes what is happening. "The evil jinns have worked their way into this chile and will eventually consume her and have complete control" Zela says to herself. Realizing this, Zela desists in trying to take Iblis from Silk for the moment because she knows that if she causes Silk to get emotional, that could trigger an opening into the young vulnerable girl's soul, which can be an open invitation for more powerful jinns

like Amineelia and Ludiah to channel into Silk, possessing her with
evil powers, and making her their new human source.

Lilli is still stuck in between confusion, shock, and fear at how
things are happening. She doesn't understand why all of a sudden
her best friend is going against Zela for a lizard that belongs to the
woman who has ruined her own life, as well as her (Lilli's) for that
matter. She looks at Silk with a questioning expression but says nada.

Zela eases off and she can see the energy that was building up in
Silk rapidly drain out, which was the desired effect. Iblis is nestled
in Silk's breasts now calm as ever. Zela looks Iblis at it smirks and
winks an eye at her. The Bird Lady knows all too well that it is Ludiah
who is inside Iblis, and her thoughts cause her to smirk back at the
gesture.

She begins talking again, not at Silk nor Lilli, to no human in the
room. She heads towards the large bookshelf next to a wall of photos,
removes a huge hardcover book that looks very familiar to Silk. It
looks just like many of the spell books and potion recipe books that
Beatrice owned.

Zela is still talking and flipping pages when she stops at a page
then stretches the book out for Silk to grab. Silk reluctantly grabs
the book, looking at Zela quizzically, then looking to Lilli as if for
reassurance. She then looks down at the page that Zela had opened
to. She begins reading and it all starts coming back to her as
everything that she had studied several nights at Beatrice's about
the evil guardians of hell sent to earth, Ludiah and Amineelia. It's
like deja vu to Silk. She looks up at Zela confused. "But I told you
already that I already know all of this stuff. How God send His
most powerful and experienced angels Gabriel and Michael from the
Heavens to battle a clan of three-thousand jinns who were lurking
outside the gates of the Heavens. How Gabriel and Michael slew all
of the jinns down to the last two. The leaders of the clan—Ludiah;
General, and Amineelia; Lieutenant General of Lucifer's army. The

two were taken by a force that only God Himself could have devised, and were beheaded then thrown back into hell where Satan restored them to their regular state." I know all this. Why are you repeating what I already know?" Silk questions cockily.

Zela looks at Silk and says, "What a lie you been told. Keep on reading, chile." Silk flips the page and begins reading and realizes that she had never laid eyes on this page before. On this page, the story goes on and takes a twist, informing her in depth that after hell's soldiers had been slew, the two leaders of the jinn army had not taken an honorable demise. Their ending did not actually occur the way Beatrice had told her. Come to find out that whole line about Ludiah and Amineelia standing up bravely and challenging God was a myth. In truth, the two most powerful leaders of the jinn were about to be beheaded by the two noblest of God's angels, leaders of the silent white army, but then Amineelia fell down in prostration and started to praise and give glory to God, begging and pleading with Him for forgiveness. Ludiah looked at his partner shocked and in confusion. Skeptical of Amineelia's intent, the mighty general follows her lead and bows down to God as well. By this show of fear of God and humiliation of themselves, The All Merciful, Most Forgiving spared both of the evil jinn's lives and commanded them to return to hell at once and to not ever pardon its' gates again, nor to ever return to Earth lest they both be choked up, dragged to that very location, and God give the command for his two noble angels to behead them both—their Judgment Day. Both Amineelia and Ludiah pledge an oath to obey the command God had sent forth and thanked The Lord for His Mercy and Kindness. The Lord allowed them both to depart from the battlefield untouched, escorted out by Gabriel and Michael, with the announcement to them on their way out, "Cursed be you evil jinns, and your evil guardian, and any of mankind who follow or take any of you as friends over Me! And I am He; The Most High, The All Knowing, All Wise, Most Forgiving! Now be gone you evil jinn, cursed be you!" When the angels saw to them walking through the opening gates of hell, the intense flames blasting out fiercely, they immediately returned home to Heaven.

In pure shame and humility, Amineelia and Ludiah enter hell to the deafening screams and cries of evil jinns and souls burning, the noise much louder and more painful-sounding than ever before. This puts fear in the most fearless, most powerful jinns of hell's army. By the way it sounded and felt, they both knew that hell was angry.

When they approach the evil tree in the middle of hell and kneel down to address Lucifer, an extremely powerful, soul-tearing roar sounds, causing the two to tremble visibly. Then, a massive hideous creature appears lunging at the two with its mouth angrily, trying to attack. This was one of the many, the largest of the hell-dogs.

Lucifer: "Why have you betrayed me for Him? And why did you allow yourselves to be spared and forgiven, yet your servants who serve you, your army, became scorching dust dismantled in the atmosphere?" the devil adds.

Amineelia attempts to reply but a huge ball of fire sent her way silences her.

Lucifer: "I have made you two honorable noble leaders in my army, bestowed magnificent powers within the two of you, and this is how you show your gratitude? This is how you repay me? By prostrating to Him?"

Ludiah speaks this time.

Ludiah: "But He is your Lord as well as my Lord. He is Lord of the Worlds, Creator of the Universe... Surely, He was to destroy us if we were not to glorify His Excellence my Lord. Forgive us our Lord and grant us your will for we did not feel it would be beneficial for this army's leaders to be beheaded. We are not like humans who we trick to adore their leaders dying in battle. No, we shall live on to fulfill our Lord's commands. And you are our Lord my Lord."

Lucifer silences Ludiah, then turns to Amineelia.

Lucifer: "Amineelia, by how many angels did my army get slew by?"

Amineelia: "Two, my Lord" she answers with a defeat and shame in her voice.

Lucifer: "Two!?!" Lucifer shoots back in complete disbelief.

Amineelia: "Certainly, these two were unlike any other angels of the Heavens we've ever battled, my Lord!" she pleads.

Lucifer: "Two angels to slay three-thousand of my loyal servants?" He interjects, ignoring her plea attempts. "Have I not endowed the two of you with enormous power and strength and training, and you train my army. Haven't I given you enough for it to take only two angels to defeat an entire fleet?"

Amineelia: "Allah endows these two with greater power, strength, and ability, my Lord" she continues to plead to Lucifer.

Lucifer: "By whom have we taken such embarrassment?"

Amineelia: "By the two most powerful of the angels; Gabriel and Michael, my Lord"

Lucifer lets out an angry deafening scream which shakes all of hell, followed by a long dragons' length ball of flames, terrifying every creature in hell, even the biggest and most gruesome of them. Lucifer's rage is because Gabriel and Michael became his successors after God exiled him out of the heavens and cast him into hell. Lucifer had always been in major competition, especially with Gabriel, his biggest rival, who he hated with a passion. To hear that Gabriel is responsible for the army's slaughter infuriated Lucifer to the highest power. Critters and creatures all begin scurrying, trying to find hiding spots to avoid Lucifer's rage, all except for one creature that is; a red bearded dragon, perched on a rock stiff like a statue.

Chapter 35

Lucifer's outrage ceases and he speaks to Ludiah again:

Lucifer: "And in what position were you in prostrate to the Lord of the Heavens?"

Ludiah: "In the same position as that lizard, my Lord," he answers in humiliation, pointing to the bearded dragon.

Lucifer: "And that creature is only accustomed to that position isn't it? It cannot stand on two feet nor fight in a battle such as yourself now can it? It can't even speak a word of pity or pleading can it?" he scolds.

Ludiah: "N...n...no... N... no, it can't my lord" he stutters fearfully.

Lucifer: "So is that incompetent mute morsel worthier of my favor than my own general and lieutenant? Am I not your Lord, or is the lizard? And did I not command you to follow only me?" he blasts at his two servants.

Ludiah: "Truly my lord. But He is the Lord of the Worlds, Most High, The All Knowing, All Wise. Even you only do what Allah has permitted you to. Not even you my lord can surpass His Knowledge nor His Might" he sheepishly admits.

All the more enraged at Ludiah's answer, Lucifer sends a magnificent blast of fire, sending Ludiah rolling across the hell floor burning at the chest. Amineelia, Ludiah's lover, looks on sorrowfully, daring not to speak, move, nor show any affection as they'd been trained to do, and mainly so not to test her master's fury.

Lucifer: "How dare you insult me in my kingdom, you ungrateful little coward!" he screams at Ludiah, shaking all of hell with his authoritative voice. "Because this lizard is more competent and loyal to thee than you are, I shall make it your successor in hell and on Earth until we all cease to exist. Now, be gone coward!" Lucifer exclaims.

Ludiah: "Why my lord? Because I believe in Allah and I know that He is the Lord of the Worlds, Most High, Most Wise, All

Forgiving, and the Almighty?" the General pleads, which only infuriates Lucifer even more.

Lucifer: "Baaanished!!!" he screams as he throws another ball of fire striking Ludiah, causing him to be consumed entirely by the lizard.

Finally, able to move, Amineelia screams, "Nooo" and runs over to Ludiah in a dire effort to block him from the blast with her protective breast plate, but she is too late to save her lover. She falls down hard onto the empty floor-space where Ludiah once lay moments ago, soaking in tears of sorrow and hurt.

Lucifer: "Pick yourself up and do not despair over that disgrace," he barks at her. "I've seen how close the two of you have become over time. However, I have tailored you for a servant far more loyal and of greater courage than he, so forget about that imbecile."

Amineelia looks up in disgust at what she is hearing.

Amineelia: "No one can replace the love I bind with Ludiah, the one I've fought alongside in battle with many victories, for hundreds of centuries. You should be ashamed. You exiled him, why, because Allah exiled you, and made Gabriel and Michael guardians of the Heavens, against you?" she rebels, seething with anger.

Lucifer: "Silence!!!" he yells, but Amineelia ignores.

Amineelia: "Ludiah was lots of things, but a coward he was not. I am the one who submitted first in prostration and pleaded for mercy and forgiveness from the Most High. It was me, so if any should be punished let me fall as well. Ludiah said nothing that we don't know is the truth. That Allah is He, Your Lord, our Lord, Lord of the Worlds. For if it wasn't for His Mercy, Ludiah nor I shalt have returned. Surely, He is Most Merciful, Most Kind, and All-Forgiving" the Lieutenant continues to talk, betraying her master to his face.

Lucifer: "Very cute Amineelia ... Well, it would have fit you both to have been beheaded. Who's to stop me from beheading you now?" he teased.

Lucifer's jealousy is very real and Amineelia knows this.

Lucifer: "How can you love him more than me? Look at how affectionate you've become over Ludiah when I am your lord and master, yet I have never received such out of you. Damned is he, damn Ludiah!" he roars.

A brief silence, then:

Lucifer: "Since you feel that there is a lord other than me, why don't you go to Him and ask to be admitted into Heaven? Nay, because you come from evil, from me, so no, you will never enter Heaven's gates!" he says followed by laughter. "Nor will you ever enter Earth again. Not by 'His' authority, but by my command. You shall remain here in hell, and you will no longer have honor, your title and authority as lieutenant is hereby stripped away, nor will you have any position in my army for that matter. You will be my lowest slave-girl for all eternity. And most of all, you will never see nor touch your *lover* again. Your love will be for my loyal servants. All dignity and respect are hereby stripped from you, bitch" Lucifer declares.

Instantly Amineelia is stripped of her entire uniform and gannets. Now she lay disrobed on hell's floor, and a thick steel chain is clasped around both legs and wrists and waist. Lucifer then gives his command, and a dark hole appears and opens up. As he commanded it, the lizard, which is now holding Ludiah's soul, is swallowed up by the dark hole and casted into Earth. Before being swallowed into Earth, the jinn inside the lizard, Ludiah, turns to look directly at his love, Amineelia, with eyes which she could read that said I love you forever. Amineelia rises and races towards the lizard to catch Ludiah before he is swallowed.

Amineelia: "I love you ever more Ludiah, for always and eternity!" she screams.

As she gets within a few feet of him, the chain that rounded her bare waistline jerks, causing her to hit the ground and bang her forehead with a loud thud. She cries emphatically, heartbroken as she witnesses her love disappear into the portal headed away from her forever. When the portal is gone, Amineelia lies face-down crying.

Lucifer: "Pathetic. What a waste of emotion, because you will never greet him again" Lucifer scolds in pure disgust.

Amineelia: "Liar!" she shoots back, heartbroken, and through a face full of tears and blood running down her face.

Lucifer: "Because of your disobedience and insubordinate behavior, you will be a slave to all creatures of hell for all eternity... Queen of the damned" he declares followed by a horrifying laugh.

Suddenly, huge ugly, monstrous creatures appear around Amineelia, all with possessed looks filled with hunger for lust and perverseness. Lucifer continues laughing, deeper and louder this time and that's when all of the beasts go in on Amineelia, ravishing her naked body. She screams and cries out, trying to fight off the creatures but she is quickly subdued and forced to take the sexual punishments the beasts inflict on her—feeling, touching, grabbing, clawing, licking, fondling, and then penetrating her mouth, vagina, and anus with their male parts-and all other things sexual one could imagine. After about a decade, the pain and her crying stop, and she would grow accustomed to the thousands, if not millions, of beasts penetrating and getting their thrills off on her, that she begins liking it, performing tricks, enticing more and rougher sexual acts and punishments from the beasts-her undying love and want for Ludiah resting temporarily and she falls in love with being hell's sex slave. However, she never forgets her first and true lover, and she makes a secret covenant with him and herself to unite their love again. For now, she remains the greedy whore demanding pleasure from everywhere. Those humans that call upon her, like Beatrice, will be encouraged to like the same things.

Chapter 36

Silk is hit with a bolt of fear looking at the image of the lizard being gutted and eaten by what looks like a hawk or maybe an eagle. She jumps back, releasing the book and it falls to the floor, still opened to the same page. Zela quickly picks it up and places it back on the shelf then presumes back where Silk stands looking like a deer in headlights.

Zela: "So now ju see dey truth about matters which ju had no knowledge, and moreover, matters in which ju have been lied to concerning. Now I must ask ju again chile, do you see the power that creature there possess and the grave danger ju have put us all in?"

Silk: "What should I do then?" she replies in a worried voice.

Zela: "The best ting to do is let me have him. I will return him to the voodoo queen" she insists.

As soon as the words leave Zela's mouth, the raven from earlier that stared Silk down when interrupting her and Lilli's sex escapade, comes into the living room and lands on the ledge, inches away from Zela, staring directly at Silk's bra. The image from the book flashes through Silk's head and she stands back defensively.

Silk: "No! I will return him, you're not touching him" she states.

She moves towards the door, but Lilli beats her to it, stepping in front of her, blocking her from leaving. That's when it dawns on Silk that at the big battle of magic at Beatrice's, Lilli had gotten in it defending Zela. She looks at Lilli, then Zela, then back to Lilli putting two-and-two together.

Silk: "Wait... so you practice voodoo too? You're a witch Lilli?"

No need for her to be verbal about it, Lilli looks down at her feet with a guilty expression.

Zela: "She has been my student for half of her life, little do you know, chile... The difference is, I would never turn an innocent chile into a monster like that bitch Beatrice do" she continues.

Silk: "But... y'all are witches too. Y'all practice the same voodoo, witchcraft, and sorcery, all of the same stuff she has taught me. So how are you two any different from her and Antonio?" she questions. "And here I am thinking we were best friends, but I see I thought wrong Lillianna" she says, rolling her eyes at Lilli who's still looking ashamed.

Zela: "Don't chu dare insult me in my home you little wicked heifer. If you had of paid mind to me when I warned you to stay here in the first place, none of this nonsense would be happening. That woman and that lizard are extremely pure sources of evil, an evil like no one's ever seen before- Iblis, jinn Ludiah and Beatrice, his human endorser and worshiper of Amineelia. Now I'm not gone ask again, give it to me" the bird lady demands more sternly, holding her palm out for Iblis.

Silk, content on not giving Iblis up, steps back, her back towards the doorway, and both hands shielding the middle of her breasts where Iblis is still dug deep in between. Lilli speaks up now;

Lilli: "Silk, she knows what's right. Please just listen to her", she pleads.

Silk: "Shut up! Shut-the-fuck-up you lying ass bitch. You're not my real friend!" she snaps back at Lilli.

Then, WHAACKUP!!! Zela's open right hand comes slamming into Silk's face.

Zela: "Have you lost yo mind, chile? Watch your evil tongue in this house!!" she demands, setting Silk straight.

Silk holds her now stinging face, consumed with embarrassment and anger, but instead of challenging the elder woman, whom she knows of course is far more powerful than she is even at her senior status, she bolts through the doorway, knocking Lilli backwards as she tries again to obstruct Silk's departure. The raven is summoned by a wave of Zela's hand and a short spell, and it takes off in hot pursuit of Silk. As Silk gets out of the screened porch, the messenger pigeon that had been sent with the message for Hernando returns, flying right towards her head-on, causing her to duck her head and scream, but the bird flies right past her back into Zela's home.

A large SUV pulls up, and when Silk regains her composure, she frantically runs in the truck's direction to get on the road and exit the property. With the raven right on her heels, screaming and flapping its wings thunderously atop her head, Silk screams. Hernando exits his truck urgently holding a small box that looks like a lunchbox, and looks towards Silk in confusion, mumbling in Spanish, and reaches out for her to stop, but she shakes him and is almost off of the property.

As soon as her right foot is off of Zela's property line the raven's talons finds its grip around her bob and it yanks upward viciously, causing a painful high-pitched scream to escape her. Just when she hits the ground and thinks that she can't get away and that it is over with, a bright green flash of light comes from behind her and freezes the raven in mid-air. At first she assumes it was Iblis's work again until she looks down in between her bosoms at him and sees that he is in his normal color. She looks behind her, following the source of the light, and meets Beatrice's eyes. Beatrice has her hands up reciting a spell and looks at Silk with a menacing stare.

Beatrice: "You little ungrateful troublesome whore! How dare you be bold enough to steal from me, after every ting I've given to you? After I saved you from death? This is how you repay me? And of all things, of all the things imaginable bitch you take my dearest love, my heart." Beatrice vents.

BOOM!!! Splat... the raven explodes in mid-air into a million bloody pieces, causing blood and guts to get in Silk's hair and face.

She looks up at Beatrice in complete fear and tries to talk but can't get a word out.

Beatrice: "Look at you, pathetic. Have I not been the best teacher? You disgrace me" she utters in disgust.

Silk: "I was about to bring Iblis back to you, because Zela and her wicked birds wanted to kill him. I never stole anything, well anyone from you. I saved Iblis from being burned alive in your home."

Beatrice laughs in amazement.

Beatrice: "You saved him?... Burning alive? Ha ha ha, you are truly a mess, foolish little girl!"

Silk: "And I just saved him from Zela's killer birds."

Beatrice: "Yet I just saved your little fast ass again! What bird, dat one?" she points, gesturing to the remaining remnants of the once possessed raven.

Silk: "I think I have proven my loyalty and faithfulness to him" she stutters.

Beatrice: "To whom?" she asks, stepping closer looking wickedly possessed at Silk, daring her to say what she thinks she is about to say, while Silk holds her breasts firmly.

Silk: "Iblis. Ludiah. General of Lucifer's army; Amineelia's true love. I've proven my loyalty and worthiness to him. I am not giving him to you either now. Now that I know you lied to me."

Beatrice laughs wickedly, surprised at Silk's sudden boldness and defiance to her, but more amused by her ignorance.

Beatrice: "Ju talk so foolishly little gul. Tell me, what makes a weak, spoiled, ungrateful, ignorant little bitch like you tink you can bargain wit me ha? Ya gon challenge me aye? Give me what belongs to me or else!" she threatens.

Silk: "Or else what?" Silk responds firmly.

Beatrice: "Or you die, simple as that. The choice is yours, bitch!"

Silk : "Well, I guess you might as well get to killing, since I'm already dead anyway once the law gets hold of me."

Beatrice: "'Ju brought all dis mess, all dis trouble on your own, you little slut. But let's make a deal. I can make all of your legal troubles vanish wit one spell if you give me baby back to me. What do ju say Silky, huh? Deal or no deal?" she offers.

Silk thinks about it, heavily weighing her options.

Silk: "Deal, but I don't give him up until you have taught me the spell completely and thoroughly. Understand?"

Beatrice glares at Silk for a minute with hate-filled eyes, and then agrees to the terms. Then, two of them fly back to Beatrice's home on her broom. When they arrive at Beatrice's estate, Silk is stunned at how immaculate the house is put back together after being in flames when she'd been there earlier. Beatrice goes to open Iblis' habitat, then looks at Silk who stands defensively, arms crossed, and shaking her head *NO*.

Silk: "Nope the deal is not until I know the spell to rid me of my troubles" she states sternly.

Beatrice curses underneath her breath, irritated to the max before storming off to her bookshelf. After finding the book she was looking for, she slams it down on the coffee table and yells "sit." Silk does as she is told and sits down. Beatrice, mean-mugging Silk, eyes the center of her bosoms earnestly, which Silk takes immediate notice to and puts a hand over to shield her freakish view. At her own request, Silk washes all of the raven's blood and body parts off with warm water that Beatrice provided reluctantly.

For the next hour and a half, Beatrice teaches Silk the entire spell and everything that went with it. Feeling satisfied, Silk gets up on her feet and Beatrice excitedly leaps up on her own in anticipation.

Silk: "Are sure it's going to work. All my problems will vanish immediately?"

Beatrice: "Yeas, yeas gul, now give me what is mine. Time to seal your end of de bargain now Silky" she responds, hand stretched out to receive Iblis. "And I might even be nice enough to let you have a quick little snack before you leave" she adds, palming her vagina through her dress in a teasing fashion.

However, Silk is way more cunning and conniving than Beatrice gave her credit for. Beatrice gets no immediate response to her gesture and no compliance from Silk on her request, just an intense stare-off.

Beatrice: "Come on Silk, give him to me" she urges more, smiling wickedly. She becomes impatient with Silk's noncompliance.

Beatrice: "Bitch give him to me NOW!" she yells, energy circulating around her like lightning bolts, and then it actually causes a thunderstorm outside.

Silk, feeling in control, smirks at an enraged Beatrice.

Silk: "You want him back? How bad do you want him? Huh?" she teases, holding both hands to her bosoms.

Beatrice: "Give him to me now Silk!"

Silk: "Get down on all fours and crawl over here" she orders.

Beatrice: "WHAT!?!... Are you mad!?!"

Silk: "Nope, but if you want him back, you better do as I say now."

Beatrice: "You little bitch, you back-stabbing little cum guzzler, ooowww I will!"

Silk: "You will what, huh?" she responds, squeezing her breasts as if threatening to suffocate Iblis with them.

Beatrice gasps in fear then falls down to her knees in the quickness.

Beatrice: "NO! NO! NO! Please, please don't hurt him, please" she pleads with Silk. Silk laughs, amused at the powerful woman's vulnerability.

Silk: "Lick the bottom of my shoe" Silk instructs, lifting her left foot.

Beatrice: "What?" she asks, looking at her crazily.

Silk: "Do it and I'll hand him over right now!"

Beatrice, weakened by the situation and desperate to get Iblis back safely, complies with Silk's demands and begins to trace her tongue lightly down the bottom of Silk's dirty sneakers.

Silk: "Uh uh! Whole tongue" she orders.

Beatrice's eyes shoot daggers through Silk. If only looks could kill and Silk would be good as dead right now. Beatrice rolls her eyes then brandishes her whole tongue and begins lapping the bottoms of Silk's shoes.

Silk: "Yeas, yeas, that's it!" Silk mocks in her "Mama B" voice. She continues to coach Beatrice's shoe licking in sheer pleasure at the sight of the revenge she is getting. After about five minutes Silk's shoe bottoms are polished from the toes to the heel on both feet. Beatrice, spitting out grass and hacking up mud threatening to go down her esophagus, gets up furious, demanding Iblis back.

Silk: "Ok, so you want him, back do you?"

Beatrice: "Dats was de deal gul now unhand him!"

Silk pulls Iblis from between her bosoms, cradles him in both hands, smiles at Beatrice mischievously.

Silk: "Sorry... No deal... got cha!"

Before Beatrice can get a word out, Silk swallows Iblis down her throat, gagging and almost choking as the lizard goes down. "NOOO!" Beatrice screams loud enough for the entire bayou to hear.

Beatrice: "How could you, you little stupid bitch?" Silk finishes swallowing Iblis and then wipes her mouth.

Silk: "You ain't nothing but a lying old wicked witch that's gonna burn in hell for all eternity ... And Ludiah doesn't love you. And you will never be Amineelia no matter how much you beg him to come inside you. You cannot, and never will, replace Amineelia bitch. I will!" she eggs on.

Beatrice roars loudly in anger, hair on her head standing straight up now. She starts reciting spells back-to-back at Silk while pointing a huge ball of glowing energy at her, then finally, BOOM!, she sends it at Silk who goes crashing through the front door and out into the pouring rain and thunder. Something strange begins happening to Silk after the blast that should have, and would have, killed an ordinary human being. Little did Silk know, however, she was no longer an *ordinary human-being*. Her throat, breasts, torso, legs, hands, and eventually her entire body, all start to illuminate and glisten like flames in the rain. Beatrice comes out and apprehensively spots Silk. She tries to throw another blast at her but it bounces right off of Silk and crashes into a huge thirty-to-forty-foot-tall pine tree, splitting it in half, sending it crashing down onto Beatrice's home. Furious, Beatrice tries another spell and tries to recharge her energy to send another blast at Silk, but it's like her power got cut off, because she could no longer work her magic energy up. Silk's mouth is moving but her eyes are closed, head hung down, hair wild and frizzled now even in the rain, and she is rising off of the ground. She uncontrollably recites spells of her own, and all of the reptiles of the bayou and swamps appear around her as if possessed by her spells. Beatrice looks on in horror. Silk finishes her spell then points and yells, "Go to hell Beatrice!" a wave of energy entraps Beatrice all around, consuming her, then leads her to the swamp waters where a black whirlpool is spinning viciously, pulling her towards the mouth into a portal. She screams until she is swallowed up by the black hole in the swamp. Once Beatrice is gone, everything calms down, including Silk, and the thunderstorm also ceases immediately. The amphibians are still poised as if awaiting a command from Silk. Silk's feet reconnect with the earth, and all of the mud and dirt fall off of her body like dead skin. She opens her mouth and Iblis comes out crawling off of her outstretched tongue. The lizard returns to its species and Silk walks away, leaving Beatrice's yet again ruined estate.

Silk now feels guarded by all of the cold-blooded creatures, even the killers, like she is now their new leader, by the way they are watching over and surrounding her now; the same way they used to guard Mama B. She is exhausted and decides it's' time to go home, but not before she recites the spell she'd just tricked the voodoo queen out of before her demise. She does it and after feeling satisfied walks out into the dark glossy woods to go home and back to her normal life. Or so she thinks.

Chapter 37

Back at Zela's, Hernando is in utter confusion. He knew what he was summoned there to do, but what had him confused was the encounter with a hysterical Silk storming off of the property with a wild bird on her trail upon his arrival to the Bird Lady's home. He asks what happened, but Zela dismisses the question and ushers him inside to examine and treat Billy Ray, who appears lifeless lying on the floor. He is nearing his final breath.

Hernando: "Do you know what kind, what species of snake did this?" Zela and Lilli both answer in the negative.

Hernando: "Well, I must know in order to administer the proper antivenom. The wrong serum or too high dosage of different antivenoms could do more harm than good, and can even be fatal. There's no way you can find out this information" he explains. "Where did this happen? And how long has it been since he was bitten? I need answers, Zela."

With heavy grief and sorrow, Zela looks at Lilli with pleading eyes and says to Hernando, but looking at Lilli:

Zela: "Yes, there is a way to know which snake did this."

Lilli looks back at Zela, wide-eyed, shaking her head 'no.' She knows what Zela is asking her to do, but she doesn't want to reveal her true identity and powers to this complete stranger.

Noticing the stare-off, Hernando clears his throat purposefully, and interjects.

Hernando: "Well, we don't have much time, he'll be dead in minutes."

Zela: "Please chile" she begs Lilli through pleading eyes.

Lilli gives in and begins to recite a spell while placing both of her pointer fingers on Billy Ray's eyes, causing her to see his memories in a quick vision. That is when she sees him in the truck getting bitten by the King Cobra. She stops her magic and nearly falls backwards had Zela not caught her fall. Hernando is not looking even more confused and shocked at the same time. Lilli surpasses his looks and begins relaying all the details of what she saw in the vision. She still doesn't know what species the snake belonged to so she uses the movie "The Mummy Returns" starring "The Rock" as a reference to the snake.

Lilli: "The same snake from that movie, that's the one."

Hernando doesn't take long to answer, "King Cobra!" "Holy shit!" he shouts and then rushes into his case, grabbing vials out of it, shaking and mixing two solutions of antivenom, wrapping a clean needle and filling the syringe. He has trouble finding a good vein on Billy Ray to stick because he wants the venom into his bloodstream as quickly as possible knowing how lethal and rapidly-acting the cobra's venom is. When he does finally find a good vein, he shoots all of the antivenom serum into Billy Ray's arm.

Zela: "What's wrong? Is he going to make it Hernando?" she asks, worried.

Hernando: "He should be fine now. Just give it some time. He'll pull through. Just lucky I got here when I did, or he'd be a goner for sure. King Cobras are one of the top five most lethal killers on the planet. Fortunately, he's a pretty big guy, otherwise the venom would've taken over his entire body and killed him sooner" he explains with a thick Spanish accent.

Zela: "Thank you Hernando, my dear friend, thank you so much, she says staring deeply into his eyes, holding both of his hands tenderly.

Hernando: "De nada, senorita Zela" he replies compassionately.

He gathers his belongings, but before leaving, he prepares a couple more vials of the antivenom to leave with Zela.

Hernando: "Let him rest and give him another full dose in eight to ten hours, and give him about twenty-four to thirty-six hours for him to fully recover. You know how to reach me if you need me again, but hopefully you don't, not for this at least. Like I said, he's a big guy, so I believe he will make a full recovery" he ends with before departing.

Zela: "I sure do. And again, muchas gracias mi amigo. And tell your wife Ms. Z misses her enchiladas" she says, giving him a farewell peck on both cheeks. Hernando nods farewell to Lilli also, who shyly waves good-bye in return, still feeling embarrassed.

It had stopped storming and Hernando had already exited Zela's property when Lilli was looking out of Zela's front window, in deep thought about her best friend's reaction to finding out about her very own dark secret. This made her feel like she was a phony, fake friend, and what Silk said was all true about her. She looks out at the gloomy night at the dirt road and spots Silk wobbling, heading in the direction of the residential area. Lilli jumps up and runs to the door to try to run after Silk, to talk to her, but Zela, who was gently wiping Billy Ray's face with a wet rag, magically locks her door with a point of her finger.

Zela: "No... You have to let her go, chile. She is too far gone now", she says sympathetically with her head hung low.

Lilli drops her head also in disappointment and obeys the Bird Lady.

Chapter 38

Silk is dizzy, wobbly-legged and exhausted after the blast from
the voodoo queen Beatrice and from whatever was happening to her
after swallowing Iblis. Her walk is completely zombie-like, staggering
with every step as if drunk, however she somehow makes it past
the Bird Lady's house, out of the woods, and onto the asphalt city
streets on her own. Dark and demonic voices ring through her head.
Visions of intense battles between jinns versus angels and jinns versus
humans, scenes of hell and of evil characters she's never saw before.
She sees Amineelia bowing in prostration to Allah, then bowing
down and explaining to Lucifer. She also sees Amineelia in hell,
chains around her naked shapely body being sexually explored and
abused by the beasts of hell, all while pleading for Ludiah to still love
her and to never forget her. It is like a movie playing in her head, a
real-life play of just as the book she had read at Zela's described. The
difference now is that she feels as if she is right in it. Simultaneously,
visions of Barrika and the janitor from school in hell in intense
flames screaming, the vision of Antonio raping her, and also the
voluntary sex she had with the warlock and the voodoo queen all
envelop her mind as she staggers down the empty street. Everything
that had been happening recently all rapidly spinning in the vision in
her head, when all of a sudden, she is knocked out of her zombie-like
state by a hard object crashing into her body, sending her airborne six
feet and smashing onto the hot cement. The loud blaring of the horn
did not penetrate Silk's mind on time, and she is smacked hard by the
truck.

Miraculously, Silk is still awake, although now dizzier than she
was just a second ago, and in severe pain. She grips her stomach
trying to catch a breath, and can barely see because she is blinded
by headlights. Seconds after she is hit, a tall athletic figure comes
running out of the truck to her aid. The man's voice sounds so
familiar, but Silk is so out of it she cannot put a face on it until he
touches her head and side and she can smell his scent.

Silk: "David Beckham cologne... wait a minute... it's him!" she says in her head.

"Silk! Silk! Can you hear me? Oh my god, Silk, I'm so sorry ... Silk! Can you breathe? Hold on Silk, I'm calling an ambulance!" the man says in sheer panic mode. As soon as she hears him say that he is calling 9-1-1, Silk comes back to her senses almost immediately and regains her strength enough to respond. "Lorenzo" she calls out. He stops in mid-stride back to the truck, turns around, and runs back to Silk.

Silk: "I'm ok sweetie, you don't have to do that. As a matter of fact, please don't call 9-1-1, please don't. Just... I need you to help me up", she states with as much strength as she can muster through aching ribs and lungs.

Lorenzo looks shocked at Silk from her response, but then quickly helps her up off of the ground. He picks her up and carries her to his truck, lays her in the passenger seat, runs to the driver's side to get in, and pulls off quickly.

Lorenzo: "Silk, I can't believe you are still up and talking after that! I am so sooo sorry, I didn't see you! You came out of nowhere girl, oh my gosh I can't believe this is happening! I gotta get you to the hospital right now babe, where's the closest one?" he rambles, still excited and panicky, talking a hundred words a minute.

Silk hears most of it, but pops up and smiles when she hears him call her "babe."

Silk: "Really Lorenzo? I'm your babe now? Hehehe! I mean, I'm not saying that I don't want to be, because I do. In fact, I would love to be yours, zaddy," she says with a heavy seductive southern drawl.

This makes him smile too. He looks her in her eyes.

Lorenzo: "Yea... Look Silk, there's something I been meaning to tell you."

Before he can get another word out, Silk leaps into his lap and plants a wet one right onto his lips. He takes it in and reciprocates the kiss. He slows down and pulls over to the side of the road, puts the truck in park, and turns to face Silk. They stare each other directly in the eyes for a split second, then they rush each other's lips, tonguing one another down passionately. They don't talk, only kiss for about five to six minutes on the side of the road. He moves his hands up Silk's figure rhythmically, underneath her shirt, finding her hard nipples, grabs both of her breasts, and the more passionate the kissing gets, the harder he unconsciously squeezes them, causing her to wince in pain. "Ouch" she exclaims as she jerks back from the pain, abruptly ending the kissing session.

Lorenzo: "I am so sorry baby. Look, let me get you to a hospital to get you checked out. I think my dumb ass may have caused you a broken rib or something. I gotta get chu to" he says and then shifts the truck back into drive.

Silk stops him, moves the gear back into park, turns the ignition off and tells him straightly:

Silk: "No, I'm not going to the hospital, Lorenzo! Baby, the police and everybody think that I killed two people, and they are looking everywhere for me. I can't go to a hospital, they will find me there too easily. I'm fine, trust me. Can we just chill or go somewhere private to talk? Is that okay with you, zaddy?"

Lorenzo: "Yea, it's cool. So... what happened at the locker room today anyway?"

Silk explains very briefly what happened which surprisingly has Lorenzo very intrigued. They laugh and make jokes at the janitor.

Lorenzo: "That's what that old creepy perverted mafucka get. It's just fucked up that such an innocent, beautiful, sexy, smart girl like yourself gotta take the fall for it you know? That's fucked up forreal."

The two continue to sit and talk inside Lorenzo's truck, and he confesses to her that he has been low key crushing on her. The more they converse, and after hearing Lorenzo tell her that he does truly have feelings for her, Silk feels herself getting hotter and hotter between the legs. Then the demonic voices and the visions of Amineelia teasing and enticing the beasts that lust over her begin playing in her mind again. Lorenzo is talking but Silk is no longer listening. She is in a zombie trance-like state again, looking in his direction but not looking at him.

Silk: "Lorenzo! I love you boy! I want you! And I need you! Please take me! Take all of me!" she burst out, interrupting him talking.

What she bursts out screaming are the exact words coming from Amineelia in the vision, directed toward her lover Ludiah. The sudden outburst catches Lorenzo off guard. Silk does not wait for him to respond. She leaps up swiftly, this time landing her vagina right on top of his manhood, straddling him in his seat, and resumes to tonguing him town vigorously, moaning, purring, and breathing heavily the more she gets into it. Lorenzo does not hold back either and returns the passion.

Silk: "I'm all yours, daddy! Tell me I'm yours! Tell me I'm all yours!" she says between kisses.

Lorenzo: "You're all mine baby!"

He places his right hand on the back of her neck, right on her spot, and grabs, slightly caressing her, which causes her to climax on herself, releasing an enormous orgasm. She throws her head back, moaning super loud as she releases herself all over the inside of her panties. He pushes down on her spot controlling her head so that her lips stay on his. He makes his move onto her neck now, sucking on it passionately, purposely trying to create a hickey on her neck. This only causes her to scream and yell out in pleasure and ecstasy even more. All of Silk's grinding, moaning, breathing, and orgasms causes Lorenzo's little soldier to become rock solid. Silk feels him growing larger and larger through his jump-suit pants, where now he is poking her vagina as she sits atop of him. When he takes his hand off of her spot, she forcefully puts it right back on it. His tongue

AMPHIBIANS : THE DARK SECRETS DEEP DOWN IN THE BAYOU

143

travels down further on her body until one of her full-sized breasts finds his mouth.

He methodically circles around the areola using only his tongue, flicking at it to tease her, and then he spontaneously engulfs the whole breast in his mouth, which drives her insane. She cannot take it anymore, so she reaches to the side of the seat, finds the control arm, and pushes the adjustment button to move the driver's seat back as far as it can go. When it does not go back anymore, she quickly drops down to the floor on her knees, her feet touching the gas and brake pedals. She grabs his pants at the waistline, yanks them down past his knees, observes his swollen rod pumping through his boxer briefs, and rubs her hands methodically over it. She then pulls his underwear down past the knees as well, grabs his penis roughly, stroking it up and down rhythmically and methodically with one hand first and then with two, while moaning and purring seductively, staring his dick down the entire time as if it was a piece of meat and she was a starving lion, saliva sliding down the side of her lips. She takes her eyes off of his dick for a split second to lustfully lock eyes with him and utters, "I love you, Ludiah."

At that moment, she quickly grabs his right hand, puts it right on the spot on the back of her neck, and then as a new wave of ecstasy explodes in her again from the touching of her spot, she dives mouth wide and swallows his entire dick to the back of her throat and holds it in tight, not releasing nor coming up for air, causing Lorenzo to jump and shout in pleasure before falling back in his seat. Her lips touching his base and balls while his dick is in her mouth, her eyes locked on Lorenzo's face while his are rolled to the back of his head, where all you see is the whites in them. Without taking his dick out of her mouth, she begins wiggling and waving her tongue back and forth quickly, doing tricks on him, giving him the greatest oral pleasure he's ever had. Mind you, Silk had never even sucked a dick before, yet she is giving him a professional blowjob.

Unbeknownst to her or Lorenzo, Silk is·not herself. Amineelia is now in control. Silk is deeply into it, moaning and stroking more passionately, even growling like a hungry tiger, while moving up then going all the way down with no gag reflex, vacuuming his whole dick at a steady rhythmic pace, ultimately making a wet sloppy mess of his groin area. She goes on like this for about one-hundred-twenty seconds, which is all it takes for Lorenzo to explode all the way down her throat, causing her eyes to flicker in pleasure, rolling rapidly as she enjoys the pleasing sensation of his warm, creamy children rolling down her tongue and esophagus. "Mm! I love how you taste, zaddy!" Silk says seductively, while licking around his tip for any more cum and slurping up every drop. He jumps again from how good it feels, however, Silk is not finished yet. She pins his legs down with her large plump breasts and elbows so he cannot move and then dives on his dick again, swallowing and smothering his entire dick with saliva and sperm mixture seeping down his piece and her lips and cheeks. She attempts to come up to start bobbing her head on him again but Lorenzo cannot take anymore, so he uses what little strength he can muster up to lift her up. She protests, lips still attached to his tip as he smoothly lifts her up, causing a slurp and pop sound when her mouth finally releases him. The two of them are heaving, breathing heavily, trying to catch their breaths.

Silk: "I need you inside of me now, daddy. I need you now please, my lord! Please my lord, Ludiah! Please! I need you in here with me, please save me!" she pleads, kissing Lorenzo on his face and neck with saliva and cum coated lips, reciting Amineelia's pleads and sexual desires when she and Ludiah had last made love in a cave in hell.

Lorenzo spun his neck away, grabs Silk by both arms, and looks her in the face confused.

Lorenzo: "What? Silk, who the hell is Ludiah? What's up with you and all of this "my lord" bullshit?" Lorenzo questions to himself.

"You sure you don't need to see a doctor? Because you acting really crazy, girl. Are you taking any medication? Tell the truth, Silk."

The hallucinations, visions, and voices subside, and Silk returns back to her normal human self and out of the trance. She looks at Lorenzo dumbfounded, then gets off of his lap and sits back in the passenger seat, wiping cum and spit off of her mouth area, straightens her bra and shirt, then pulls down the sun visor mirror and straightens her hair and face while Lorenzo pulls up his pants, putting his soaked penis away, and readjusts his seat to its original position.

Silk: "My bad. I'm so sorry baby, I just got a little into the moment" she shyly admits.

Lorenzo: "Yea, you really got into the moment a lot, not just a little bit. Damn girl, you freaky as fuck. . . and I mean really freaky" he responds with a non-sarcastic expression on his face.

Silk: "I can't go to any hospital. I already told you that. Do you want to see ya girl get arrested?"

When Lorenzo doesn't answer, this angers Silk. She smacks her lips, searching him up and down for an answer, but he just stares back blankly. Silk blows her breath in annoyance, and Lorenzo gets a full whiff of his own ball juice and children.

Silk: "You know what, just take me home bruh, that's what chu can do. I don't have time to sit here while a ma'fucka judge me and trying to treat me like I'ma weirdo, naw um good bruh. Take me home right now, bruh!" she demands, full of frustration.

Lorenzo: "Whoa whoa whoa, time out, errt! Wait, who's judging you, Silk?" he rebuts. "Look, I'm really sorry for being so inconsiderate. I know you going through a lot right now, and I'm being an asshole for suggesting the hospital again", he concedes.

Silk: "A big one", she jabs back with emphasis.

Lorenzo: "Ok I deserve that one baby, but don't chu ever think for one minute that I want to see you rot in anyone's filthy jail or prison. Never that, baby. I'm sorry, but you got me all wrong, Silk. I'm not judging you at all. It's actually kind of crazy of me to be saying this, but I think I'm falling in love with you, girl!" Lorenzo confesses in sincerity, causing Silk's hazel eyes to water.

Lorenzo: "I really do Silk. I... I love you" he affirms.

Silk: "Do you mean that or are you just saying that because I sucked the soul out chu just now?" she questions him, watching his facial expressions skeptically while still massaging his semi hard dick through his shorts.

Lorenzo: "Baby I would not say it if I don't mean it from the bottom of my heart. I am in love with you, girl!" he states sternly.

Silk: "Oh, I love you too Lorenzo" she returns, blushing, wrapping both arms around his neck.

He returns the hug, wrapping his arms around her waist which again sends her jumping back in pain. "Oow, ouch!" she shouts.

Lorenzo: "Damn, I'm sorry baby, are you okay?" he asks worriedly.

Silk: "Yeah, it's coo, I'm alright. Just could use some medicine for the pain and some ice. Can you take me to my house now, lover boy?" she requests, followed by a flirtatious wink.

Lorenzo: "Oh hell no! Absolutely not" he objects. "If the jakes are looking for you, then you'd best believe they've already got the crib on lockdown." He states before Silk can respond. "As a matter of fact, I do remember seeing a gang of twelve all in armored army-looking trucks rushing toward your ward. You most definitely not going back home, not under my watch, baby." he asserts.

Looking seriously turned on by his assertion of masculinity and bravado, and loving how he takes charge, Silk runs her hand through his hair, down the back of his neck, to his shoulders while purring seductively.

Silk: "So where are you gonna take me to then, my hero? You come to save lil ole me, is that what it is? Mmm, you so sexy, big

zaddy. Go ahead then and save me. Save your princess from the evil
dragons with the army trucks then, my handsome knight in shining
armor!" she says, cheerfully.

The two of them burst into a fit of laughter as he puts the truck
into drive and dips back into the streets, taking the poorly lit back
roads to be discrete, avoiding any high traffic streets.

Chapter 39

Essance is worried sick. She tried phoning Silk and Lilli since
leaving school to no avail. She sits in Felix's car outside one of his
many trap spots, the same spot he'd taken the girls to the day before,
a nervous wreck.

Her and Silk's parents have been calling and texting her phone
every five to ten minutes seeing if she'd linked with Silk or Lilli, and
each time her answer was "No." She and Felix had been tearing the
streets of New Orleans apart in search of Silk and Lilli until Felix
opted for a quick snack break, "code word for a smoke session." He
urges Essance to hit the weed, and she persistently protests, but then
she falls into the peer pressure and hits the blunt four good times.

Chapter 40

Lorenzo is a street-smart kid, and knows that Silk needs to be out
of the city for a minute, so he makes the two hour drive to Tallulah,
a small city north of New Orleans. He pulls into a cheap low-key
motel, gets out and pays for a room, then pulls his truck up in front
of door number thirteen, the number on the keycard that the clerk
gave him. He shuts the truck off and wakes Silk up, who is snuggled
up in the passenger seat resting peacefully. He grabs his New Orleans

Saints jacket off of the back seat, gets out of the truck, goes around and opens Silk's door, and places the jacket around her to cover her up so that her face could not be seen. He then quickly ushers her to the room and opens the door.

Once inside, Silk takes off the jacket and heads straight for the bathroom. Lorenzo turns on the television and searches for a good channel. He walks to the small desk next to the bed and grabs a brochure with a restaurant menu, local stores, gas stations, etc. "You hungry Silk?" he yells out to her. "No, I'm starving, baby!" She responds from behind the bathroom door.

Lorenzo: "Well look, I saw a market up the road there on the way over. It says here that they are open for about another hour. I'ma go grab some chicken and sides, is that cool, baby?" he asks.

Silk: "I already can't wait" she responds, flushing the toilet and washing her hands. She rushes out of the bathroom as if she were going with him.

Lorenzo: "Wait ma... I think it will be safer for me to handle this one solo, you know what I'm sayin'? With your face all over the news I can't risk anyone spotting you and tippin' you off to 12. I can't lose you, not like that, love." He states this last part sincerely, pulling her head into his chest.

Silk: "That's right big daddy, way to be on point wit it" she says, looking up into his eyes mesmerized. "I'm trippin all the way, huh? I like how you, ya know, protecting me and what not, but I really don't think we gotta worry about po po or anybody coming after me. I mean, we way out of da city, ya herd me, so nobody knows I'm here, besides, I kinda took care of that already," she states, referring to the spell that Beatrice taught her before meeting her demise at the clever hands of Silk.

Lorenzo: "What chu mean, ma?" he asks, looking quizzically and full of confusion.

Silk: "I mean you don't have to worry about it baby, no one is looking for me anymore, those problems are gone" she states boldly. "Look baby, just gook" she says, noticing that he still is completely confused. "I will stay here and wait for you to get back with the food. Then I will explain everything to you in full detail while we eat, okay?"

Adoring her cute smile, he accepts that and kisses her on the lips. Before he leaves out of the room, Silk stops him. "Oh wait," fetching some dollar bills out of her bra. "Will you grab me some feminine products and laundry soap so I can get fresh?" she requests, handing him a crumpled twenty-dollar bill, but he pushes it back to her.

Lorenzo: "Keep it, ma. I'll take care of yo lil fine behind."

Silk: "Make sure you grab some caps too, because baby, I got something real special in store for you when you get back, papi!" she says seductively with a wink and a smile.

Lorenzo: "Let me hurry up and get back then" he says while running out of the door. "Do you need anything else?" he asks before parting the doorway.

Silk: "Strawberry soda!" she answers, giggling at him by how quick he is running to get into the truck to go there and back after she mentioned more sex.

She's not sure he even heard her as fast as he got in, started the truck and was off. She closes the door smiling and thinks to herself, "I think I wanna marry this man and have his babies. Mrs. Sanchez. Wait. .. what is that boy's last name??? Bahahaha! Silk you crazy as hell bitch, you don't even know the mane last name" she says out loud, followed by hysterical laughter.

She then lay on the bed, still wrapping her head around what was happening. She begins to ponder about her parents and siblings. "They must be worried sick about me so much that maybe they done put an APB out on me. I better call and let them know not to worry." She thinks about the spell and reassures herself that everything is good. "All of Mama B's spells work properly" she reasoned in her head. She rolls over on the bed closer to the desk, picks up the room telephone, and dials her twin's cell phone number. Her and Essance are identical twins, born three minutes apart, and have been extremely inseparable since day one, so she feels it imperative to call her twin before calling her parents. Essance answers on the fourth ring not really sounding like herself. She is all goofy and giggly when she answers, "Hello" in mid laughter.

Silk: "Damn Stink," she responds (calling her twin by her childhood nickname) "must be a good damn joke that got chu bustin' up like that, I wanna hear it."

Essance: "What... what did you say? Wait, who is this?" she replies, and then takes a deep breath in shock when it registers whose voice it is, calling her from a number she didn't recognize. "Wait... Silk? Silk, is that you? Oh my god, I been... well everybody had been worried to death about you, oh my god, I can't believe it!"

Silk hears loud rap music blaring in the background, so she knew her sister could not be at home. The music gets turned down and Silk can hear muffled voices in the background, then silence.

Essance: "Silk... Silk, are you there?"

Felix: "Is that her? That's her? Gimmie the phone!"

Silk lays there looking up at the ceiling with a grin on her face as she listens to her twin and Felix scuffling over the phone. Just as Silk is about to speak again, Essance starts objecting loudly, saying, "NO!... wait Fe Fe!", but before she could finish, Felix had successfully relieved her of the iPhone. "Hello", Felix hops on the line, voice sounding husky and winded.

Silk: "What's up with you lil big head ass boa? And what chu got my twin out chea so late for woe? Wer'z y'all at anyway woe-day?"

Felix: "Look, check it out mane, now ain't the time fo all da playin games and da fuckery ya herd me? Ya ass is in real deep shit wit dem folks down her ya herd me? They got da whole city on smash lookin fo ya right now, ya herd me. I'm talkin' bout ward to ward ya herd me! Shit's real tight right now, ya done got da city on fire, ya herd me, like it ain't never been before, ya herd me!" he explains excitedly.

Essance: "Give me my phone back Fe!" she demands again, but Felix refuses.

Felix: "Hol on, wait! Chill out, bruh!"

Essance: "Let me talk to her Fe, damn, stop playin' na, gimmie my phone boy!"

Felix: "Gimmie got shot in da ass and robbed by a mongoose, now watch out na, Stink, damn, lemme finish mane!"

Essance keeps asking for and trying to snatch her phone away from him to no avail, and Felix ignores her and continues talking to Silk.

Felix: "I know you ain't out an about cus they'd been done snatched ya lil ass up, so you need to stay put up wherever ya at, ya herd me. And don't talk to nobody or tell nobody ya location, ya herd me! Matter-of-fact... we been on this here line too long. Stay low and keep ya eyes open, ya herd me. And we love ya, Silk. Call on a different line and let us know ya aight, ya herd me, and make ya calls short, ya herd me, fifteen seconds or less ya herd me. And whatever ya do mane, don't go to da crib and don't call there either, ya herd me!

Aight we love ya shawty, be safe, one" he ends with before hitting the red button.

"Wait let me ask her" Essance blurts out, but before she could finish, the line goes dead and the call is disconnected. This leaves her pissed, because she didn't even get to ask her twin any of the gazillion questions she had stored in her mind for her. Silk was a little pissed as well, because she barely got a word in herself and she didn't get to ask Essance about how the family is doing before Felix hung the phone up in her face. However, she soaked in every word he spoke.

Silk places the receiver back on the base and contemplates calling Essance's phone right back, but decides against it. Then she gets to thinking about how frantic and worried both Essance and Felix both sounded, and knew that things weren't as sweet as she'd thought. She hops off of the bed, grabs the TV remote, and turns it on to the channel 4 news station. She looks at the screen in disbelief as she faces the reality of her life: there, her high school photo is plastered on the news below what read:

WANTED FOR SUSPECTED DOUBLE HOMICIDE. IF SEEN CALL 9-1-1 IMMEDIATELY. ARMED AND DANGEROUS.

The news reporter was going over a segment on the story and the investigation's progress. Silk grabs her hair in frustration and confusion. "How could this be happening? Why didn't the spell work?" she questions out loud. Instantly her nerves start going into overdrive, so she begins pacing the small room looking around at everything suspiciously when it finally dawns on her:

Silk: "That bitch tricked me... "

Chapter 41

Essance punches Felix hard in the arm and starts cussing him out.

Essance: "Why-the-fuck you do that for, stupid ass? I wanted to talk to her and see where she was at and if she aight! I need to know where my sister is and know that she is okay! What-the-fuck is wrong wit chu bruh?"

Felix: "She is okay, don't chu see that if she wasn't, den she never would've called? Now chill the fuck out mane, damn!" he yells back at an angry Essance. "Silk should've never even called from any numba that can be traced how hot they is on her!" he continues.

Essance: "See, naw woe, I don't care, I'm calling the numba back! I gotta make sure she's safe and not in the streets" she states as she opens up her recent calls in her iPhone.

Felix snatches her phone away before she can hit the call button on the number Silk had just called from, and throws it in a pocket of his cargo shorts.

Essance yells and instantly starts wrestling with him on the couch over her iPhone, demanding he give it back to her. She tires quickly after a moment's struggles, the effects of the potent marijuana she had smoked a short while ago taken its course on her now. Feeling lazy and uncoordinated, she throws herself on top of him in an effort to pin him down and reach in his pocket for her phone. She has on a short skirt, so her reaching over him, bent over the way she is, causes her skirt to rise up exposing her curvy light brown thighs and her Victoria Secret panties. Felix, with the mixture of weed and Hennessy, gets turned on as he gets a peep at Essance's plump butt cheek popping up out of the skirt, and as she continues wrestling him for her phone, her pussy lips manage to show themselves sliding out the sides of her panties. He licks his lips looking at the back of her head, which is in his lap from his view, and he starts to get aroused and mischievous.

Chapter 42

After learning from the Greene family how close the twins Silk and Essance are, detective Valorie had decided that it would be best to put a tail on Essance, being as though she is Silk's twin and she was one of the last people with Silk before she allegedly killed the school janitor. An unmarked undercover Chevrolet Trailblazer followed Essance and Felix all around town, with additional unmarked police units assisting so that covers wouldn't be blown, and rested on the two at Felix's trap spot in the Seventeenth Ward of New Orleans. This particular area is the projects, known for gangbanging, drug dealing, pimping and hoeing, murder, bootlegging, and all sorts of other crimes. Inside of the undercover police vehicle, officers are equipped with all of the latest in high-quality spy and intel technology, normally used in narcotics surveillance operations. One device is a small box with a microphone that can pick up sound waves five blocks away from where they are parked. They listen in intently on Felix and Essance. The IT officer is nodding off, but jumps up when he hears Silk's name being repeated. He turns up the volume and listens closely, getting the other officer's attention and snaps his finger when he realizes that Essance is on her cell phone talking to Silk.

The officers in the unmarked Trailblazer radio in to detective Valorie to inform her about the phone call, and confirm that from the conversation heard, Silk made the call to Essance. "Ten-four. Does anyone have the phone number of Essance Greene?" Detective Valorie announces over the radio. "Negative" the Communications Unit, known in the police community as "COMMS", responds. Detective Valorie, who is back downtown at the New Orleans PD headquarters, tells officers in the field, via radio: "Stand-by. I'm going to make a call to the house to see if I can get the number from the parents, so stand by until further notice, I repeat stand by!" "Copy that, ten-four, standing by" was the response she got.

Detective Valorie races to her desk, finds the Greenes' home phone number, and dials it using her desk phone so that the call could be recorded. Lashunda answers on the first ring, anxious to hear any good news. Detective Valorie identifies herself, lets Lashunda know that they have not yet located or apprehended Silk, but that they do believe she is safe. When asked by Lashunda how they knew Silk was safe without knowing where she was, Detective Valorie informs her about the recent call that Silk made to Essance and asked if she could get Essance's phone number so that she could call to see if Silk is ok, if she's safe, and what she said. Feeling the need to protect and find her baby, Lashunda gives Detective Valorie Essance's cell phone number, and requests that she calls her back notifying her the second she knows anything new. Detective Valorie agrees and hangs up after thanking Lashunda.

Detective Valorie gets back on her police radio and lets the Comms team know that she has acquired Essance's number. She airs it over the radio for them to do a database sweep to pull up the phone's information. Comms comes back informing Detective Valorie and other officers that Essance's phone is active through T-Mobile and that they could ping Essance's location now using her phones' signal from the Command RV. They also inform Detective Valorie, only after she'd asked, that they had no access to the information stored in the phone's call log. Apple's strict policy on privacy blocked the police from being able to get into the personal information stored in Essance's iPhone. Detective Valorie knew from experience that she needs a judge to issue a search warrant to be able to obtain vital phone records, and she also knew that even with a warrant she probably still wouldn't get in the phone through Apple. She also knew that she doesn't have time on her side to do all of those things. Although it is Friday night, and the court was closed, and although she knows it's a long shot, she had to go for it. She sits at her desk and begins drafting an application for a probable cause search warrant; which she'd use as a phony search warrant to get Essance's phone if she couldn't reach a judge this late. Fifteen minutes later and she is done typing the warrant and is on her way to the printer, cell phone in hand calling her supervisor for assistance in acquiring a judge's signature on the warrant. The chief of police informs her that he will see what he could do, although the request was a long shot being it so late in the night. Slightly satisfied at this response, Valorie ends the call with her chief, grabs the single-paged warrant, heads back to her desk, and retrieves her black leather jacket and handheld police radio set. She signals to her partner, Detective Billy Bob, who is leaning back in his desk chair, stuffing his mouth full of Popeye's chicken breasts. He gets startled when Detective Valorie waves the phony warrant in his face, taking him out of his deep sick infatuation with the fried chicken, and he hits the floor hard, extra crispy chicken still in hand.

Detective Valorie rushes him on as she makes her way to leave the department. He grabs his own radio set, jacket, and his bucket of fried chicken and staggers after her. Over the police radio, Detective Valorie alerts all of the active special response units and S.W.A.T. teams to prepare to conduct a sweep in the 17th Ward projects, and to be on standby, awaiting her arrival. All units confirm their orders over the radio.

Billy Bob hops into the passenger seat of their assigned unmarked Dodge Charger, supercharged with extra hemi power, involuntarily opting not to do the driving. Valorie rolls her eyes and mumbles a few obscenities under her breath, in complete disgust at her partner, who shoots her a slight grin. "I heard that," he teases. They ride in silence, all except for the loud crunching and smacking Billy Bob is doing on the greasy chicken.

Detective Valorie: "Can you glut any louder? God! I can't even hear the radio!"

Detective Billy Bob: "Somebody needing a little TLC lately huh? Ole man ain't cleaning ya pipes no more sugar? Oh, how sad. But don't worry, Ole Billy Bob hear a getcha back squirtin' and queefin' just right sugar plum!" he shoots back, teasing Valorie even more, and purposely trying to strike a nerve in her.

It works because he gets a good cursing out from her the whole rest of the ride to the target location, which is about a fifteen minute long cussing out.

Chapter 43

Essance: "Felix, come on bruh, stop playin' with me! Give my damn phone back now! Silk is probably trying to get through right now."

Felix: "Girl quit wit the bullshit. You know Silk not dat damn stupid now. She smart and playin' safe which is a good thang, ya herd me! Just sit back and chill out, mane" he says, the last part he puts on his deep smooth voice, which Essance instantly catches on to, making her complexed face turn and look at him with an alert, curious expression now.

He lights another Backwood full of Kush and blows smoke in her direction while resting a hand on her lower back. Hearing Felix sounding so flirtatious makes her feel awkward, especially now that her full attention is on him, instead of her iPhone. It's at this moment she realizes that her skirt has risen from the back and that her whole ass and panties are exposed to her childhood friend. Instantly, she jumps up to pull down and straighten her skirt, then she stares at the floor with her arms crossed over her breasts feeling embarrassed. Felix senses her thoughts so he moves in to relax her, to get her back comfortable.

Felix: "Come her, sit down and hit dis piff, mane" he offers, smiling while extending the smoking Backwood to her.

She pokes her bottom lip out like a defiant child, but takes the spliff and plops back down into her original spot on the couch, one leg crossed underneath her butt, and begins choking on the exotic herb again.

Felix watches her lustfully as she inhales, holds the smoke in, and chokes. Coughing heavily on the weed. Felix chuckles at her.

Felix: "Damn baby-lungs, ya aight, ma?" he asks.

Essance stops coughing abruptly and shoots him a serious look:

Essance: "What's wit all this 'lil mama' shit bruh? Nigga I ain't one of ya lil thot ass groupies ya got round her chasin' ya bruh, ya herd me. What cha call ya self doin, tryna test me now or something huh lil bitch?" she states, playfully punching him in his arm.

She pulls on the weed again, taking an even harder hit this time, and chokes her lungs out again.

Felix: "My fault, Stink. I don't mean no harm, ya herd me. But let me be real wit cha doe. I been feeling ya fa years now, but I just ain't really know how to tell ya dat, ya herd me. I mean, you, me, Silk... we all grown now, ya herd me. And you done grown up to be one hell of a lady, ya herd me. Like... you so beautiful, and ya body is amazing, and I can't even lie, I got forreal feelins fa ya, Stink. Ya make me feel weird, ya herd me. In a good way. Like... all tingly inside and shit, ya herd me" he confesses.

Essance: "Mhmm... well what was all dat about yesterday with you and Silk back there in dat room together then huh? I guess she make you feel the same way then huh?" she counters, with a suspicious look, and then takes another hit of the wood as she waits for his comeback.

Felix is quick with one too, so quick and fast and so smooth that before Essance knows it she lay on the couch with her legs across his lap. He continues charming Essance, reminiscing on childhood memories that they share. One time in particular he rehashes; the time that they experienced their first kiss at an after-school program. Thinking about the kiss makes Essance feel all mushy inside. Felix, playing off of her response, uses that experience as leverage to say that the two of them have always had chemistry. "So, let's quit playin' these games now that we are both grown and mature, so let's hook up" he states. Essence is staring deep into Felix's eyes now, searching his soul for any hint of bullshit, because she is somehow loving the game he is laying on her. She is intrigued because this side of Felix, this Dr. Smooth, she has never seen before, so to her surprise, she is actually turned on, something she never thought in a million years would be the case.

She does not answer his question, she stares at his lips for a couple seconds, looking mesmerized. She can't deny that she had secretly been noticed how handsome Felix had grown up to be as they'd gotten older. Also, she has always been attracted to the hard, hood niggas in the neighborhood, and that, she knew by now, Felix most certainly has always been. Felix puts out the Backwood, sets his clear cup of Hennessy down on the coffee table, and then goes right in, planting a wet kiss on Essance's full lips. She jumps out of her trance, starting to object, but the feeling going from her chest to her stomach and down to her knees and then to her vagina stops her from pushing him off. She taps both of his shoulders a few times, then lets her hands rest on them as his tongue makes its way in her mouth. She relaxes and then joins him in the tongue dance. Essence is hot and wet and completely caught up in the moment. This is the best kiss she's ever had, and the feelings are tremendous. "Oh my god... what is going on? What the heck am I doing? Stop him Essance stop him... No wait... Damn this shit feels so good... Okay now boy! Damn Felix know what he doing. I didn't know this nigga could kiss like this... shit!" Essance rambles on in her own head as the kiss happens. Out of nowhere, she climbs up on top and straddles Felix, lips never separating. Touching, feeling, rubbing and grabbing all over his slim muscular upper body as his hands explore every inch of her slim-thick zaftig. He eases his hands down and around her waist, cupping her round plump ass cheeks, causing her to moan and breathe heavier. He lightly smacks her ass, causing it to jiggle, and cups both cheeks, this time squeezing tighter, methodically rocking her body, making her clit rub against his lower abdomen. With his big hands covering her ass cheeks, he is able to slide a finger under her panties, finding a soaking puddle in her panties, and he is easily able to glide his finger to her tight pussy hole.

Essance jumps again, but then she eases her muscles, not slowing down on the French kissing, arches her back so that her body is in better position to let him in, and then she moves her hips up and down, applying pressure so that his finger may enter her insides. Now she is grinding on his finger as he works it in and out of her, still gripping her ass cheek with his other hand as they continue making out on the couch.

After about four minutes, Essance climaxes all over Felix's fingers and hand, grabs her around the waist and lifts up off of the couch holding her in the air, tongues still dancing on one another's. He carries her, holding her up by her ass cheeks, in his bedroom, lays her on the bed, and then dives right back in on her wet lips, and then to her neck, and then down to her C-cups, kissing and sucking rhythmically on her breasts. Then he moves further down her torso, causing her to wiggle and giggle. "That tickles" she laughs out uncontrollably. As he moves down to her navel, she really starts to heat up. "No! We need to stop Fe Fe, we friends" Essance says in between kisses and moans of pleasure. He ignores and keeps going on past her waistline with his tongue, tasting her body. She arches her back, lifting her ass off of the bed, and he cups her breasts with both hands as his head remains in between her thighs. He takes his time tracing her waistline with his tongue causing her body to shake, and talking in tongues she feels so damn good.

He then begins to go lower, kissing and licking her inner thighs, all while staring up at her eyes. He feels enough is enough and gently pulls her panties to the side and starts feasting on her love box. After a minute of getting her soaking wet, he pulls her panties all the way off of her body, and completely smothers her pussy with his mouth, causing her to have an orgasm, screaming and gripping the bed sheets and she releases again on him. Loving how she tastes, he takes in all of her juices.

Felix continues eating Essance out for about five to seven minutes in all sorts of ways, with the final position being her sitting atop his whole face, riding and grinding on him, leaving her sweet juices running down his mouth onto his cheeks, neck, and ears. After climaxing from the oral about four times already, Essance reaches the height of her orgasm and she squirts all over his head, getting her juices all over his shoulders, chest, and arms. She falls out in pleasure and exhaustion while still squirting. She had never experienced anything so good before in her life.

Felix gets up, takes off his pants and boxers and tries to get on top of Essance, but she jumps back against the wall, sitting up in a defensive position. She raises a hand to his chest to halt his advance.

Essance: "Wait... what chu think you doin?"

Felix: "What chu mean baby? I thought... " he replies, looking confused.

Essance: "You thought what? You was gone go inside of me without protection? Boa what chu been smoking on? It ain't that Kush. Can't be just tree if you think I'm finna sit here and let chu inside of me without a condom" she cuts in sternly.

Felix: "Yea you right, Stink, what was I thinkin?" he admits, as he smirks and gets off of the bed.

Essance: "You was thinkin' about how you wanna get beat up in ya own spot, sir" she caps back sarcastically.

Felix: "Ha ha ha, you funny as hell, Stink" he responds, and the two of them share a laugh.

Essance: "And quit calling me that, not uh, not while we're doing this. Shit feel weird anyway, and you calling me that only make me feel weirder... "

Felix: "My bad" he replies while rummaging through the dresser drawers in search of a rubber.

Essance: "It's just... I mean... I just couldn't have saw this coming. Like... that I'd be making out and making love with my best friend in the whole world, like... It just doesn't seem real for some reason. Is it real Fe, or am I just dreaming?"

Felix: "Making love? Holdup, we ain't even really started yet, girl, what chu tom bout some 'making love?'"

Essance: "Yes, making love, that is what this is gonna be, so I hope you don't think you finna "fuck" on me like you do one of them skeezerts y'all got around here, because that's not hannen sir!

Nope, no sir, you not finna just blow Essance's back out up in here tonight, no buddy. Sorry not sorry" she snaps.

Felix: "Yea you right, ain't none of that finna go on with you tonight. Tonight is gone be special. Something memorable. So I'ma save that rough shit for another time, sweetness" he replies, followed by a wet kiss on Essance's lips which causes her to grin mischievously, biting her bottom lip and staring at him seductively.

She can't help but to admire how sexy and strong her best friend is.

Essance: "Ok, but after this, are you officially my man or what? Cause you know I don't get down like that. If I give you my precious goodies, we are together, playboy" she boldly asserts, raising an eyebrow for emphasis.

Felix: "Fasho... no doubt. You is my ole lady starting tonight. No question" he answers hesitantly, caught off guard by Essance's bluntness.

Essance: "Good. Now can I have my dang ole phone back?" she asks, holding her hand out with a bright seductive smile.

Felix: "Now ya really reaching, baby, you reaching" he teases, smiling back.

Essance: "Ugh... you is so irritating bruhhh I swear!" Essance quips back and they both share another laugh. "Hurry up, boy, what is taking you so long? You gone mess around and have to get dis juice box back drippin in a second as long as you takin" she entices, looking down at her pussy seductively.

Felix: "I'll be right back, lemme go see if my kin folk in da other room got one I can use" he replies, putting his boxers back on:

Essance: "Nigga what chu mean use? It betta be still in the wrapper and the wrapper betta be sealed bust! Fuck wrong wit chu mane?... Don't get cho ass stomped up in here bitch playin' wit me like that!"

Felix: "Come on now, baby, don't insult me like that. Be right back" he states, laughing off her attitude. "Hurry up" Essance yells at his back as he leaves out of the bedroom.

Felix: "Quit trippin" he yells back from the hallway.

Felix leaves out in a hurry, runs down the small hallway to his cousin-in-law Skip's bedroom and busts in the room unannounced to loud rap music and strong weed in the air.

Skip: "Damn bitch don't chu know how to knock?" he barks at Felix, pointing his Glockl 9 at his bare chest for emphasis.

Felix: "Aye bitch stop playin' wit me forreal" he responds, smacking the gun away from his chest. "Aye I know you got an extra jimmy up in dis bish I can get up out chu real real fast cutty?"

Skip: "Extra? Let chu get? Ain't a got-damn thang up in here free partna, so I can't let chu get shit, and ain't no got damn such thing as a extra nothing! Now I got what cha lookin fo woe, but chu gotta pay da man just like err body else round dis ma'fucka", he demands, showing off his mouth full of golds while rubbing his fingers together indicating he is talking dollars.

Felix: "Look at me cutty, do it look like I got some dollars on me right at dis moment?"

Skip takes a long drag at the wood and pauses, holding in the smoke while looking at Felix sideways. He blows the smoke out, coughing and chuckling at the same time.

Skip: "Shidd ... show coulda fooled me bitch, walkin round dis joint lookin like a male go-go dancer, nigga! Ha ha ha! Shidd, shouldn't you be on ya way to somebody's bachelor party or sumn, nigga? Ain't no pole out there, but come on in here hoe. Ha ha ha! While I'm sittin' up her tryna charge you, it looks like I need to be

payin' you for the entertainment" he remarks, jokingly examining
Felix's body.

Felix: "Mane quit wit da bullshit bruh" he snaps back in an
annoyed tone. "I got shawty waitin' fa me in the room, you gone look
out or what?" he asks impatiently.

Skip looks past him at the door to Felix's room then back at him
with a quizzical look on his face like he didn't believe what Felix said.

Skip: "Wait, you mean to tell me you nailing dat lil fine ass lil
cinnamon thang, that lil twin skeet I saw you chillin on da couch wit
earlier. She got da twin sis right? One dat Wood walked in on you
wit yesterday in ther huh?" he asks in a flurry.

Felix: "Yea bruh, that's her now wassup?" he asks, growing more
and more impatient and annoyed with Skip.

Skip runs to his dresser drawer, rips off two Trojan Magnums off
of the strip of twelve, comes back to the doorway, and extends his
arm out to give them to Felix, but when Felix reaches both condoms
Skip snatches back, stopping him from getting them.

Skip: "Whoa whoa woedy calm down now, slow ya role playboy!
Take one" he instructs.

Felix: "But you grabbed two for me ... I mean... what the fuck?"
he replies in confusion.

Skip: "Naw naw woedy. I grabbed two for 'us'-—one fo you and
one fo me. We finna have a party up in dis bish, all on that lil fine
piece of meat you got up in ther."

Felix: "Naw bruh, dis ain't that type of party ya herd me. Not this
time ya herd me. Not this one woedy!"

Chapter 44

When Felix leaves out of the room, Essance takes advantage
of this small window of opportunity to dig through Felix's shorts'

pocket and retrieve her cell phone without him knowing. "Ha ha ha, sucka," she mocks as she gets up out of the bed and quickly locates his shorts on the floor of the poorly lit bedroom. "Damn!" she exclaims under her breath due to how heavy the shorts are. She goes in the left pocket and pulls out Felix's LG phone with a blue and black case around it. She puts his back in the pocket and feels in the right-side pocket where she instantly feels her iPhone. She gets ecstatic and quickly pulls it out and kisses the screen. As she is about to put his shorts back on the floor where they were, she hears a vibration followed by a bird chirp go off in the shorts' pocket. She turns the shorts, looks at pocket, and sees a blue screen light flashing. Against her better judgment, she allows her curiosity to get the best of her, so she grabs his phone out and looks at the screen. When Essance sees what is on his screen, she gasps and damn near chokes at the picture with the incoming call signal flashing. She sees the name *Big Daddy Long Pipe* and a picture of an extremely muscular built man with a lot of tattoos with long hair slicked back past his shoulders standing naked, flexing while clutching his erect penis. Essance makes a daring move and presses 'Answer'. She puts the phone up to her ear and just listens. What she hears makes her gag, threatening to vomit. "Aye baby, what chu doin? Say, I'm in the area and I wanted to stop by and get a sample of dat peanut butter box. I know it's been a minute and you probably been needing Daddy Long Pipe in ya system, so have dat ass and mouth ready for Big Daddy when I get there. I'll be pulling up in about fifteen. Don't make me wait longer" and the man hangs up. Essance drops the phone, frozen in bewilderment, and just stares at it in pure disgust. She sticks her tongue out as if not wanting it to be a part of her mouth anymore after hearing that Felix's tongue has been on that mystery man's dick and shakes her head.

As disgusted as she is with what she's just discovered about Felix, however, for some reason, just to dig deeper and be nosey, she picks the phone up again. She unlocks it on the first attempt after guessing what the most typical password would be for her best friend to come up with. "His Granny's birthday" she guesses to herself. She quickly enters 6-19-41 and the phone unlocks.

She shakes her head at how simple Felix is. "Sooo street smart yet so dumb" she mumbles quietly. First, she checks the call log and contacts, seeing a bunch of females' names, some of which she knew from school and the neighborhood, and guys names, which she guesses are most of his homeboys, or maybe not. She comes across the contact named: "Bae Trey."

She clicks it out of suspicion and looks through the text messages where Felix and this Trey dude are talking to each other like lovers instead of homeboys. She covers her mouth in disgust when she reads:

Trey: I love what you did to me last night boo. Oow that mouth of yours is a work of art chile

Felix: you know how I do it bae anything to please my favorite niggae

What Essance sees when she goes to Felix's stored photos and recorded videos almost causes her to faint. There are real live sex photos and videos of Felix wearing a blonde wig having sex with multiple men and teenagers, but none with any females. From looking at the videos, you would think that he was auditioning for PornHub or something. Felix is taking and giving it up in the mouth and backdoor. Felix in the video getting hit from the front, back, side-to-side and even riding dicks, all while screaming and moaning for more in his deep manly voice. Unable to stomach anymore, Essance puts his phone back into the shorts' pocket. It starts vibrating again indicating another incoming call but she doesn't even dare to look at it this time. She is too turned down and disgusted for any more surprises. She shakes her head while putting her bra and panties back on, repulsed at the thought of her almost was about to let Felix go inside. She feels super nasty for kissing him passionately in the mouth, letting him eat her out, and was almost about to go down on him had he not been so thirsty to get the nookie, after what she'd just discovered in the photos and videos of him. "Glad I didn't, thank you Jesus" she says underneath her breath, shaking off the thought and straightening herself up. She heads for the bedroom door and reaches for the handle when Felix dashes back in, out of breath and kind of sweaty, still in his boxers. He looks at Essance questionably. "What chu doin baby, I got one, see!" he says, smiling, showing her the Trojan Magnum condom.

Essance: "Good for you. Now go on ahead and call one of your lil boy freaks to put it on and use it on you cus it ain't happening with me, now move!" she states sternly, looking at him in pure disgust, as if she didn't even know the individual standing before her anymore, she takes a few steps back to create some distance.

Felix: "Girl, what the fuck is you talking about? Wassup with cha all of a sudden?" he counters, confusion and disappointment etched on his face.

He quickly glances around the room and notices his cell phone light is flashing in his shorts pocket. He mentally kicks himself in the ass once he notices that Essance has her own phone in her hand. Now he knows where she got her information about his indiscretion. "Fuck" he whispers and runs over and retrieves his phone. Looking at his face when he saw what is on his screen says it all, and confirms what Essance already was suspecting: it's *Big Daddy Long Pipe* calling back. He hits the END button then goes through his phone history to see what all exactly Essance saw and discovered about him.

When he discovers what she has went through and seen he looks up at her in tons of shame and embarrassment. He opens his mouth to start trying to explain but Essance cuts him off:

Essance: "No, I don't want to hear it, I don't want to know any more than what I do now... just take me home right now Felix, and just forget that any of this ever happened. Or, matter of fact, you know what, just drop me off at the bus shuttle. I don't want to be the reason you keeping *Big Daddy Long Pipe* waiting to pump dat got damn tree up yo ass nigga... Yuck," she states unapologetically, with a disgusted expression on her face.

Felix is stuck in disbelief at how quickly the situation has changed.

Essance: "Hello! Did you *not* hear me? Earth to the meat lover! Hello! Take me away from here! NOW!" she demands.

Essance is screaming, face almost turning red. Felix tries to shush her, constantly looking back down the hall where he'd just come from. However, it was too late to shush her. A second later Skip's door opens, releasing a big cloud of weed smoke along with rap music blasting. Skip steps out and into the hallway, peering down at Felix and Essance. He smiles widely, gold teeth blinging, and makes his way towards them, shirtless, with a limp is his walk, feeling as though he was 'Pimpin Kin' himself, clutching a bottle of Southern Comfort. Felix looks and feels weak and perplexed now that his deep dark secrets were exposed. He wonders if Essance will tell anyone about them and the whole world would know.

Skip: "Yeaaa lil nigga! That's what I'm tom bout right ther, move this party on into the living room so we all can have room to enjoy," he chants, approaches the two in the living room, staring at Essance's body from head to toe, like she is a healthy impala to a hungry lion.

He sets the bottle of whisky on the table and rubs his hands together, licking his lips like he just knows that he's about to get it in on Essance. He starts making his chest jump rapidly by flexing his chest muscles and showing off his six-pack all in an effort to entice Essance to get all on him so he can hit it first.

Essance looks at him with an annoyed, uninterested smug on her face, then she looks back at Felix and demands again, "Felix, drop me the fuck off, NOW!" Felix starts to put his shorts on, but Skip moves in on him and grabs the shorts, easing them down with one hand.

Skip: "Wait... hold up... naw ain't nobody goin no wher, this party just getting started, lil baby," he says, eyeballing Essance lustfully.

He unbuckles his belt, allowing his pants to fall down, revealing his throbbing dick underneath his boxer briefs. Essence instantly closes her eyes and turns her head, shielding her face with her hand to block Skip out completely. Then it dawns on her; a piece of one of the videos she'd skimmed through in Felix's phone.

She realizes that Skip is one of the dudes in the video that Felix was dancing naked on while he threw dollar bills and pitched quarters at him. Skip was the first to pull his dick out while Felix was on all fours dropping down low, and he is the one she saw shove himself into Felix's mouth violently, then turned him around and did the same thing to his ass with no remorse. She couldn't believe how Felix could take what he took. Skip was stroking the young man fast and rough as if he was trying to damage Felix. She couldn't believe it. This dude was acting like he was in some real pussy. To make matters worse, he then calls his guys in to run a train on Felix and they do. The images haunting her mind causes Essance to look at both Skip and Felix in pure disgust.

Skip attempts to reach in and touch her backside, but she is too quick. She smacks his drunken hand so hard and fiercely, causing him to jump, then she pushes him in his chest with full strength, causing him to fall back clumsily and trip over his pants that were around his ankles.

Skip: "Oh shit... bitch... what the fuck," he screams from the ground as he falls.

Felix is taken aback, looking from Essance to Skip in confusion, not knowing what to do.

Felix: "Woedey I told you this wasn't that type of party... chill out mane" he states sheepishly to Skip.

Essance: "No, this most definitely ain't 'that type of party' punk! Don't chu ever put cho filthy ass, faggot ass paws on me again bitch! I'll kick yo gay ass, bitch! You dick in the booty ass bitches will never be able to fuck with this. Y'all don't even want no woman anyway, y'all would rather fuck each others' brains out" shaking her head in disgust, "Fucking disgraces. Bitch-ass niggas like y'all are an embarrassment to black men. And the Bible say that fuck boys like y'all are an abomination ... two wasted souls. And to think I could trust you, Felix. Take me home right now" she snaps, then demands Felix again.

Felix, looking dumbfounded and confused, and feeling insulted, but he knows she is right.

Felix: "Yea... I'll take you home, Stink. Let me get my... " he begins but Essance butts in:

Essance: "Mhmm, hurry the fuck up, nigga! And what I say about calling me that name huh? Those privileges of your's are dead now" she snaps again.

Skip: "Lil nigga, you gone let this bitch treat chu in yo own house, in front cho own folk woe?" he gets up off of the floor in rage and screams out.

Essance: "Yea... the same folk dat love taking his ass hole and mouth for joyrides for quarters, huh woe?" Essance shoots back.

Both Skip and Felix's anger grows the more Essance insults them, and Felix starts letting Skip influence him to take charge -—to be the man and take control of the situation, to put the bitch (Essance) in her place. With Skip in his ear and Essance still throwing insults at him, Felix is fed up, so he snaps. He rushes Essance, who is still shouting out insults and name-calling, reaches back and slaps the shit out of her, sending spit flying out of her mouth and sending her flying 2-3 feet, landing hard on the couch. She lets out a faint whimper from the pain and grabs her face.

Before she could get up to react, Skip and Felix are on her like lions, ripping her shirt, grabbing her bra and skirt off, grabbing her legs, arms, neck, and waist, attempting to maneuver her into a good position while stripping her of all of her clothing.

Essance screams and kicks and apologizes, pleading for them to stop, but the men wouldn't let up, looking demon-possessed. Skip is laughing at her now pleading for mercy, encouraging Felix and rooting him on as he pulls away at her skirt and panties while Felix holds her upper body down to stop her struggles, stuffing her face into the comer of the couch to muffle her screams. Essance is crying hysterically, apologizing and begging them not to rape her as she feels air from the back hit her ass and pussy, knowing now that Skip had gotten her panties off and that she was now exposed to him. Neither attacker pays any attention to her pleas.

Felix: "Who's the bitch now, bitch?"

Skip: "Yea, this is what I'm tom bout, woe. We finna tear dis lil mafucka up right chea", he cheers, looking down at Essance's ass and pussy. "I'ma fuck dis bitch in her tight lil ass hole too now since you called me a booty-bandit. I'ma make that ther statement true today bitch", he announces while laughing, then he takes a long gulp of the Southern Comfort and passes the bottle to Felix who does the same.

Skip licks three of his fingers, then puts them down in between Essance's legs and starts rubbing in her butt hole to get it wet while stroking his dick with the other hand. Essance is screaming, still pleading for them to stop and to not rape her.

Essance: "Please y'all I am sorry, do not do this. This is rape! I'm sorry Fefe, I didn't mean it! I'm sorry, man. Please don't! Oh my God, please don't rape me, I'm so sorry!" she begs.

She feels her pleas are dead and feels Skip's wet fingers playing in her butt, and she begins to feel hopeless. She feels Skip's penis slapping up against her ass cheeks and realizes there is no more use in pleading, because they are about to do it. Frozen in fear and shock, she braces herself for the penetration. Just as Skip is steering his dick towards Essance's ass, the whole front door of the apartment comes crashing in, flying into the living room.

"FREEZE! New Orleans P.D.! Get the fuck off of her, and put your hands up! On the ground now! Do it now or I'll roast your dirty black ass!" one of the officers screams at Felix and Skip. They both comply immediately with the dozen or so S.W.A.T. team officers who hand their long guns drawn and ready to kill. They both release Essance and get onto the living room floor.

Chapter 45

Once Felix and Skip are both on the floor and subdued in handcuffs, a female S.W.A.T officer runs over to aid Essance while the rest of her team do a clearing sweep of the rest of the unit. "Hey are you alright, mam? Are you hurt anywhere?" the officers ask Essance.

Essance: "No I'm not hurt, but thank you! Thank you so much for saving me!" Essance cries out joyfully, eyes filled with tears of relief and grace and gratitude.

Police Officer: "You are so welcome, sweetheart. Don't worry, they won't ever be able to hurt you again, that's what we're here for, to save lives, hun. Alright, what's your name... are you Essance Greene?" the female officer asks compassionately while helping Essance to her feet and grabbing what torn pieces of clothing were left from off of the floor.

Essance: "Yes, I am", she answers, still crying and too shaken up to even bother about asking how the officer knew who she was already, or how and why she was there to find her.

She is just so grateful that her cries and pleas were heard by the right people, and that she was rescued. And who better to come to her rescue than the police, she thought to herself. "Thank you Lord Jesus, thank you" she whispers to herself looking up towards the heavens.

Six or seven officers all yell out their locations, followed by, "clear" as they check the entire apartment. "All clear" the lead S.W.A.T. officer announces. Seconds later Detective Valorie comes rushing in, putting her pistol back into the holster. She mean-mugs Felix and Skip, who are both on the floor swearing at the officers searching their persons in an effort to convince them that they did "nothing, nothing wrong". They are unaware, however, that the police had the entire thing audio-recorded, and would be submitting it all to the district attorney's office to prosecute them both on rape, attempted rape, kidnapping, assault and battery, and attempted murder on Skip, due to the fact that he is listed as being HIV positive and he knows it. A shit load of additional charges including possession of controlled substances, felon in possession of a firearm, providing alcohol and drugs to a minor (Essance), coercion by use of and threats of force, and check forgery would also be added at a later date to both men's laundry list of felony charges.

Detective Valorie walks right past the two men. Skip tries to stop her.

Skip: "Ms. V, come on mane, you know you know I would never touch no lit guls now", he tries to plead.

Detective Valorie: "Oh yea, then why in the hell are your pants down to your ankles, and why is your AIDS-infested dick out?" she caps back.

Skip begins to try to swear at Valorie, but the bottom of Detective Billy Bob's cowboy boot lands right in his mouth, causing him to fall back viciously with a now-busted bloody grill.

Detective Billy Bob: "Fucking ass-wipe, done got your triflin' ass AIDS blood all on my boot now. Sum-bitches cost me five hundred dollars a pair, now you done went and got your AIDS blood all on

em, you faggot piece of dog shit you" he rants on and smashes the
half full bottle of Southern Comfort on the back of Skip's head. "You
done gave my boot AIDS, bitch! That's alright cus I know you got
some drug money round this raggedy dump somewhere, I can smell
it. You buying me a new of boot you ugly sum-bitch. Matter of fact,
you gone buy me a brand-new pair, you boy-loving sissy-fied, toad
sucking sum-bitch you, ya hear!" he screams at Skip.

"Hey, watch it! What cha do that for, that was evidence" the
lady S.W.A.T. officer who initially aided Essance says, referring to the
bottle of whisky Billy Bob broke on Skip's skull. Billy Bob shrugs his
shoulders.

Detective Billy Bob: "She ain't drank none of it, no way. Sides,
there's plenty of evidence in this shit-hole to indict the whole damn
projects. Sure as hell enough to put these two creeps away forever" he
asserts confidently.

Detective Valorie: "Can you still try to keep your temper at bat,
and preserve and not destroy as much evidence as possible, please?"
she requests nicely.

Detective Billy Bob: "Alright" he replies reluctantly.

Detective Valorie: "Thank you" she adds sarcastically.

"Yea, if you need something to hand out an ass-whoopin with,
use this," says another female officer as she approaches with her
bouton out, followed by two forceful swings, clubbing both Skip and
Felix across their faces, dropping them both.

"Hey that's a good idea. Why didn't I think of that? Do ya
mind?" Billy Bob says, and asks for the bouton which the officer
gladly hands over. "Thanks," Billy Bob says, then begins wailing down
hard on Felix and Skip with all the power he could muster up until
he became winded. He bends down to catch his breath, still looking
at the two men groaning in pain and agony. "Give me a hand over
here, will ya", Billy Bob says to the remaining officers in the room. As
if on cue, all of the S.W.A.T. team officers begin beating the shit out

of Felix and Skip, who scream and plead for them to stop. While the beating is going on, Billy Bob puts on latex gloves and goes to the back of the unit to search for drugs, money, weapons, more money, and any other contraband he could find.

"Do you have all of your things, sweetie?" Detective Valorie and the female S.W.A.T. officer asks Essance before walking her outside of the unit to get her some medical attention and away from the crime scene. "Yes", Essance answers. As she walks out with the police officers, she glances at Felix in disappointment one last time before exiting. She feels sort of bad for him because of the way he is being beaten so viciously by the cops. It reminds her of all of the cases of police brutality on young Black men and women that you hear about in the news and in her community. But she quickly pushes the feelings of remorse and sorrow out of her mind when she looks down at her ripped up clothes, and puts her hand on her face and feels the stinging pain from him slapping her so hard. She then feels like he is getting his fair share of karma, and that worse is coming. She forgot about all of the years of friendship they had. What makes her hate him even more is the fact that not only was he just about to rape her with his sex partner, kinfolk, or whoever Skip is to him, but the fact that he knew Skip has AIDS and could have passed it onto her. "Or did Felix know? Doesn't matter at this point, but damn was it a close call", she thought to herself. "Fuck you faggot mutha-fuckas", she yells and spits right on their faces as she is walking out the door. Detective Valorie and the officer then usher her outside. The female S.W.A.T. officer radios in a code, requesting an ambulance on the scene to pull up, which arrives in seconds, to render medical aid to Essance.

Chapter 46

The man "Big Daddy Long Pipe", a senior member of the local section of Blood Gang sat parked in his vehicle puffing a Cuban cigar and witnessed the entire police raid of Felix's and Skip's unit. He had tried phoning Felix to warn him about the S.W.A.T. armored combat vehicle parked on the next block and all of the police presence surrounding the projects, but his calls got sent to voicemail. Being currently on parole after serving ten years straight in prison for a murder-by-drug overdose (heroin), Lenard Wilson III knows to stay inside his Lincoln Navigator behind tints if he didn't want to go back to Louisiana State penitentiary. From the looks of how they are set up and their movements, he concludes that the police are indeed targeting Felix's spot.

He sits and watches and sees when they kick the door in. He sees them bring Essance out, although he doesn't know who she is, without any handcuffs on, battered looking, and with torn pieces of clothing falling from her top, heading to the back of the ambulance as it pulls up. "What the fuck?" is all he could say at the chaos he witnesses unfold.

Chapter 47

Silk is on the bed biting her fingernail, nervous and anxious as hell. Lorenzo slides the key in the door and enters the room, causing Silk to jump up in paranoia. He has several bags, including the bag of hot food in his hands. Silk tries to fake up some courage, hopping up trying to play it off like she wasn't really scared shitless by him opening the door. Truth is, she was shitting bricks when she heard the lock turn.

Silk: "Finally! Oh my gosh, what took you so long to go right up the street?"

Lorenzo: "My fault baby, I'm not a good shopper when it comes to female stuff. I would've called to ask you but didn't have the number to the room phone, so I just ... "

He stops talking, because he notices fear etched on Silk's face. The way she is standing there looking: like a frightened child who just saw a monster under her bed, gives it all away. He quickly sets the food on the table and the rest of the bags on the TV stand and gives Silk a questioning stare.

Lorenzo: "What's wrong with you? Are you okay? Something bothering you, baby?"

Silk begins to stutter her words and her hands and feet begin to fidget, which starts to make him nervous. He knows something is wrong, because not only is Silk not looking at him, but she is not talking like her normal self. He puts his hands on her shoulders and shakes her a little because she is talking so incoherently that he can't understand her at all.

Lorenzo: "Silk, what is going on? Calm down... Why are you acting like this all of a sudden, baby? Sit down and talk to me... Tell me what's wrong?"

She calms down enough to talk to him.

Silk: "They're still out there... they're looking for me... they're gonna try to kill me, baby!" she says, leaning on his chest and starting to weep deeply. Lorenzo doesn't know what to say. All he can do is comfort and soothe her as much as possible, so he holds her closely, gently massaging her back and shoulder.

Lorenzo: "Shhh ... it's gonna be okay... I got chu, Silk. They gotta find you first to catch you" he states sincerely.

Silk: "But what about when they do catch me? I can't run forever. .. What about when I get caught? Are you gonna stay with me or will you get ghost?" she asks seriously, looking deep into his eyes.

Lorenzo: "No, I will not leave you, and I'll be there the whole way!" he answers, causing Silk to smile, followed by a passionate kiss.

Lorenzo's words provide a spare few moments of relief, and the kiss warms her up again: his soft lips, his touch, and his cologne. A faint erotic wave of electricity shoots through her spine and down to her toes. She opens her eyes, looking deep into his, and with a mischievous grin she asks: "you didn't forget the caps, did you?" He laughs and replies:

Lorenzo: "No I did not, are you crazy? But slow down though, tiger, go on in there and get yourself together (nodding his head towards the bathroom). Take care of yo business, then let's eat, and then we can get it in, okay baby?" he instructs dominantly.

"Yes zaddy", she answers in her most seductive, sultry southern drawl, letting the word 'daddy' roll off of her tongue, while eyeing him lustfully.

Silk: "Do you know I love it when you take control of me, lil daddy?" she states as she wraps her arms around his neck, standing pelvis up against his pelvis. "I really love it when you demand me to do something ... when you say it wit authority ... I love dat shit zaddy! I really do" she says in her most sweet, sexy, innocent voice.

She kisses him on the lips again, he grabs her plump ass cheek causing her to release a soft moan followed by giggles. They break it up, she grabs the bag with the soaps in it and opens it up, inspecting the contents. She opens the top to smell the Dove body wash and inhales deeply. She loves the fragrance. "Ahh... " she says as she walks to the bathroom to take a much-needed hot shower. She also sees that Lorenzo grabbed 200mg Ibuprofen and 200mg Motrin, so she takes two pills out of each bottle and pops them. She then goes into the bathroom and gets naked, then comes back to the doorway of the bathroom completely naked. "Lorenzo", she purrs seductively, teasing him. He comes around and is star-struck when he sees her perfect Coke bottle-shaped zaftig standing there naked, looking extremely appetizing. He licks his lips, she blows a kiss at him and shuts the door, giggly playfully.

When Silk gets into the shower, Lorenzo sneaks back outside of the motel room, glad that Silk didn't ask him to come get in the shower with her, which would ruin his plan. He goes to his truck and retrieves the other bag of merchandise he purchased while out, which is what took him so long, and the bottle of *Dom Perignon* wine.

He moves fast but is also careful not to drop the expensive wine on the ground. He makes it back inside the room silently, waits a second to make sure Silk is still occupied, and when he hears the shower water running and her singing Mariah Carey's hit 'Hero', he lights in to getting the room set up in decorations to make this, their first (and maybe last) night together as special and romantic as possible. The chicken meal got a bit cool over time, so after making their plates, he put them in the microwave that is next to the TV stand. In record timing, everything is set up perfectly. He is finished and anxious, so he knocks on the bathroom door. "Baby you ok in there?" he asks. "I don't know... maybe you should come in here and see if I'm okay, lil daddy", she replies playfully. He looks at the room once more to make sure he didn't miss anything.

Everything is right and the plates of delicious food are still steaming. He decides to go in so he can see her giggling and also so he can get clean. He opens the door and the steam hits him instantly. Silk opens the shower curtain smiling and giggling mischievously. "Hey zaddy. Are you my lil hero?" she asks. Again, mesmerized by her flawless body and gorgeous face, Lorenzo quickly strips out of his clothes and hops in the shower with her. "I was wondering when you were gonna join me, handsome" she says, as she scoots over to let him in. "Here daddy... let me wash you up... I got this", she says, grabbing a washcloth and lathering it with soap. "Ima get chu shiny clean", she adds while grabbing and stroking his manhood with a soapy hand. He leans back against the shower wall as she strokes him rhythmically harder and faster. He feels himself getting quickly to that point and stops her with a passionate kiss, however, she doesn't let go of him, she holds his dick, pumping it gently while returning the kiss. He turns her around, her ass now up against his hard dick, and starts kissing the back of her wet neck and shoulders, hitting her spot (the bite marks), causing shocks of ecstasy to shoot through her, making her moan and start to scream energetically, and making her knees buckle. He stops her from falling, catching the weight of her body by cupping her plump breasts in his hands. "Damn, you aight baby?" he asks with a laugh. "Stand up", he says. As her head comes back up he catches her eyes rolled back, letting him know that she is nearing an orgasm. Not wanting to have it all end in the shower, he stops kissing her neck. "Baby... so are you gone get a brother clean, or do I gotta take care of it? Here... give me... " he asks and then reaches for the soapy rag in Silk's hand.

When he attempts to take it from her, she bucks up, backing her plump, soft, wet booty into his, causing him to slide back and into the wall. She backs all the way up, sliding with him until his back is against the wall and her ass cheeks are pressed up against his dick and balls. With her back against his chest, he looks down enjoying the view so much that he just wants to say 'fuck it' and take her ass down right there under the hot shower water. Her slim waist and peach-shaped ass cheeks are spread because of his dick pressing in between them along her crack, his balls snug tight in there as well, feeling the warmth of her wet-ass pussy, dick tip touching her lower back. Silk's body is so right she could be a supermodel any day. "No... I got chu daddy... Let me take care of this" she moans out, then bends over right in same spot, her backside never leaving his dick, and begins wiping down his thighs and legs and to his feet. She comes up his body slowly with the rag, her body still on his, not turning around, and that's when Lorenzo notices the red marks on the back of her neck. Upon closer inspection he looks and mouths out, "What-the...? Are these teeth marks on your neck baby?"

Caught off guard, Silk doesn't have an answer right away. She spins around quickly and takes a step back with a nervous embarrassed expression on her face. She looks up at him dumbfoundedly and asks, "What?"

Lorenzo: "Those marks on the back of ya neck... Are they teeth marks?"

Silk: "Um... Yes... No... I mean... No... Uh... Yea..." she stutters, trying to formulate an explanation without having to reveal the truth to her love.

She knows she is going to have to come clean about everything she's experienced within the last couple of weeks, however, how the subject has come about surprises her. She is not prepared. Lorenzo can tell that she is uncomfortable and he doesn't want to make her uneasy or unwilling to express herself completely to him, so he moves in to soothe her. When he attempts to put his arms around her body to hold her, she eludes him by stepping back, under the water, getting her hair wet, looking down shamefully. "Silk... baby... I'm sorry... I didn't... " he begins, but Silk extends her hand with the rag in it, giving it to him to take. He accepts it and Silk is still silent, not making eye contact. "Baby, we don't have to talk about it right now. Whenever you're ready you can tell me, aight?" Lorenzo assures, gently raising her chin up so that their eyes meet. "I'm not here to hurt you, baby. And I promise I will not judge you, okay? Trust me, Silk. I got chu, but I need you to be one-hunnit with me, and I promise to be the same with you, okay?" he adds followed by another slow, wet kiss on her full soft lips. This is the first kiss where Silk doesn't return anything. Her lips do not move, even when Lorenzo sucks on her bottom one to get her to react and join in, but she does nothing. Silk stands there under the running shower water, letting it pour down her face, an emotionless, almost trance-like expression on her face. She really wants to speak, to give him an answer, letting him know that she agrees, but for some reason, the words won't come out of her mouth. He stops kissing her, leaving her mouth slightly open and letting her lip hang, and the shower water dances off of them. Feeling somewhat defeated, he finishes washing himself with the washcloth. As he does so, Silk watches him intensely, thinking about the promise he just made to her.

Silk feels deep down inside that she can trust him, and that his words are true. She doesn't want to lose him. She loves and adores him, all of him. What she needs to tell him, she feels, is not only embarrassing, but humiliating; to tell him that she had intended on giving her virginity to him - she had even dreamed about how it would happen, but instead her dream was crushed the day Antonio raped her, and that's how the bite marks got on her neck. It ate her up now more than ever, because here she is naked in the motel shower with the man she dreamed of being with and being her first, but she was no longer a virgin. Looking at him made a couple of tears escape her eyes, which get mixed with the shower water. She tells herself to pick her head up, to be strong, and to just tell him the truth. She trusts him. Admiring his athletic body full of soap bubbles, he turns around facing her and catches her looking at his backside.

Lorenzo: "Can I get under there with you?"

Silk: "Oh... yea... I'm sorry ... I was just... Come on over here, lil daddy" she says in her soft sweet voice, pulling him over.

She steps to the side to let him rinse himself, and gets caught in the eye with some of the soap that the water shot off of his shoulder. "Ah", she squeals as the soap burns her eye.

Lorenzo: "Aw damn, my fault. .. are you good, baby?"

He reaches up and turns the shower head to spray on Silk's eye

Silk: "Hehehe... thank you lil daddy... you so sweet to me bae... why?" she asks, wrapping her arms around his waistline, looking up at him with innocent cat eyes.

Lorenzo: "Because you are special to me Silk... very special... and I want to prove that to you... from now... for the rest of our lives, till we die" he states sincerely.

His words cause Silk's heart to melt inside, more tears daring to fall from her searching eyes. "Come on... let's get out of here so I can show you", he says. He turns off the water, steps out and grabs him a dry towel and wraps it around his waistline, and then he grabs the big velvet one he bought for Silk at the store. She carefully steps out of the slippery shower and walks into the towel while Lorenzo holds it open. Wrapping it around and tucking it in, "thank you Iil zaddy", she purrs seductively. Lorenzo smiles.

Lorenzo: "You ready, babe?"

Silk: "Yea... I am, bae."

Chapter 48

He opens the door slowly, and what Silk sees is unbelievable. Her eyes are as wide as the planets when she sees the room. Stunned would be an understatement to describe the way she feels. The room is a complete transformation of what she left out to when she went into the bathroom. She is frozen in the doorway of the bathroom, mouth gaping, eyes marveling over the designs of the decor and ornaments -—the red and pink rose petals leading from the bathroom door to the bed and scattered all around the room; full roses with stems purposefully placed on the TV stand, night stand, and one in the middle of the table which had a red table cloth, two candles burning, a bottle of wine in a small bucket of ice, two plates with delicious-looking golden-brown fried chicken, baked macaroni and cheese, fried cabbage and greens, cornbread, and in the middle next to the win sat a quart-sized bowl of gumbo. On the bed is assorted, heart-shaped, chocolates with an arts and crafts made sash that had Silk's name on it. Everything is fabulous, many candles burning in all the right places around the room. Lorenzo sure did his thing with this one. He could be an event stager the way he staged this room so good.

Lorenzo stands behind Silk, allowing her to soak in the amazing job he did to make the night perfect for the two of them. She puts both hands up, covering her mouth and nose, as she surveys the room in complete awe. Lorenzo eases up behind her, rests his hands on both sides of her hips, and whispers in her ear:

Lorenzo: "You like it, boo?"

Silk: "I love it! I love it daddy... Oh my god... I have never seen... I never had anyone do anything like this for me before... oh my god... baby, thank you! I love you! I love you so much Lorenzo" she cries out in joy and excitement. "I can't believe you did all this... How...? When... ?"

She questions, but he shushes her and nudges her forward to enter the magic environment. She walks out smiling from ear-to-ear, gazing with star-twinkle eyes, musing over all of the beautiful scented candles and decorations in the room. She picks up a rose petal from the bed and closes her eyes as she inhales the invigorating smell of it, complimenting her senses. Her eyes roll back in satisfaction for a second, then they fall down on Lorenzo, who takes his towel off, lets it fall to the floor, walks square up to her, wraps his arms around her waist again and replies, "I love you too, baby", and then begins kissing her passionately. Her towel threatens to fall off of her body, but she stops it and breaks up the kiss against his wishes. "Let's eat this food before it gets cold and goes to waste, ok lil zaddy?", she suggests, giving him a final smooch on the lips, and he agrees.

They both dry off completely, Lorenzo was faster at it. He had dried himself completely and put on clean boxers and joggers he always kept in his truck for when he went to practice or to work out at the gym, which he did both religiously. He is halfway dressed when Silk looks in the store bag.

Silk: "Where's my laundry soap at so I can wash my dirty clothes?"

Lorenzo: "In the other bag in the closet... but look... don't worry about that right now... take care of that later."

Silk: "So what am I supposed to do? Sit here at the dinner table naked in a wet towel?"

Lorenzo: "Hmrnm ... that would be sexy as hell", he teased, looking to the ceiling as if picturing it.

Silk: "Shut up, silly", she laughs, followed by a playful punch to his chest... "Forreal though, that wouldn't be lady-like and we know that I'm a classy girl", she vogues, primping her wet curly hair up while staring back at her reflection in the wall mirror. "Forreal, bae?"

She looks at him awaiting an answer, but he goes to the closet looking for something. He turns back to her holding something behind his back.

Silk: "What's back there, lil daddy? I see you got more and more surprises... I'ma have to start calling you Mr. Surprise, huh, bae?" she jokes.

Lorenzo: "I told you I got chu baby, nothing but the finest for the finest lady... my lady"

He brings his arm around, and in his hand, he reveals a cherry red strapless dress and puts it up to her body, checking her out. Again, Silk gasps in shock, full of surprise.

Silk: "Oh my god! It's so beautiful, baby... I love it! Thank you! I love you daddy... you making me feel so dang ole special."

Lorenzo: "That's because you are special to me, Silk... You really are." She looks up at him in complete love, smiling.

Silk: "Let me go put it on... I'll be right back, lil zaddy."

She hauls off back into the bathroom and shuts the door. Minutes later, she exits the bathroom again, dress hugging her frame perfectly as if it had been painted on her. She had done her hair in a neat bob atop her head. Now it was his turn to look star-struck and in awe at the beautiful young lady he is with. Silk was a beautiful and attractive young woman and she knew it, she just is not all stuck-up about it; she is very humble.

She stood there for a few seconds to allow Lorenzo to soak all of her image into his soul— posing for him, looking like a supermodel, only better and more natural. She interrupts his fantasy moment:

Silk: "How do I look, lil zaddy?"

Lorenzo: "Baby... you looking edible right now! Forget the chicken, forget the mac and cheese, forget the gumbo and fuck the corn bread, I want to taste you, sweet thang!"

Silk: "Really... ? Hehehe... I would like that, but a bitch need some food, some real grub... I'm hungry, lil zaddy... can you feed me now? I'll feed you later", she says seductively.

Pulling himself together, Lorenzo responds, "Yea... you right, baby... ok come on, let's sit down and eat." He watches her ass the whole entire time she walks out and to the table. "Damn!" he says to himself. They each take their respective seats. Lorenzo opens the bottle of Dom and fills both flutes. He is about to bless the food with a prayer but Silk has already dug into her plate, tearing away at her drumstick and forking portions of the baked mac & cheese in her mouth.

Lorenzo can't help but chuckle at her.

Lorenzo: "Dang, girl, slow down... that food ain't gone nowhere."

Silk wipes her mouth, swallows what's inside, and replies, "Yes it is gone somewhere ... right in here," motioning to her stomach, which was on empty until now. Lorenzo laughs again at her sense of humor, and then he joins in with her feasting. He kills two full plates, plus half the bowl of gumbo. Silk can only hold down one plate and a small portion of her bowl of gumbo. She is full and satisfied as she sips the fine-tasting wine. She admires his elegant taste. Although she's never tried wine in her life before, or any alcohol for that matter, she knew that it was unique, top branded, and expensive, because her parents keep some in their wine rack in the basement.

While Lorenzo finishes his third cornbread muffin and gumbo, Silk admires him eating, and thinks that maybe now would be a good time to talk; to talk about everything.

Clearing her throat and taking a deep breath, Silk begins:

Silk: "I really do appreciate everything you have done for me tonight, forreal, lil zaddy. The food was on slam... I love my dress... the set is so... you know... the mood is so romantic, so perfect..."

Lorenzo: "Yes, that's exactly what this is... most def..."

Silk: "I know right... I just... I can't even find the right words to explain how I feel... but thank you... And most of all, thank you for not judging me. I really love that about you. Now I don't know how serious you are about when you say you want me to be ya ole lady, but... I know I want you.... And I'm not perfect... but I will try my best to be the woman for you, ok zaddy?"

Lorenzo nods his head in agreement.

Silk: "Now tonight is very special for us, and I want this night to be the beginning of our future together ... but first I gotta lay all of my cards on the table for you, daddy... you deserve that from me."

Lorenzo wipes his mouth with a napkin, watching intensely as Silk speaks, adoring her beauty.

Silk: "Please do not judge me, daddy please don't... you been doing good so far, don't change that, ok?"

Lorenzo: "I'm not... I'm here for you... trust me, baby... I love you."

This reassurance causes Silk to blush hard as a tingle rolls down her legs and up her thighs. She takes another deep breath and then begins:

Silk: "Some things happened to me like a month and a half, maybe two months ago, that turned my whole entire world upside down in what feels like overnight. So, there's this bayou down there by where you found me at when you ran me down with ya truck (smiling playfully, rolling her eyes at him, and grabbing at her rib cage for inference) ... Anyways... "

"I'm sorry", Lorenzo whispers.

Silk: "I have been fascinated with this part of the bayou since I could remember. My Ma Ma used to live in a house nearby, but she passed a few years ago."

Lorenzo: "I'm sorry to hear about your loss, baby."

Silk: "Thank you... Yea, Ma Ma and I were really really close. I was a little girl, and used to love being with her, and she took good care of me too. We were together so often, I thought she was my mother for a good minute. But I used to go down there by myself; first started when I was only seven years old. Everything about it just fascinates me: the water, the trees and other plants, the animals. Oh my god, the animals... The way the sunset looks so pretty out there... but most of all, the peace it brings me when I'm out there. That's where I go when I need to be alone; when I had a bad day at school, done got into it with Barrika, family getting on my nerves at home, or when I just wanna see something amazing, because believe it or not, it's mind-blowing how wildlife coexists."

Lorenzo: "Sorry to interrupt you, baby, but you said when you had troubles with Barrika, right? The big guh that was found butchered in the girls' bath... "

Silk: "Yes, um hmm, that's her... um yea... and yea you are excused for interrupting me, sir," she replies before he can finish his question. She smiles at the last part and he returns the gesture.

Lorenzo: "My bad... when I heard you say her name, it just stuck out like a sore thumb to me. But I do have to ask you... What happened in that bathroom, baby? Are the rumors true?"

Silk waits a moment before responding to his question, looking deep into his soul through his eyes. She knew it was coming the moment he mentioned Barrika's name.

Silk: "Barrika and I haven't saw eye-to-eye since she moved here from Alabama. It was the fifth grade when I first met her, and that is the first time I ever got into a fight with someone other than my twin... and ever since then the two of us been beefin'. I would usually have to fight her on my own, because Essance is not a fighter at all, and Lilli used to get picked up most of the time by her folks. But a few months ago, me and Barrika gets into it again, or should I say Barrika tried to take property from me again that didn't belong to her, and I wasn't going. So we fought, and once again she gets the best of my lil cute butt, and my forearm got all scraped up on the ground and I was bleeding and dirty, so I go down to my chill spot down at the bayou. I wash off all of the blood and dirt and whatnot in the river water. Well ... my lil dumb butt forgets its gators that live in them there waters, and gators love them some blood and fresh tender meat to eat." (smiling). "So, next thing I know, I look up and the gator is like 5 or 10 inches away from taking my cute lil face off" (placing her hands on her cheeks for emphasis), "but then I feel someone grab me hard and snatch me out the water. Turns out the person who saved me from them gators' stomachs is the voodoo queen herself; 'Mama B' ... well, I think err body else know her by Beatrice ... you know who I'm talking bout?"

Lorenzo: "I've heard the stories about her... but you know I am still the new face around here, so I don't know her personally... But anyway, continue."

Silk: "So Beatrice rescued me, and you know I'm feeling grateful that she was there to save me from being gators' brunch, so I talk to her, and you know, sort of befriend her... That's when she introduces me to voodoo, witchcraft, sorcery, and all that magical stuff. So, I stop going to the bayou to look at the wildlife, but to start visiting her more, and I learn a lot... I start liking it."

Silk continues revealing everything to Lorenzo; all of the things her and Beatrice discussed, including him; the spells, potions, history and secrets of voodoo; about catching Beatrice and Antonio (Beatrice's first cousin, the warlock, and her sex-slave master) doing the ritual, and their debate on whether to let Silk go home with their secret or not; Zela and how she warned her to stay away from the two evil cousins, and about how she ignored those warnings; the day Antonio raped her, how she was thinking about him (Lorenzo) and was looking at love spells to use on him, and how terrible and hurt she felt about not losing her virginity to him like she'd dreamt of and planned on doing.

Silk explains that that is why she acted so crazy with him the day in the school parking lot in his truck. She tells him about the voices, the flashbacks of her being raped, evil visions; and she explains to him how the teeth marks got on the back of her neck. She shows him so that he can see clearly. While he closely inspects the marks, Silk explains what happens to her body now whenever contact is made by herself or anyone else on that spot; the visions, the chants, and extreme sexual arousal. As she explains the visions come at her full force, causing her to relive the whole rape incident in her head. She begins crying hysterically. Lorenzo leaps up from his seat and wraps his arms around her, consoling her. She grabs his arm, sobbing into it. Still weeping, she apologizes to him; feeling guilty for not having her virginity to give to him.

Lorenzo rubs her back and soothes her with assurances that he would be by her and that it wasn't her fault. She is still crying and feeling guilty. He lifts her up, carries her to the bed, and gently sits down on it with her. He gets back up, grabs their flutes and the bottle of wine, and refills them both. Silk kills the flute in one gulp, looks at the flute on the desk, then at the bottle, knocks the flute on the floor, and grabs the bottle of Dom and takes a long swig. "Better?" Lorenzo asks, smiling curiously. "Yea... a lil bit," Silk replies with a silly giggle, the last two tears falling off her cheeks. Lorenzo scoots closer to Silk, reaches up and wipes her tears with his pointer finger. She looks so beautiful but it pains him to see her so hurt, so broken.

Silk sniffles and smiles, letting him know that she appreciates his gesture. She clears her throat and then begins:

Silk: "There's something else I need to tell you. Promise me you won't judge me or turn against me for it?"

Lorenzo looks deep into her eyes and shakes his head indicating that he won't.

Silk: "Say it... I want to hear the words come off your lips... Say you promise."

Lorenzo: "I promise, baby... I'm not going to do any of that, ok? Trust me, please. Now what's up?"

Silk takes about fifteen seconds before responding to clear her thoughts so that she can speak properly what she needs to tell him. She wipes away the remaining tears, closes her eyes, takes a deep breath, and then clears her throat.

Silk: "Well, I told you already how bad I felt after Antonio violated me. I told myself that I would never go back to that house, let alone go back around Mama B or Antonio, but for some reason though, the next day I felt the need to go over there more than ever. So, while I'm explaining to Mama B how bad and angry I felt about her cousin violating me, she switches the whole thing on me; acting like I told him, or like I wanted Antonio to rape me.

Lorenzo rubs the small of her back to comfort her as he can hear Silk getting emotional over the traumatic incident. "It's ok, baby... I'm listening ... you're good, baby, he will never hurt you again", he says sternly. Silk continues telling him what Beatrice had fed to her about her (Silk) dressing provocative for men to lust over; Antonio's actions being part of their rituals; how Silk voluntarily gave herself

up (an illusion that she tried to brainwash Silk with). She explains
to him how she began to believe what Beatrice was saying so she
dropped the whole rape scenario and started practicing and
performing voodoo rituals with both of the cousins, and about the
night that they all engaged in a drunken threesome. She describes all
of the details precisely as the visual images of the night replay in her
head. Rehashing the events gets her pussy moist.

Chapter 49

Sort of taken aback by the confession, Lorenzo remains neutral.
"So... did you like it? I mean... did you enjoy them? I mean him?" he
asks with a skeptical confused expression on his face. Silk sits silently,
stopping herself from stuttering. She is trying to find the best words
to answer his question, because she feels that there is no way no how
she can lie to him now after everything that's happened. She feels like
she owes him the truth, so she must tell it like it is. She toys with her
fingers while looking at both of their feet.

Silk: "I honestly... I did like it at the time, I'm not gone lie... but...
I was also not in my normal state of mind, ya heard me... I was out of
my body, like literally."

Lorenzo: "So wait a minute... you let them get you drunk first?"

Silk: "No, no, no... the potions, remember? I'm not a big fan of
alcohol nor threesomes, Lorenzo. I was really messed up in the head.
That day was just too much for me, and so Mama B told me to drink
it to take away my pain and worries and to lift all my burdens off of
me, so I believed it would, so I drank it. Mama B is normally always
on point with her mixes and the things they cure you know, so I
trusted her word."

Lorenzo: "Whoa, whoa, whoa! Wait a minute Silk... I'm sorry to interrupt you, but please tell me how in the hell could you trust some old bitch that practices voodow, voodoom first of all... "

Silk: "It's voo-doo, fool" she interjects.

Lorenzo: "Ok, I'm sorry again... voo-doo. But how could you put any amount of trust into anyone who practices that stuff first of all? And second, she let her old perverted-ass cousin rape you, then she throws all the blame on you; making you feel all guilty and shit, and tricking you into believing that the shit was ok? I mean... I just don't get how you could feel comfortable after that alone. I mean... shh... What made you go back, baby? After the magic tricks I would've been done with going anywhere near them swamps and bayous. So... what kept you going back, Silk? And why didn't you tell anyone, Silk? Huh? Your parents? The school? Your friends? Me?"

Silk: "That's what I am trying to tell you, daddy... I don't know why I went back. I don't even know why I became her friend. I guess I felt like it was the least I could do... I mean come on now, she is the reason why I'm even sitting here having this conversation with you right now... Baby, I... I just cannot explain to you, to myself, to nobody what possessed me to go back. You're right... Like you said, after I saw the magic the first time, I was spooked to death and I told myself then that I wasn't ever going back... but it's like for some reason, I don't know... it's like she put a spell on me to keep me going back to her... like I was possessed or something."

She stops talking, thinking hard about what she had just stated.

Lorenzo: "What... what is it, baby?" he asks in curiosity of her abrupt silence and the trance-like expression she's gone into.

"Possessed", Silk mutters to no one in particular. That's when the light bulb in her brain goes off.

Silk: "Mama B put a spell on me to keep me coming back... the 'Return Spell'. I read about it in one of the chapters of the spell books she taught me out of. No matter how strong a person is or how hard

you try to resist it, the powers of the spell will always win and you
will most definitely return. It's the same with any spell. That's what
it has to be... she used it on me so I could go back... so they could
control me... seduce me."

Lorenzo looks on at Silk in shock, not speaking a word as she
explains her rationale. He is trying desperately to piece together all
of the information Silk has laid on him.

Silk: "They wanted to get me out of my body to cover up him
violating me the way he did. His spell... I try... I tried to yell... to scre...
scream ... f... f. .. for ... hel...hel...help... b... but" she stutters, breathing
heavily, nearly gasping for air.

Seeing Silk struggling, looking distressed, and speaking as if she
is about to go into convulsion, Lorenzo places a firm grip on her
hands and speaks to her gently.

Lorenzo: "Silk... slow down, take your time, baby, you're ok,
ok...? I'm right here... talk to me."

Silk: "I tried to scream for help while he was on top of me. I
tried to yell to the top of my lungs for someone... anyone... for you
to help me... to come in there and get him off of me, but no sound
came out of me. My voice box wouldn't work. And he was reciting
some sort of chant or spell that I ain't never been taught before, and I
just felt so weak and helpless because nobody ever came. I wanted to
tell someone so bad, but every time I was 'bout to, her voice would
ring in my head threatening that if I told anyone, I'd die... and I'm
too young to be dying, so I kept my mouth shut till now. After that
incident and Mama B taking up for him, I didn't trust her no mo!
She was supposed to look out for me and protect me... so I thought.
But now I see that I only have me for protection."

Lorenzo: "Naw baby... you have me now. You understand me?"

Loving the confidence and conviction in his voice as he spoke,
Silk smiles joyfully, lifting their clasped hands and rubbing the back
of his on her soft brown cheek.

Silk: "And Zela, 'The Bird Lady', tried to warn me about those two from the jump, but my dumb butt ain't listen. Being a fool for those two. I didn't see but now I do see how evil they are, and how they only wanted to ruin me all along. That same night that we had sex, right before I drank the potion, Mama B tried to tell me not to hang with my bestie, Lilli... called her a trouble-chile . My dumb butt so brainwashed, really believing her, got to acting shady towards my best best friend since the mud woe. Whole time Lilli really love me and want to protect me. So earlier today I find out that my best friend is also a witch, and that Zela is her teacher. I can't... can you believe that daddy?"

Lorenzo: "No... but I can't say that I'm surprised... She is a lil weird acting... weird looking, too."

The two of them burst out into a fit of laughter and his joke, and then he adds:

Lorenzo: "But naw, before moving to the N.O. I heard a lot of stories about the people practicing voodoo, so that's why I ain't surprised, ya know? Shit is still crazy as hell though."

Silk nods her head in agreement. She then relays all of the events of the day, starting with the school janitor, then the magical battle between Mama B and Antonio versus Zela and Lilli. She explains what new found truth Zela had revealed to her about the evil jinns and the significance of them and Beatrice's pet lizard 'Iblis.' She admits to being enticed and possessed by the demons now. This puts Lorenzo on edge now. Finally, she tells him about her final interaction with Beatrice; learning the spell to erase all of her problems, how she played Beatrice, and then swallowed Iblis and the jinn Ludiah, and lastly about how she had the power to cause the swamp to swallow Beatrice up. She ends the recount with her getting hit by his truck.

By the time Silk is done revealing all of her secrets to Lorenzo, he is in a mix of feelings; fear, suspicion, curious, intrigued, and nervous all at the same time. Silk is happy on the inside because she finally got everything off of her chest, and who better for her to vent to than the young man she fell in love with the moment they locked eyes in the school hallway. She has a neutral expression on her face, gazing at him, awaiting his response. They both sit silently for a moment.

Silk: "So... what are you thinking about me, daddy?" she asks, breaking the silence.

Lorenzo: "I don't know Silk... I mean... I don't know what to think."

Silk: "See, that's why I didn't even want to tell you in the first place, because I knew you'd get to looking at me all different."

Lorenzo: "Silk , I'm not looking at chu any different. I mean, it is just not the usual for a girl to tell me that she loves an evil spirit, demon, or whatever it is, so much that she swallows it, and now it's walking around living inside of her. It's just..."

Silk: "Ok, but now you're judging me... didn't you just make me a promise that you wouldn't do that shit, daddy? Huh? Dayumn!" she wines in frustration.

Lorenzo: "Silk, no... you got it all wrong. I'm not judging you."

Silk: "Yes you are!"

Lorenzo: "Look, lil mama... all of this you just laid on me is brand new to me... very weird, by the way."

Silk stands up. She is hot now and about to go off.

Silk: "So now I'm weird, huh, Lorenzo? See mane, I knew I shouldn't have let nobody get me so weak and open like this, I told myself. .. I don't know why I don't listen to myself. I know I couldn't trust no... "

Lorenzo: "Baby look... stop it now! Look... I am not judging you. If I felt some type of way I would have sprinted my ass on up out of here by now, don't chu think? I'm right here still trying to get you to see that I care about you a whole lot, and that I am really here for you. Why can't chu see that, huh, ma?"

He reaches for Silk's hand as he says this last part. She pulls away, pouting her lips out, her eyebrows brunched together from her frown.

Lorenzo: "Come on baby, look... I'm sorry, ok...? You know I didn't mean to offend you, you gotta believe me. I'm here for you, and I'm falling for you, lil mama."

He cups her chin with his hand, turning her face to face him. He leans in and places a soft, tender kiss on her pouty lips, causing her to go from angry to a silly kiddy smile; the smile of a kid who'd just gotten their way with something. He looks at her and smiles also.

Lorenzo: "You're such a brat, you know that?"

Silk playfully pounces on top of him, knocking him back onto the bed, straddles him, and while grinning mischievously says:

Silk: "I'm your brat though, right, lil zaddy?" She plants a wet kiss of her own on his lips.

Lorenzo: "No question, baby"

Silk: "Promise not to turn on me or use anything against me, daddy."

Lorenzo: "I promise, baby."

Silk: "And promise me you won't leave me. That you will protect me." A split thought and then he answers:

Lorenzo: "I promise... but when the law catches up with us, baby, I don't know if I'll be able to fight the government's guns and shit, ya feel me? But I will be there... "

Silk: "Stop... don't talk like that. I don't want to hear that... ain't nobody gonna lay a hand on me or you daddy, ok?" she states matter-of-factly.

Lorenzo: "Ok, ma."

Without another word, Silk dives into him, letting their lips lock, devouring each other's, and their tongues dancing magically under the candle lit room. The kiss becomes extremely passionate, especially for Silk.

Chapter 50

Essance is taken away from the projects in the 17th ward that Felix had brought her to by ambulance, heading to St. John's Hospital in downtown New Orleans to be examined thoroughly. Detective Valorie rides along with Essance in the ambulance while her partner, Detective Billy Bob, trailed in their unmarked squad. The lady S.W.A.T. officer had returned to her unit in the combat vehicle, awaiting further directives from Detective Valorie. As the EMTs begin doing their work on Essance, checking her vitals, injuries, and getting her personal information, Valorie knows she must use that open window of opportunity to acquire Essance's cell phone.

Detective Valorie: "Here, why don't you let me hold that for you while they get you all hooked up... just so it's not in anyone's way."

Essance looks at her skeptically, not trusting the police detective. Instead of giving it to Valorie, she sets her phone down beside her on the stretcher bed.

Detective Valorie: "The ride can get quite bumpy in these things you know... It'd be a crying shame if that iPhone 10 falls and breaks the screen or something on this steel floor... Just saying", she persists.

Female EMT: "She's right. You should let her hold it, baby."

Detective Valorie: "It'll be with you the whole time. I am not leaving you, sweetie."

Essance reluctantly gives in, feeling as though they had made a valid point. She doesn't want her brand-new iPhone 10 getting damaged in any way, so she eases up a bit. She knows that she is safe now after the close encounter back at the projects with her ex-best male friend and his homeboy; possibly being raped, and by one who is a confirmed AIDS carrier. Just the thought of what almost happened makes her nauseous, and the bumps and shaking that the ambulance is doing isn't making things any better. Detective Valorie observing her, notices Essance's body posture.

Detective Valorie: "Get her a bag, she's about to puke!"

The EMTs respond immediately, and just as one gets the vomit bag over Essance's mouth she lets loose, barfing into the bag.

Detective Valorie: "Are you ok sweetie?" she asks, sympathetically.

Essance nods her woozy head, answering that she is ok, looking fatigued and drained, and then continues barfing into the bag. She fills it up so quick that the EMT has to grab a fresh bag for her.

Detective Valorie: "You've been through so much, you poor girl. Your parents are probably worried sick, and we should let them know you are on your way to the ER and why. I don't have your folk's number handy on me right now. I left it on my desk at the ole office. Is it ok if I look in your phone for your mother's phone number? I just think it's only right to let them know that you're fine and not to worry about your pretty little self, ok, sweetheart?" she says smoothly.

Without a word, Essance nods her head in compliance. This is all the opportunity Valorie needs to get into Essance's cell phone, with Essance's permission, making it a legal search, and get the number that she'd talked to Silk on. She knows it's dirty and conniving for her to take advantage of Essance's vulnerability in this unfortunate predicament, however, she also knows she doesn't have much of a choice nor time if she is going to locate and apprehend her real target --—Silk, which in her mind, there is no question about that. She was going to do just that. This little move was all in a day's work to her. She turns the iPhone on and asks Essance to enter the iCloud password. Essance is sweating profusely and breathing heavily, her breath reeking of cognac.

Detective Valorie: "Honey, have you been drinking any alcohol while you were with those heathens?" she asks as Essance enters her password.

Essance: "A little Henny ... Not a lot... maybe... two to three shots I think... " she answers honestly, after she unlocks her iPhone and hands it back to Valorie without making any eye contact.

Female EMT: "Well, that is too much for a chile you size, honey."

Detective Valorie: "Ok, so what do you have your momma saved as in here, sweetie?" she asks, pretending as she really searches through Essance's call history.

Detective Valorie already has Lashunda's house and cell phone numbers stored in her own cell phone, so she doesn't bother looking. Instead, she locks her eyes on the last call made to Essance's phone, and based off of the information the IT specialist team had given her, she is certain that the phone number with the 318 area code was the call from Silk.

Essance: "Mama dear."

Detective Valorie: "Ok, thank you... Up, here we go."

Detective Valorie pulls her own cell phone out, acting as if she is putting Lashunda's phone number in to call her, but really, she is entering the suspected number from the call log that she believes is to be made by Silk.

Detective Valorie: "Got it... I'm making the call now", she says once she has the number locked in.

She exits Essance's call log after deleting the memory of the phone history so Essance doesn't find out. After shutting Essance's phone off, on her own cell phone, she sends a text message to her partner who is still trailing the ambulance with the contact that reads: 'Suspect phone number'. Essance is so out of it she doesn't notice Detective Valorie doing all of this.

Female EMT: "Are you allergic to any medicines that you know of, honey?" Essance shakes her head no.

Female EMT: "Ok, I'm gonna put you on an IV bag so you don't dehydrate from throwing up so much body fluids, and I'm gonna put a dose of this medicine to calm you down and help you to relax your stomach, ok?" she explains sincerely, rubbing Essance's arm for comfort.

Detective Billy Bob texts Valorie back with: "You little red fox! (smiley face emoji). Good work... relaying over to COMMS now... stand by. Valorie shakes her head, annoyed at his flirtatious comments. Instantly she hears Billy Bob's voice air over the police radio, so she quickly reaches to the small of her back to lower the volume so that Essance doesn't hear him announce the newly obtained information on Silk. It works, because Essance doesn't hear a thing.

Detective Valorie then finds Lashunda's house number in her contacts and places a call to her to inform her of Essance's whereabouts and status. Lashunda answers on the second ring, anxious for an update on Silk. She is hysterical when Detective Valorie informs her that the reason for her call wasn't regarding Silk, but instead is about Essance. Valorie does her best to calm her by affirming to her that Essance is doing fine and is in safe hands now, and that she is on her way to St. John's. Lashunda asks if she could speak to Essance, but when Valorie looks at her she is drifting asleep on the stretcher bed; the effect of the medication put into her IV.

Detective Valorie: "She's been given some medication to relax her, so she's kinda out of it right now... but you can talk to her right away most definitely when you get up to the ER, ok. mam?"

She says her goodbyes to Lashunda and hangs up the phone. Another text had come through from Billy Bob which read: "Location found. Tallulah motel on Highway 65, room 3. Units en route in N.O. and Tallulah squads on location with perimeter on standby. Your orders, doll?"

Detective Valorie responds in a text: "10-4. Do we have surveillance set up? Positive ID confirmed? Standby until I arrive. ETA 30 min appr."

"Copy that, 10-4 doll", Billy Bob replies via text. Valorie looks at her phone and shakes her head in pure disgust at the man's persistence.

Detective Valorie: "Where are we at on an ETA?"

Ambulance Driver: "Less than a minute... Pulling into the dock in 30", he answers, then turns off the sirens.

Detective Valorie: "Make sure this iPhone stays with her, and let the hospital know as well. And no visitors for this patient except immediate family because of an ongoing investigation, ok?"

She then prepares to exit the ambulance and hop into the squad with her partner. The EMTs all nod their heads in confirmation, jotting down Valorie's directives onto Essance's medical sheet. Before Valorie exits the truck, she rubs Essance's thigh.

Detective Valorie: "Hang in there, sweetheart... you'll be fine."

Valorie then jumps out and hops in the passenger side of the unmarked charger and immediately asks for updates.

Detective Billy Bob: "Yup, so room is registered under the name 'Lorenzo' ... high school senior, attends the same school, star athlete, plays both wide-receiver and point-guard, straight-A student, drives a 1999 Chevy Tahoe, moved here about a year or so ago from Minneapolis, Minnesota, and he's super hot, and yea, fits the perfect description of a young hottie like Silk's boy crush."

Detective Valorie: "The ID confirmation?"

Detective Billy Bob: "Negative ... more squads have arrived at the scene... COMMS too... and they talked to the clerk, says she ain't seen no guh, just him. He checked in, looked the room over quick, then headed back out, up to the market to grab some grub likely, cause he returned with food bags."

Just as he finishes, the COMMS team comes over the police radios: "8952 to all units, we have confirmed a female occupant in the suspected room... sniper has spotted female figure that matches suspect's description in the room... I repeat, we have positive ID, suspect is in sight."

Detective Valorie: "10-4, all units stand by, ETA 1 hour , 20 minutes... this is lead Detective Valorie Sanchez, I repeat, STAND BY ... over and out."

All officers on the scene at Silk and Lorenzo's motel in Tallulah reply with, "10-4, copy that, over and out."

To Be Continued...
Epilogue

The Comms team wasted no time at all filling Detective Valorie and her partner in on all of the information they had acquired while awaiting the detectives' arrival -—they had set up the microphone they'd used in the 17th Ward to listen in on Essance and Felix, and confirmed that they were actually sitting on Silk -—they had tapped into Silk and Lorenzo's motel room telephone as well, plus they had pinged Lorenzo's cell phone from a nearby cell phone tower powered by Verizon. Detective Valorie takes in all of the new information and thanks the officers. The next person to approach her is another detective from her department -—Detective Faudeau, 20-year veteran of the NOPD, 8 years as detective in the violent crimes unit/hostage negotiator. Detective Faudeau wanted to know what Detective Valorie had in mind for an apprehension plan. He offers to make a call into the room, but Detective Valorie rejects. She sits silent for a moment, contemplating an alternate method.

Detective Valorie: "I want Lorenzo out of the room when we go in."

After receiving the phone call from Detective Valorie, Lashunda goes into a frenzy until DeAngelo is able to calm her down using an ice pack to her lower back, the spot that always relaxes her.

Once she is relaxed, she explains what the phone call was about, and why she is freaking out. Revealing what was happening causes DeAngelo to go crazy now. Instead of unnerving DeAngelo the way he'd done for her, Lashunda urgently races to Zay Zay's bedroom and frantically dresses her in a pair of flower shorts, a Hello Kitty t-shirt, colorful mitch-matching socks, and a Hello Kitty snapback.

Roberta, Lashunda's eldest child, comes out of her room talking on her cell phone, her usual activity, walks past Zay Zay's bedroom, but stops and enters the room when she notices her mother moving with urgency to get Zay Zay together.

Roberta: "Mama, what's? What's going on? Where are you and Zay Zay going? Did they find Silk?" she asks, sounding very concerned.

"Ah si, yes, Mr. Sanchez, this is Elizabeth calling from de front desk... Um, I'm so sorry to disrupt you, I know it is very late and you are probably sleeping, but the reason for this late call is very urgent and requires your attention right now," the caller informs Lorenzo, in her thick Spanish accent.

Lorenzo: "Well, what is it?"

Elizabeth: "Well you see... I checked you in, and I completely forgot to have you fill out our vehicle registration form to ensure that your vehicle is safe for your stay, and so you won't have to worry about it getting towed. I am sure you don't want that, Mr. Sanchez, and neither do I," she urges.

Lorenzo: "No, I do not, so... what do you need? My license plate number or something?"

Elizabeth: 'Uh ... no sir, actually, I am gonna need you to pull back up to the office, fill the vehicle registration form out completely, sign and date it for me, please" she explains.

Lorenzo: "What the fuck? You got to be kidding me... Woman, it is 2:30 in the morning," he complains.

Elizabeth: "I know, sir, and I am very very sorry that I have to have you get up out of bed... I apologize, it's completely my fault, because I forgot to have you fill it out earlier ... And yes I know it is 2:30 in the morning, and again, I truly apologize, but I think you gonna be more angry than now if your vehicle gets towed this morning when the tow company does his 3:30 to 4 o'clock sweep, so please sir, hurry over to the office, it will only take up about five minutes, not even."

Lorenzo: "It's ok... no problem, mam... I'll be right there," he answers as he slides off of the bed, blowing his breath. "Can you please have all the papers ready so I can just come sign and leave?" he requests, clearly irritated.

Elizabeth: "Oh si, si sir, absolutely ... and again, I' m very sorry sir. Ok then, see you soon, adios," she ends with before hanging up, nervously looking out of the front window at the Comms.

ABOUT THE AUTHOR

Lannon L. Burdunice was born January 2, 1991 in Minneapolis, Minnesota to Louise Wesson and Leonardo Burdunice Sr. Lannon is the father of two brilliant children. He is an author, songwriter, musical engineer/producer, and screenwriter. Lannon is also a recording artist and performer who goes by the stage name 'Wykeeta', however, those career endeavors have been put on hold because he is currently incarcerated at the Minnesota Department of Corrections-Stillwater Facility, serving a 40 year sentence, after he was wrongfully convicted of second-degree murder on May 8, 2018 by the Hennepin County District Court. Lannon is in the process of appealing his wrongful conviction, and he is representing himself in the litigation process. Upon his release from prison, Lannon plans to pursue his career goals of being a serial entrepreneur, book author, music engineer/producer, songwriter/recording artist/performer, and film producer. He also aspires to embark on a lifetime journey of humanitarianism around the globe. Lannon gives special thanks to everyone who indulges in this novel.

For more information about Lannon's wrongful conviction and the fight for justice, please visit, www.freelannonb.com[1] and follow Lannon on social media:

facebook.com/freelannonb
twitter.com/freelannonb
instagram.com/freelannonb

---

1.   http://www.freelannonb.com

www.ingramcontent.com/pod-product-compliance
Lightning Source LLC
Chambersburg PA
CBHW031952010726
47493CB00007B/2173